THE REBUILT MAN

WILLIAM BEECHCROFT

D0286515

B

BERKLEY BOOKS, NEW YORK

THE REBUILT MAN

A Berkley Book/published by arrangement with
Dodd, Mead & Company

PRINTING HISTORY
Dodd, Mead edition published 1987
Berkley edition/April 1988

ISBN: 0-425-10752-3

A BERKLEY BOOK ® TM 757,375
Berkley Books are published by The Berkley Publishing Group,
200 Madison Avenue, New York, NY 10016.
The name "BERKLEY" and the "B" logo
are trademarks belonging to Berkley Publishing Corporation.

PRINTED IN THE UNITED STATES OF AMERICA

10 9 8 7 6 5 4 3 2 1

THE REBUILT MAN

He lay in bed with a bandaged head. He didn't know where he was or who he was.

He asked the woman at his bedside, ". . . You a nurse?"

"I'm your wife, Don," she said.

He'd never seen her before . . .

OTHER BERKLEY BOOKS BY WILLIAM BEECHCROFT:

IMAGE OF EVIL

"A terrifying yarn!"—*Los Angeles Times*

CHAIN OF VENGEANCE

"Frenzied . . . the story proceeds with consuming excitement . . . Bravo!"

—*Publishers Weekly*

"A Grade-A effort from start to finish!"

—*San Francisco Chronicle*

—1—

He struggled awake through billows of nausea. The taste in his mouth wasn't the sourness of last night's liquor; it was the frightening medicinal bite of chemical.

That terrified him.

There had to be more to this than awakening in an unknown place. He'd come to consciousness in strange places before, hadn't he? Then he had discovered he was in a hotel room on a business trip. He guessed that was how it had been.

This was different. A hell of a lot different. He could not recall one damned thing leading up to this awakening into total unfamiliarity, not one clue to explain the alien aftertaste . . . the impression that his head had been jammed full of cotton . . . the numbness of his face.

He lay on his back, eyes clamped with the fear of what he might find when he opened them. He slid his right hand upward along the weave of a blanket, then over the turned-down edge of a sheet, then up his neck and along his stubbly chin. The fingers felt deadened, as if he were wearing a rubber glove.

They found . . . a bandage? God, yes! Beginning just above his right ear. His fingers moved upward along webby gauze to intersect stiff adhesive tape. Sweat broke beneath the gauze, and it stung.

Whatever he lay on began to tilt. Or was the motion only

apparent, within his brain? He tried to open his eyes. Failed. Some gluey residue sealed them shut.

He moved the hand downward, touched a spiky eyebrow, found the sealed eye, and rubbed crust off the tangled lashes. He urged the clubby finger upward.

The eyelid cracked open. He stared into blurry brown. Was this blindness? He inched the unwilling forefinger across the bridge of his nose.

The nose wasn't there. It had been replaced by a great blob of adhesive-strapped gauze. He willed the finger to move another hard-won inch. High on his left cheek was a third dressing, this one smaller.

He fingered it, still staring upward into umber fuzz through one eye. The left lid, too, was crusted with sticky granules. He forced the clumsy finger to work at it. Then the eyelid snapped open.

He felt bursts of cold air against his lips and tongue. He was panting. Sweat made his back itch against what he assumed was a bunched sheet and unyielding mattress. He struggled to make sense out of the earth-tone blur above him, began to focus his eyes vaguely, then stared at a ceiling of mahogany inlaid with a honey-toned starburst pattern.

The intricately crafted ceiling began to drift. He nailed his stare directly above him. The ceiling stopped its nauseating shift.

The bed he sprawled in seemed gigantic, with a cherry headboard high as a hedge towering above him. Not a hospital bed. Not a hospital room.

He panned his eyes slowly rightward, along the ceiling to its ornately molded juncture with expensive grass cloth on the walls. The top of a paneled door swam into his vision. Two doorways, the far one larger than the other. Probably the room's entrance. The other a closet? Or bathroom. Now he saw a delicate upholstered chair and an elaborate three-drawer chest. Antiques.

He inched his head the other way. Slowly, so that it wouldn't start the spinning again. His gaze traveled back up the wall, across the incredible ceiling work, found the wall molding opposite, then a huge bay window with leaded glass, and lush, velvety green drapes held open with green rope tiebacks. The ivory shades were half-drawn.

There was daylight out there, but the room wasn't bright, because outside the window he could make out a shadowed wall of rough-hewn red stone blocks. Another building? Or an ell of this one?

In the farthest corner hulked an imposing mahogany dresser, five drawers with a gilt-framed mirror on the wall above it.

He dared raise his head an inch or so. The vertigo surged, then receded. A polished parquet floor extended beyond a vast maroon, cobalt, and cream Persian carpet. He sank into the pillow, exhausted by his minuscule effort. There was much more. He could feel it. He would have to bend his neck against muscles already protesting.

It hurt, but he turned his head again. Into wavering focus drifted shoes. Shiny navy-blue pumps with pointed toes. High heels. Surely not his. Then he saw that the shoes were not casually cast on the rug's fringed border. The legs crossed at the ankles; strong legs, well shaped. In hose with a bluish tint. His eyesockets throbbed, but he forced his stare higher. To the navy skirt, with hands folded in its lap. White blouse and demure string tie.

Her face was nearly as white as the blouse. He squinted for better focus; made out a squared chin and determined mouth. Straight nose and fine, high cheekbones. Full, delicately arched brows—then the remarkable hair, lustrous and shiny black as a crow's wing. She sat in a red-leather wing chair.

He worked his throat against chalky dryness. "Are—" His voice was a squeak. He swallowed, tried again. "You a nurse?"

The eyebrows rose. He couldn't read her expression.

"I'm not a nurse, Don," she said in a voice that sounded husky with concern. "I'm your wife."

—2—

He would have been willing to swear on any denomination's bible that he had never before seen this woman. That alone scared the hell out of him. Add to it the facts that the name she had used—"Don"—didn't mean a damned thing and that he had no inkling what he was doing in this remarkable room. The effect was devastating.

Holding his head hard left to stare at her hurt like hell. He eased back to neutral and stared straight up.

"You called me 'Don,'" he managed.

"Of course, darling." He heard the swish of her skirt, then she stood over him. A frown disrupted the creamy smoothness of her forehead. "It's the anesthetic, Don. It still hasn't completely worn off. You'd best get some normal sleep."

Surrender to sleep could cost him the toehold on sanity he'd managed to this point. "No. Not sleep now." God, that had sounded like Pidgin English.

Her fingers were cool on his hand. "I'd better get Dr. Horger."

He must have dozed despite his effort to remain conscious. Abruptly, a pudgy man in a white coat, with its pearl buttons straining over a blue shirt and slightly askew burgundy-and-silver-striped tie, bent over him. He hadn't heard the man enter the room.

"Ah, Mr. Franklin. How are you feeling?" The

scrunched features were set in jowly putty; the blue-chip eyes in suet sockets. He had an unctuous fat man's voice.

Mr. Franklin? He was Don Franklin? The name meant nothing. "What in hell am I doing here, Doctor?"

"You don't remember?"

Don Franklin began to shake his head. He groaned at the sudden pain. The doctor's perspiration, not quite masked by expensive shaving lotion, didn't help.

"Post-operative headache, Mr. Franklin. Don't try to move around quite yet. It will pass." The doctor pursed wet lips. "Exactly what do you recall, sir? Do you know where you are?"

Don tried to concentrate. Nothing.

"Or why you are here?"

"No." His voice cracked. "I don't remember one damned thing."

"Oh, come, Mr. Franklin. You obviously recall words. You're using them. The alphabet? A, B, C, D—" He nodded encouragingly.

"E, F, G."

"Two and two?"

"Four."

"You see? Your mother's name?"

Blank.

"I see. Your birthplace? Wife's name?"

"I—" Stinging moisture broke under the dressing across his forehead and dampened his chest, the cold sweat of fear.

The doctor gestured. "Mrs. Franklin."

She drifted into Don's view, gliding as people do in the presence of the very sick.

"Selective amnesia. He seems to have blanked out his own past. A psychiatrist could find that interesting, but I strongly recommend building physical strength before he faces that sort of ordeal."

"Rest?" she asked. "Just simple rest?"

"He's obviously suffered severe trauma, Mrs. Franklin."

"Damn it!" Don lifted a protesting hand, heavy as a brick. "Include me in the conversation, if you don't mind. What the hell has happened to me?"

She leaned over him solicitously. She smelled of woodsy

musk, and her vivid green eyes were intent on his. "An accident, darling. We were on Route Thirty, driving to Lake Algonquin. To a client's homesite. A truck ran a stop sign. We are both very, very lucky that we weren't killed. Don't you remember any of this?"

"Nothing. Nothing at all. What's happened to me?"

"Facial lacerations," Dr. Horger offered quickly. "Fractured nose. You're quite fortunate. Your wife, of course, was even luckier. Not a scratch."

"Well, thank God my wife—"

"Lori, darling. I'm Lori." He caught her quick glance at the doctor.

Horger said, "You're lucky to be alive at all, but you're even more fortunate to be in the Horger Clinic near Lake Arandaga, west of Albany, in upstate New York. To your great benefit, the police elected to send you here."

Don struggled to grasp what he was talking about.

"This clinic of mine specializes in plastic surgery, Mr. Franklin. I dread to think what an M.D. in any of our regional emergency rooms might have done with that face of yours."

There was self-satisfaction in Horger's tone that Don found . . . What? Nonprofessional?

"But my loss of memory, Doctor. What—?"

Horger waved that aside. "Temporary, sir. The effects of lengthy anesthesia, following severe trauma, are unpredictable. Rest, perhaps an extended recuperative period with Mrs. Franklin, should speed recovery."

The doctor's bland assurance was unnerving. Don had the creepy feeling that something was being withheld, something they didn't want him to know.

The cottony nausea had receded enough to permit him to move his head more freely. "This is one hell of a room, Doctor. All this for plastic surgery?"

"Ah, Mr. Franklin. You, too? Another uninformed denigrator. No matter. You'll appreciate my work when the bandages are removed. But your question is appropriate enough. There is another adjunct to this establishment, the highly profitable one of weight control."

"A fat farm? You're running a fat farm here, too?"

"We prefer the term *health enhancement*. But my true vocation is the readjustment of nature's carelessness, and of course, the repair of grievous tissue damage. As in your case, sir."

Horger moved to the carved-cherry footboard. Beneath his jacket, his ponderous belly rested on the footboard's cornice. The fat doctor brushed his hand across his glistening upper lip. Why did the man sweat so in this cool room?

"Now that you've had a chance to relax, Mr. Franklin, let's try again. Your mother's name?"

Still a total blank.

"Where were you born, Mr. Franklin?"

Don compressed his lips. Beneath the cheek bandage, stitches picked.

"Your home address?" Horger's voice was casual, but Don detected a tense undercurrent.

His own voice quavered, "I can't answer any of that. Isn't there some way you can . . . jolt me back to reality?"

"Oh, there are certain experimental techniques, but when selective amnesia is the result of severe cranial trauma, I strongly advise rest, relaxation. The brain has a remarkable capacity to heal itself. I'm optimistic."

Horger glanced at the chronometer on his thick wrist. "I'm afraid I'm overdue elsewhere. You are making splendid progress, sir. No need for undue concern. Mrs. Franklin, a word with you, please."

Alone in the overwhelming room, he began to miss her. Or miss her presence; anyone's presence. He diverted his concentration away from such self-pity and reviewed what he knew about Donald Franklin. Then a cold wash of helplessness rippled through him as he realized he had not recalled one solitary personal fact on his own. It all had been coached input.

Then the woman—Lori, damn it!—returned. He cleared his throat. "What was that all about?"

"Finances. We'll have to make up the difference between his charges and the Blue Cross, Blue Shield coverages. But he's not going to charge me for my room."

"Your room?"

"I'm next door, dear. He said this is the slow time of the year, and the room would be empty otherwise. He seems decent enough, don't you think?"

"He seems offhand, superficial, and nervous."

She took his hand in both of hers. "Give him a chance, Don. All this will work out. You'll see."

Something was missing. Something in her voice, as if she had gotten her lines right but they lacked conviction. Could he be more damaged than they dared tell him?

The room went gray. He slept, her hands still holding his.

—3—

He felt like a first-grader. Even dumber. Surely there wasn't a first-grader in the nation who had to ask his teacher, "Tell me who I am."

"Donald R. Franklin," Lori explained with studied patience. "The *R* stands for Roberts, your mother's family name."

"Donald Roberts Franklin," he repeated slowly. "What's her first name?"

"Leala was her given name."

"Was?"

"She's dead, Don. Four years ago, of abdominal cancer."

He felt no loss. This was classroom learning.

"And my father?" He was half-sitting now, the ornate head and footboards having disguised an electrically adjustable hospital-bed frame.

"He's gone, too, Don. He didn't want to go on after your mother died. He never did enjoy retirement, after forty years in the printing business. His heart gave out."

She had pulled her chair close. Her earnestness was almost touching.

"His name . . . Lori?" Easier this time. "What was my dad's name?"

"Phillip. Phillip James Franklin. When he retired, he was vice-president of Carlisle Press." Her voice was softer than her determined face, he thought.

"Where? Where did they live, I mean?"

"Pittsburgh. You were born there in nineteen forty-four."

"I take it we're still in the year nineteen eighty-four."

For the first time she smiled. She had even little teeth, brilliantly white. He was struck by the satiny perfection of her mouth.

"Yes, it's still nineteen eighty-seven. April seventeenth."

"Five days."

"What?"

"I've been here five days. The last date I remember is the twelfth."

"Do you remember what you were doing on the twelfth?" Her tone seemed abruptly tense.

"An appointment . . . something about lunch?"

Her ebony eyebrows drew together briefly. Then the creamy forehead smoothed. "You remember the date but nothing at all about what happened that day?"

He tried to force his brain around its wall. No use. "Only the date." The grass cloth shimmered, returned to focus.

"Don, are you all right?"

He waved a weak hand. "I'm okay now. Tell me about you."

"Lori is for Lorraine, darling. With two *R*s, one *N*. Née Lorraine Frances Shannon." The gorgeous eyes searched his. "Oh, Don, doesn't any of this strike some memory chord?"

"I'm sorry, Lori."

"It will. I'm sure it will." She squeezed his hand. "Philadelphia."

"Philadelphia?"

"That's where I was born and grew up. My father was Joseph John Shannon, a construction foreman. Mother's name was Margaret. Margaret O'Connor. Solid Irish Catholics."

" 'Was'?"

"Both of them are dead, Don. We're a pair of orphans."

"Any brothers, sisters?"

"None on your side. I have a sister, Peggy. In Montreal. She was a flight attendant for United until she married Sam

Roseman. He's in the raincoat business." She made a little grimace. "My parents weren't too happy about that. He's not a Catholic."

"Were they happy about us?"

"You're not a Catholic, either, darling. They weren't much more delighted with a failed Episcopalian than they were with a conscientious Jew."

"But now they're gone."

"Three years ago. A six-car crash in the fog on the Schuylkill Expressway."

"Children?" His mouth was parched. None of this struck the tiniest spark of familiarity.

"They have two."

"Who?"

"Peggy and Sam."

"I meant us."

The vibrant eyes dropped. "You don't remember anything at all about us? Those awful tests? The damned thermometer? All that embarrassing procedure we went through for nothing?"

"Lori, I can't recall one blessed thing about you, myself . . . us. Nothing at all."

She brushed the back of a cool hand against his unbandaged cheek. "It will all come back. I know it will."

"I sure hope so. Oh, hell, I'm sorry. My face hurts. My head is stuffed with wet wool, and everytime I draw a blank, it scares the daylights out of me."

"Don, I realize that." She withdrew her hand slowly. "Will you be all right if I lie down for a while? I was a little shaken up, too. I'm still not quite back to normal."

"Sure. Sorry. I've been thinking only about myself."

She kissed the exposed area of his forehead below the bandage. "Don't be discouraged. It's all going to work out."

"Lori?" His call was a pathetic croak.

She turned back.

"What do I do? How do I make a living? You said we were on our way to see a client."

"To inspect a client's homesite, Don. You're an architect. Get some rest. We'll talk about it later."

Ergo that Lake Algonquin business. Pieces were falling into place, but how many more ends were loose?

"Could I have something to drink? Maybe ginger ale or a Coke?"

"I'll have the nurse bring something. See you for lunch."

The nurse showed up ten minutes later, a white-clad block of a woman with her blue-striped cap perched on straw-straight orange hair. The plastic name tag on her low-slung bosom read J. OAKFORD.

"Here's your ginger ale. Can you manage it by yourself? Need anything urgent, hit the button there on the night table. Otherwise, lunch'll be up in an hour."

She had the voice of a police matron, but suddenly he didn't want her to leave.

"You've been in here before?"

"In and out. You been sleeping a lot."

"They tell you what's wrong with me?"

Wrong question. It turned her off like a switch. "Get some rest, Mr. Franklin." Her voice was ice.

"Damn it, people keep saying that."

"Do it, then." She shut the big noiseless door behind her.

He sucked on the bendable plastic straw and let the cold bubbles percolate down his throat. They were real, but how much of the rest of this was?

In contrast with the grandeur of his isolated mansion, Elmo Horger operated out of a spartan office tucked away in the rear of the main floor. Lorraine had been impressed with the magnificent carved-oak front doors and the breath-stopping great hall, now a huge lobby, its parquet floor strewn with oriental carpets, each of which framed a conversational arrangement of antique chairs and settees. This was obviously an establishment for the financially untroubled.

What she had found abysmally unimpressive was Horger's office. The chrome-and-green metal chairs were cold and uncomfortable. He had a pastel-green steel desk. A steel desk! Worst of all was the slitty, narrow-slatted Venetian blind across the inadequate window set too high in the yellow plaster wall. The only up-to-date touch was the Bogen intercom terminal on the table behind him.

She sat primly in the frigid grip of his damned clearance-sale chrome. The air-conditioning unit beneath the window was running overtime, though New York State's mid-April was comfortably cool. She took a flat red box of Sherman's Casinos from her purse, queen-sized brown cigarettes with gold filters.

"Do you mind?"

"Not at all. I'll join you. Oh, no, thank you. Not one of those." He fumbled under his white jacket to pull forth a phallic chunk of a cigar. It took the flame from his gold Dunhill lighter hard, finally caught, and produced eye-stinging smoke.

He leaned back, cocked his cigar in his right hand, and contemplated the acoustical-tiled ceiling.

"I'd say it has gone exceptionally well, don't you think, Mrs. . . . ah, Franklin?"

"The jury has barely retired, Doctor."

"Oh, come, come. We're right on schedule. He's doing beautifully. He will be discharged in another few days. You are to trust me, Mrs. Franklin."

Was she transmitting antipathy so strongly that even his self-centered receptors could pick it up?

"You are to trust me as long as you are in this institution," he said. "After that, success will depend entirely on you." He stuck the cigar into his lips' wet O and slowly turned it. Then he took it out with an audible little pop. "You and the Pyremisine, of course."

"The Pyremisine. How dependable is it, Doctor?" She exhaled a bluish cloud of her own in his direction.

"Close to one hundred percent in controlled test usages. Of course, we can hardly consider the environment con-trolled once you leave here."

"You underestimate me."

"I suspect that is mutual."

"We each have our specialties," she said.

"Yours interests me." He reinserted the cigar in the glistening pucker.

"You do your job, I'll do mine." She glanced around the unappealing office. "Why this?"

"Our austere surroundings?" He chuckled and leaned toward her confidentially. "I hold all staff consultations in here. They are brief and to the point because this is not a comfortable office. And my people find it difficult to insist on budget increases and raises when they are in this atmosphere. You understand?"

You cheap son of a bitch, she thought. But she offered a smile.

"My personal quarters are quite a different experience," he said. "Might you care to have a look?"

She stubbed out her Casino in the clunky glass ashtray on his desk, a single, hard stab.

He sat back. "While you are here, Mrs. Franklin, you may as well enjoy yourself. Surely you must be bored by your reclusive residency upstairs. Every meal with a vegetating husband? I would be delighted were you to join me for dinner tonight in the staff dining room. The fare is far more attractive than the carrot spears and broccoli in the main dining hall, I assure you."

"Thank you, but I will continue to join my husband in his room for all meals."

"Your husband." He shrugged. "Of course." The cigar dropped an untimely ash that exploded in a gray cascade down the front of Horger's white coat. He slapped at the offending smear.

"I trust we understand each other." She uncrossed her ankles to stand. Horger grunted to his feet with her.

"A pleasure to have you here, Mrs. Franklin. I'm sure you are finding our several services A-one."

"Hawaii," she said abruptly. "That's essential, you realize."

"Why Hawaii?"

"Because of its isolation."

He studied the cigar. Then he looked up at her again, his eyes bemused.

"Aloha, Mrs. Franklin."

—4—

On the third day—actually the sixth, they'd told him, but the third in his consciousness—Don was able to sit up with no vertigo at all. He had only a sensation of needle pricks at the perimeter of his upper face, nose and cheek repairs. Much more the nose. At times, with no warning, the nose throbbed like hell.

What a shot he must have taken. Probably straight into the steering wheel. Forehead slammed its top arc, nose flattened on its hub, cheek smacked the left side.

"Breakfast, darling. How are you this morning?" Lori—radiant in pastel blue trimly cinched at the waist with wide, navy patent leather—with tray in both hands, butted the door wider for Nurse Oakford, also tray laden.

"First," Oakford insisted, "this." She set the tray on the foot of the bed, popped a bitter thermometer in his mouth and fingered his wrist. "Normal enough," she announced after the standard silence. She moved the tray to his lap, then he watched her broad rump disappear out the door.

Lori had placed her tray on a small table she'd moved to her corner chair. "Cantaloupe, darling, and raisin toast," she announced brightly. "Your favorites."

They were? Give it a chance, Franklin, he told himself as he sipped the coffee, rich in translucent blue-and-white china.

"Just what was I doing when—" Because he recalled

17

nothing about it at all, he had trouble even saying it. ". . . When we had the accident?"

She nibbled delicately, swallowed. "You were standing on the brake, darling."

"Come on, Lori, damn it!" Was she trying to be funny? "I mean the job at that lake."

"The residence at Lake Algonquin, Don." Her voice sounded tightly controlled.

"Oh. Yeah." It had come back to him, but only what she'd told him yesterday. If she asked him to name the client, he would be at a loss.

Her even teeth nipped another corner off the toast triangle. "Abner will take over the project. Don't worry about it, darling."

She had filled him in on the firm last night. Franklin, Jellicoe & Associates, in Baltimore. A twelve-person, privately owned operation. Mostly residential work with occasional commercial commissions. She had already notified Abner Jellicoe, had briefed him on the problem, and he would cope. For an indefinite period, Lori had assured Don. No problem there. Don sipped his coffee. No problem there, but plenty of problem here, Jellicoe.

In their mid-morning discussion, ninety minutes later, Dr. Horger assured him tritely, "The mind is an amazing organ. An amazing organ, sir. You mind if I smoke?"

Without waiting for a yea or nay, he fished a blunt cigar from the shirt pocket beneath his clinical coat, wet its rounded end, then pumped his cheeks against the flame from his lighter. Acrid smoke boiled ceilingward. Horger sank into one of the armless chairs and tilted it back on its slender rear legs. The cigar came out with a faint pop.

"My advice, sir: rest and recuperation. Some place where you and your wife will be entirely by yourselves. The Caribbean, perhaps. Or, say, Hawaii. Yes, why not Hawaii? Wonderful restorative climate and atmosphere in Hawaii, Mr. Franklin. Have you ever been there?"

Don shook his head. He could do that now without sickening consequences.

"Ah, that's my prescription, then. Three, perhaps four,

weeks in Hawaii. Not Oahu. Too congested and nerve-wracking. One of the neighboring islands, I'd say."

"The Kona Coast." Lori's sudden input drew a speculative glance from the putty-faced doctor.

"The Kona Coast?" he echoed.

"On the Big Island. It's . . . I've heard it's a wonderful blend of new resorts and old Hawaii. Off the main tourist track."

Horger puffed thoughtfully. "Sounds ideal, Mrs. Franklin. What do you say, sir?"

Don was startled by the sudden request for an opinion. They both looked at him expectantly. He shrugged. Some response.

"What a wonderful suggestion, Don. We've wanted to visit Hawaii, but something always seemed to get in the way. Now there's nothing to stop us, is there?"

Only the lack of reality. But wouldn't that be the problem wherever he went from here? Why not Hawaii, if she was so set on it?

"It's settled, then. I'll get right to work on the arrangements." She seemed childishly delighted to have something substantial to occupy her time.

"Our telephone is at your disposal, of course, Mrs. Franklin." He was a big "of courser," Don had noted. The very soul of cooperation was Elmo Horger.

"When do you think he will be able to travel, Doctor?"

"Perhaps in a few days he will be up to the automobile ride to Albany County Airport. From there, the air travel should not be overtaxing if you are able to secure first-class tickets. More leg-and-seat room, greater attentiveness on the part of personnel . . ."

Again they had reverted to consideration of the pathetic sack in the bed as if he were inert filler. Damned if he'd just lie here and take it.

"My wallet," he demanded.

"No need, darling. I'll handle all the details."

"Lori, please get my wallet and whatever else was in my pockets." He had just been struck with the idea that such personal effects might prove the impetus for real recovery.

"I'd best be about my routine," Horger announced in his

wattly voice. "If you do want your husband's personal effects—"

"*I* want them, damn it!"

"Certainly, darling. Doctor?"

"Whenever you wish, Mrs. Franklin." At the door, he gave her a deferential—or was it faintly mocking?—little bow.

Don had to go to the can, but he hated to. Not because of the bathroom itself. In fact, it had a pleasant decadent ambience with its big porcelain tub raised off the tile on cast-iron lion paws, broad basin on a fluted column, and a toilet on a raised marble platform as if it were a true throne.

What had gotten to him was the merciless glare of the fluorescent ceiling fixture. Yesterday he'd looked like death barely resuscitated. Bloodshot gray eyes squinted at him from huge areolas of blue brown bruise. God, what a pair of shiners! With those eyes and the stark-white gauze of his three bandages, he'd looked like a Heidelberg loser without the glory. The bathroom had slowly rotated in yesterday's vertiginous drift.

Now, though, the palatial sink, vitreous throne, and iron-clawed tub stayed nicely put. But the return of full balance made the bandaging all the more blatant. He was a raccoon-eyed mess!

He brushed his teeth with an unfamiliar red-handled Oral-B, thumbed a strange can of lime foam, and shaved with a Gillette he couldn't recall having seen before yesterday. Three days of beard—they'd told him six, and yes, it could be—came away with painful pulls. When he returned to the museum of a room, Lori had made the bed and turned it down.

"Wouldn't you rather be in your own pajamas?" She held out a pair of light greens with white piping. He took them and turned back to the bathroom.

"For heaven's sake, Don. We've been married eleven years."

He felt stupid, stripped off the fetid gown, stood naked. She busied herself with the pillows, but he felt exposed.

The fresh pajamas were cool against his skin. He sat on the bed, swung his legs under the sheet and blanket. The banked pillows were welcome after his modicum of exertion.

"Tell me about us, Lori." What a ridiculously pathetic request.

"About us?"

"I don't remember one blessed thing about myself, or about you. I feel so damned . . . inadequate."

She sat prettily on the edge of the bed, trailed her fingers down his sleeve. "Where should I begin?"

"Where we began, I suppose. When we met. Where we met. How we met."

"It was in New York, at the Metropolitan Opera."

"We met at the Met." How could he recall a nickname yet forget a whole life? "You're kidding."

Her smile was dazzling. He'd never seen prettier teeth—that he could remember. "It was winter. January. After the performance, it was impossible to get a taxi in the snow. Then a limo splashed slush all over my legs. You came out of nowhere, grabbed my arm, and pulled me into the street shouting, 'Pregnant woman!' That got attention—and we shared the taxi. I was staying at the Essex House, on a buying trip for Wanamaker's. That's where I was working then. You were at the Plaza. So we were almost neighbors anyway. Will you ever forget that weekend, darling?"

"I'm afraid I have."

"Oh, God! I'm sorry." She squeezed his hand. "It's so hard to get used to. But I'm really trying, Don."

She was more appealing when she was vulnerable, when she dropped her crisp officiousness.

"I gather it was quite a weekend."

"We took in New York like two tourists—the ferry ride to see the skyline, the Empire State observation platform, Rockefeller Center. We did everything."

"Everything?"

The green eyes danced. "That, too. The second night. By then, I hadn't an iota of virtuous hesitation left. You were a big, handsome, self-assured architect. I wanted you like sin, and it was wonderful sin."

"Virtue to the winds on a January weekend at the Plaza. Or was it the Essex House?"

"Your room at the Plaza. I remember it overlooked Central Park. A storybook room for a storybook weekend." She gave him a quirky little smile.

"I keep hoping for a flash of something familiar. Maybe a glimpse of how you looked then or words already heard. It's no damned use, Lori. It's like I have no past at all." He grimaced. "I wonder if this is how a thinking robot might feel?"

The flawless iridescent-coral lips twitched. Abruptly, she stood. "I'll get your wallet."

Following the directions of a jogging-suited, young male staff member in the office area, she found Horger at the observation window of the indoor pool. Beyond the wide glass rectangle, a dozen clients splashed and shrieked in the crystal water, like liberated schoolgirls. The fluorescents in there were pink-tinted, Lori noted; no doubt to impart a healthy glow to the palest-skinned urban matron. Except for the butter-haired supervisor, trim as a starlet in her orange HORGER CLINIC emblazoned swimsuit, sizes had to range from stuffed twelves through jiggly eighteens.

Elmo Horger's watery blues were riveted to a hyperactive brunette whose purple maillot threatened to split like a grape skin with every thrash.

"Doctor?"

He started visibly, recovered quickly. "Do you happen to have a swimsuit, Mrs. Franklin? You should make use of our pool. Or may we lend you a suit? Size ten, perhaps?" His eyes appraised her openly.

"Thank you, but I'm not here for a vacation. I'd like to get Mr. Franklin on the road as soon as we can safely do that."

"Of course." Horger turned back to the window and clasped his hands behind his back, the cigar in his grip. It made a stubby and somehow lewd tail behind his medical coat. "Ah, my wonderful white whales," he murmured. "How they love to be steamed, soaked, sweated, starved, then returned to husbands who probably are as gratified with this brief respite as are they." He swung around, hands still locked behind his heavy buttocks. "We'd better begin it tomorrow."

He'd thrown her with his sudden change of thought.

"Begin it?"

"The daily Pyremisine therapy. Surely you have noticed his assertiveness this morning."

They stood in the apple-green ceramic-tiled hallway that connected the pool building with the locker room addition to the old mansion. The turflike carpeting, a darker green, crunched beneath the thin soles of her Italian pumps. The tang of chlorine nipped at her sinuses.

Apparently, he couldn't take conversational silence. "I enjoyed that tender little episode after breakfast, the story of your New York tryst."

"Is the monitoring so damned necessary?" she asked sourly.

"You find it inhibiting? If we are to control his recovery, I'm afraid it's essential."

"There's no chance he might find the mike?"

"None, my dear. It is built into the wall behind the bed." He inserted his cigar into his meaty smile and rotated it slowly. "Are you quite sure you wouldn't enjoy the use of our pool? The thundering herd will be out of there shortly. You would have it all to yourself."

"About the Pyremisine, Doctor, when we leave here."

"You will be given a supply adequate for at least three weeks. It will be in the form of hundred-milligram tablets. They are quickly effervescent in liquid. It does have a slightly bitter taste, but coffee masks it nicely. You realize how vital the medication is, of course. Without it, everything we've done here could fall apart."

She was silent. He detached his cigar with that repellent pop. "You don't think much of me, do you, Mrs. Franklin?"

"I think it's unfortunate that Dr. Krupas had to leave so abruptly."

"He considered his work here done, and he was needed elsewhere. Come, your husband wanted his wallet; we'll give him his wallet."

The wallet, keys, change, and pen were in a manila

envelope in Horger's steel desk. He handed her the packet and perched his rump on a corner of the hard-rubber desktop.

"Don't underestimate me," he said in a voice that was as much plea as warning. "Judge me when the bandages come off."

"It's not the mechanics I'm worried about. It's your followup to Dr. Krupas's technique."

"The only concern now is the medication. The dosage will begin tomorrow. You'll see a change." He contemplated the cigar's ash. "Aren't you finding your stay here tedious? We could drive into Cloverdale this evening. A quiet drink, some music."

She'd had it with this fat medical mercenary. "Call off your campaign, Horger. I'm not interested. Go sleep with your cigar. All my hours here belong to that man upstairs."

He grinned wetly. "You're such a good soldier, Mrs. Franklin."

Sitting up without assistance, Don opened the manila envelope and dumped its contents on the blanket. Lori, knees drawn up in her corner chair, busied herself with a magazine, but he sensed that she was watching him.

The wallet was reddish cowhide, a fairly new Pierre Cardin with the stylized *P* encircled in an embossed corner. Eight twenties, ten tens, three fives, seven ones. Two hundred eighty-two bucks for a trip? It looked like he traveled a little light, until he found the credit cards: American Express, VISA, MasterCard, Deardorff's International, Shell, and Texaco. All neatly imprinted with DONALD R. FRANKLIN.

There was more. A Maryland driver's license, its small red-and-white card encased in hard plastic, his photo taking up most of the left-hand side. So this was what he looked like under these bandages. An even, sober gaze from level gray eyes. Slightly furrowed forehead rising to thinning dark hair. A longish face.

Behind the license in its plastic window there were a Maryland AAA membership card and a Continental Insurance card. From that pocket, he also dug out a compact clutch of business cards, nice-quality off-white stock with raised blue letters. FRANKLIN, JELLICOE & ASSOCIATES, 26th and Howard, Baltimore MD 21218. DONALD R. FRANKLIN, AIA, precisely centered. Phone number, a 301 code, lower left.

"Nothing," he muttered. "Not one item here means a thing to me. Wouldn't you think I'd have a hint of recall? A wallet is a pretty damned personal thing."

She glanced up but said nothing.

He fingered the key ring, a split-steel circle on a leather tag embossed with a script *F*. Two car keys for a Chrysler product, two brass keys he assumed were house and office keys, and a smaller key that probably fit his desk.

The pen was a slim, gold-plated Mark Cross ballpoint. He stirred the loose change. Not an echo of familiarity here.

"Don't let it throw you, Don." She had the perception of a shrewd psychiatrist. "I'm sure you'll feel differently tomorrow."

She was sure as hell right about that.

—5—

When he awoke the next morning, he felt more like himself. Pause for laughter, Mr. Franklin. More like what self? In the bathroom mirror, the reflection of an enigma looked less like a panicked raccoon, more like the Polaroid on his driver's license, allowing for the three obscuring bandages.

Breakfast, grumbled in by the heavy-bodied nurse, was a step forward: pineapple juice, a Belgian waffle with syrup, bacon, and coffee. He had already begun when Lori carried in her tray. She was dressed in a pants suit of some flowing rose fabric.

"I'm sorry. I didn't wait. Pretty hungry today. And I'm glad to report that I've managed a bath, and I'm feeling a hell of a lot better. You think Fat Elmo might let me wander around the premises?"

The coffee was stronger this morning. He added another spoonful of sugar. An Albany paper was on his tray. For the first time since the accident, he found himself at least moderately interested in the outside world.

For not-quite-forty minutes. Then a lassitude began to engulf him, a state of comfort and detachment he hadn't felt since he'd been here. He let the paper drop across his abdomen and lay back against the banked pillows.

"Don?" Her voice was remarkably musical. "Are you all right?"

"I feel . . ."—he concentrated on the elusive words—"fine. Just fine."

"You're sure?" She moved her chair close to the bed. "Listen to me, Don."

"I'm listening."

"Let's check your short-term memory, all right?"

"Sure, let's check." He felt a sense of inebriation in this magnificent room, with a gorgeous woman who appeared so concerned that it struck him funny.

"Be serious, Don. Listen to me. What was my maiden name?"

He grinned hugely because she was going to see how incredibly smart he was. "Sharon. No . . . no, it was *Shannon*. Lorraine Shannon. Pretty name, honeybun." She looked great this morning. He felt a new excitement, a stirring.

"Good, Don. Very good. Where do you work?"

"Franklin and Jellyroll." He couldn't suppress a giggle.

"Be serious, Don."

"Jelly . . . Oh, Jelli*coe*. That's it. Franklin and Jellicoe and somebody else . . . I've got it! Franklin, Jellicoe and Associates. How'm I doing?"

"Fine, darling. I think you're ready for new information. Concentrate now. See if any of this is at all familiar."

He squeezed her hand. She really was a pretty thing.

"You were born in Pittsburgh in nineteen forty-five. Graduated from Lawrenceville prep—"

"I went to Lawrenceville?" Had he heard that name before?

"You graduated in nineteen sixty-two, then went to the University of Pennsylvania, class of sixty-six. Doesn't any of this strike some sort of responsive chord?"

"Nope," he said with a grin.

"Don, be serious," she insisted. Then she led him through his two-year army stint—all at Fort Meade—his early career with a New York real-estate-development firm, his switch to a Baltimore-based consulting-engineering group, his meeting Abner Jellicoe on a shopping center job, and the decision to depart Central Engineering Associates to establish an independent firm with Abner.

"I'm no dashing knight, am I?"

"We don't live in the dashing knight era, darling, and that's enough for one morning. Now read your paper."

Horger bustled in a few minutes later, spattered unctuous good mornings, and took Don's face in pudgy fingers. He turned him left, right, up.

"So," he murmured.

"So, what?" Don echoed with the damned inane grin.

"So I think we can remove the bandages." He pressed the bedside call button. The nurse appeared promptly, bearing a plastic tray.

The alcohol-drenched cotton was cold against Don's forehead. Then the cloying pressure of the bandage lifted. He felt cool air where it had been.

The cheek bandage came off as easily. The wad of gauze across his nose was more troublesome, secured as it was by so many adhesive strips. It, too, finally gave way under Horger's dabbing with the soaked cotton.

From the tray, the doctor offered a small mirror. "I invite you to view the results, sir."

Don saw the face on the driver's license, but with changes. His forehead was smooth now. And the nose . . .

"I must confess," Horger said as he watched Don run tentative fingers across the now unfurrowed brow, "I took advantage of the opportunity to erase some of the ravages of time. No additional charge."

"The nose job was another fringe benefit?" If so, the good doctor should have stayed with foreheads because the nose was off-center, canted several visible degrees to the left.

Horger bristled. "If you'd seen what I had to work with, sir, you would be more appreciative. When the swelling is completely gone, the effects of reconstruction will not be so pronounced, I assure you. In the future, you might consider wearing your seat belt."

The cheek work appeared routine but not as neat a suturing job of what must have been a nasty laceration. All in all, except for the off-center nose, the work did appear to be that of a skilled surgeon. Maybe he had underrated Fat Elmo.

"I guess I owe you thanks, Doctor." Don found himself grinning stupidly again.

"No need, sir." Horger took gauze and adhesive from the tray. "The nose does require a minor bandage for another day or two." His fingers patted the new smaller dressing in place. "There you are. Fit to travel."

"Travel?"

"Around the facility. Not quite yet around the world." Horger took the tray from the night table and handed it to the silent nurse. "If you need anything, merely call. Mr. and Mrs. Franklin, have a nice day."

Horger, Don thought, was a perfectly capable and reasonable professional. Why had he been so put off by the man until today?

"Your robe is in the closet, darling. I'll change my shoes. Be back in a minute."

"We're going somewhere?"

"You heard the doctor. We're going for a walk."

Why not? He scuffed into his slippers and ambled to the closet. Tottered might be more accurate. Why would that be? He'd been able to walk normally to the bathroom earlier this morning.

The big closet's interior smelled of cedar. In the light of the overhead bulb, he found his burgundy robe on a wooden hanger, its pocket emblazoned with an embroidered *DF* in white silk. Did he go in for such affectation?

Lori had brought him the robe yesterday, so he hadn't yet investigated the closet. Through vision a trifle wobbly at the edges, he inventoried a navy blue blazer with brass buttons, a tan sports jacket of nubbly raw silk, a light blue blazer with mother-of-pearl buttons, and four pairs of slacks—tan, a gray, and two blues. The clothes of a stranger, but so what? He pulled the robe from its hanger and put it on.

"Now you've gone to the other extreme, for God's sake!"

Horger made little patting motions. "Keep your voice down, *please!*"

"The man's on a high—a stupid, euphoric high. Couldn't you see that? A hundred milligrams is too stiff a dose."

"You're a doctor now? Confine yourself to your own specialty, my dear." Horger's voice oozed like cold honey. "His emotional surge is temporary, I assure you. Once his system adapts to the dosage, he will come out of the clouds and light at a manageable level. There is a necessary degree of well-being even in a balanced dosage, you understand. Without it, the medication would be ineffective. But you will have no trouble gaining control."

"I hope so, Doctor. For your sake as well as mine."

"Now, there is no call for threats. I know what I am doing." He gestured across the lobby, toward the rank of tall windows in the east wall. "The weather is beautifully warm. Walk him around out there. He'll soon simmer down to the desired reaction level."

She rushed from the stairway landing to her room, changed into flat walking shoes and washed down an aspirin. Don was sitting on the bed when she rejoined him. They emerged slowly onto the broad balcony outside the room. He whistled softly at the impressive architectural sweep of the broad staircase and the huge lobby below, but she could see that he was preoccupied with keeping his balance. Horger had better be right about the side effects diminishing.

They made their wobbly way to a small elevator at the end of the balcony adjacent to the stairs. He was doing better now, she felt, no longer thrusting a supporting hand to the balcony's balustrade or against the wall by the time they reached the elevator.

"You okay?"

"Legs are like rubber. Head's spinning a little, but not as much now."

"The doctor said some exercise will help."

"I hope to hell he's right."

The car descended slowly, stopped. She had pushed the button labeled EXTERIOR, and the opposite wall, also a door, slid open on to a concrete walk and a wide lawn still a weak green in the late upstate spring. Beyond the grass, rising like a palisade, loomed a dense woods mostly in bud. A sprinkle of new leaves showed lettuce-green against the dark branch mass.

They walked through a splash of warm sun toward the front of the building, past the massive red stones of the east wall. The deep-set mortar joints and rough-hewn block faces gave the place a fortress look. She decided it had been designed to intimidate. Small wonder it had appealed to Elmo Horger.

A straggle of other mid-morning strollers passed, soft heavy women in vivid slacks or shorts that strained to contain the bulges of too many martini-laced lunches.

The lawn in front of the main building stretched a hundred yards down a gentle slope, a broad sweep planted here and there with groupings of ornamental shrubs. A reddish paved drive curved through the lawn's close-cropped grass to a parking circle at the main entrance. There was a staff-and-visitor parking area at the lawn's far edge.

"Sun feels good," he offered as they slowly followed the walkway around to the big front entrance.

"If you keep improving, we'll be out of here soon. Then it's off to Hawaii, darling! A day in Honolulu to pull ourselves together after the flight, then the Kona Coast."

He stumbled on the broad bottom step. She caught his elbow.

"I'm not so sure I'll be fit to travel." He looked startled at having been so clumsy. "And can I just duck out like this? Drop everything and go?"

"I told you, Don, Abner Jellicoe is taking over your work until you are fully recovered."

She opened one of the big double doors and maneuvered him into the immense lobby. They couldn't afford to have him questioning details. She would have to call for the reinforcing action.

He had finished his breakfast and was paging through the scant financial section when the enervating euphoria crept through him again. Not so overwhelming this time—it didn't prompt the giggles—but for long, fuzzy seconds he failed to realize she was saying something to him.

"The phone, Don. It's ringing."

The odd whirring broke through. The squat little phone on the bedside table *was* ringing.

"Mr. Franklin?" Male voice. "This is the front desk. There's an Abner Jellicoe down here, who would like to see you if you are up to having a visitor."

Lori was curled in her chair with a copy of *Town & Country*. "It's Abner Jellicoe," he told her in a stunned voice. "Here! He wants to come up."

"For heaven's sake, how nice of Abner. Surely you'll see him."

"I . . . . Okay, send him up." If this wasn't the damndest situation. He couldn't remember what Abner looked like, let alone a single business detail Jellicoe might want to discuss.

Thank God I soaked in that swimming pool of a tub this morning and shaved, Don thought. His eyes wore paler shadows now, and the surgical repairs had noticeably lightened.

Lori opened the door to Jellicoe's soft tap. "Abner! It's so nice of you to come!"

They embraced awkwardly, the guy's right hand encumbered by a gift-wrapped package.

"Don! For Pete's sake, Don!" Jellicoe deposited the package on the night table, then reached out with both hands. He was right out of Brooks Brothers in banker's gray with a button-down blue-striped shirt and a gunmetal tie with tiny red anchors.

The two-handed approach was so corny that Don had to suppress a laugh, managing to make it a grin that he hoped passed for delight at seeing a business associate—one who he couldn't for the life of him recall ever having seen before.

Jellicoe's hands were cool with a trace of moisture. Again Don came close to laughing. Wasn't this a bit on the sappy side, two grown men holding hands, one of them with a battered face and a memory as faulty as a malfunctioning computer, the other an impeccable understudy for Errol Flynn?

Damned if Abner Jellicoe *didn't* look like a poor man's Errol Flynn, at that. In Flynn's good days, before he'd begun to come apart. Same chiseled profile and knowing eyes, same natty mustache. The problem for Jellicoe, who obviously enjoyed the resemblance—why else the carbon-copy lip hair?—was the purple thumbprint. Just below the corner of his right eye. A birthmark? It was the diameter and color of a Concord grape.

Don let his hands drop. Jellicoe took the chair Lori had pulled to the bedside for him. He hunched forward, hands clasped between his knees.

"I can't tell you how shocked I was—we all were—when we heard about this. And happy to hear from Lori that it's going to work out okay."

The guy wore a damned heavy shaving lotion. Cinnamon. Don wondered if Flynn had gone in for that kind of thing. "The job in—Where the hell is it?"

"We're talking about you, Don. The hell with the Lake Algonquin house, as far as you're concerned. I'm taking that over. No problem. We're concerned about you, fella."

"I'm okay." I can remember Errol Flynn's mustache, but I can't remember you, old partner. "I'm fine."

"All he needs is rest, a vacation, Abner." Lori stood at the foot of the bed, her hands resting on its ornate cornice.

"You mentioned Hawaii on the phone. That sounds great, Don. Take all the time you need."

Clichés for the sick. But that beat a conversation about the firm.

"Anything I can do for you? I'm on my way to Lake Algonquin right now. To see Hanrahan."

"Who?"

"Your client, Edgar Hanrahan. All he needs at this stage is the preliminary on-site discussion he was going to have with you. No problem. Well . . ." Jellicoe rose, a grinning rapier in tailored gray. "I'll get on up there. Oh, the package. Your weakness, Don. Be good now. Take it easy on the mai tais."

"The what?"

"In Hawaii."

"Oh, yeah. Thanks."

"Lori, good to see you again."

At the door, she got a peck on the cheek.

"Wasn't that sweet of him? To take the trouble to come here. Aren't you going to open your gift?"

He picked it up with fingers that wouldn't quite coordinate and broke open the taped metallic-green wrapping. A get-well card lay atop the bronze Godiva-chocolate box, a cartoon of a leering nurse with an immense hypo poised. Inside was the bold lettering, DON'T WANT TO NEEDLE YOU, BUTT GET WELL SOON.

Not very funny, and he didn't recall a single face to go with any of the scrawled names: Shelly . . . Herm . . . Mike . . . Dave . . . Sal . . . and five more, all meaningless, except Abner's. But he had just seen Abner.

"Oh, *God*, Lori! I just . . . I can't . . ."

She reached down, took him in her arms. He pulled her close, crushed her soft breasts against his chest.

The damned incongruous giggle threatened to engulf him. He choked it back. It gushed out, anyway, an idiot's gurgle. Then he was blinded by tears.

—6—

"I've got to get him out of here."

Horger made tents of his fingers and gazed at her over their peaks. "Why the urgency? We are doing very well. The nose dressing can be dispensed with tomorrow. The scars are healing as planned. The Pyremisine dosage seems to have stabilized."

"Didn't you hear him yesterday? The hysterics? He fell apart in my arms. Laughing, crying. I wasn't sure how to—"

"I thought you handled it very well, my dear. The man was caught up in a clash of emotions. The Pyremisine had suppressed what would have been considerable apprehension at encountering his business partner in his current disorganized state. The induced euphoria resulted in an emotional contradiction that had to be released. Well handled, Mrs. Franklin. Well handled, indeed."

"Nevertheless," she said with more control now, "I do feel that we must move forward promptly."

"The dosage needs time for precise balancing. The scars—"

"The scars are not that important."

"The one on his cheek is. The medication level is vital. At the outset of dosage, it can produce a feeling of giddiness. We're past that now. Sustained dosage should promote the essential dulled, submissive state. We should be certain of the exact level before he's released to you."

She took a Casino packet from her purse, selected one of her slim brown cigarettes. He lunged across the desktop and flicked his Dunhill. Her eyes never left his.

He sighed hugely and stood. "Well, I will miss the conversations from Room Three. But you are quite correct. The schedule calls for his release not later than the day after tomorrow. If you insist on gaining a day, I suppose no great harm will be done. Unless, of course, you wish to reconsider my invitation to—"

"We leave tomorrow." The son of a bitch never gives up, she marveled coldly.

"It has been interesting working with you." He opened his office door and offered her a mocking little bow. "Have a nice vacation, my dear."

Remarkably, Don felt exhilarated by the long complex flight. To a point. That point was not quite an hour west of the California coast.

On awakening this morning, he'd been buoyed by the realization that he was about to escape these elegant, yet confining, walls. He shaved, noting again the rapid improvement in his appearance. The coloration around the eyes had faded to no more than a shallow gray that could have been brought on by fatigue.

The small nose dressing had been removed yesterday by Horger's surprisingly nimble fingers. Only a reddish razor-thin line remained on the left side of the markedly angled nose. Most of the reconstruction work, Horger had told him with no reticence, had been accomplished from the inside.

The scar on his cheek was another matter, and Don was not pleased. A surgeon who could rebuild a flattened nose and leave virtually no scars should certainly be capable of suturing a simple cheek laceration without leaving this two-inch cicatrix that no amount of healing would obscure.

Well, no doubt he was lucky to be alive at all. He dressed rapidly, his balance reassuringly good this morning, and chose the navy blazer and the gray slacks.

She had come in as he knotted his tie. "Good, you're ready. Breakfast downstairs, darling, then we're on our way. I'll come back up and pack for you."

"I'm no invalid."

She kissed him lightly. "Don't push it, Don."

They ate with Horger at a corner table in the otherwise deserted staff dining room.

"Ah, sir, how are you feeling this morning?" the pudgy doctor burbled. "Pleased to be out of here, I'm sure."

"You could put it that way." Don found himself consistently uncertain of Elmo Horger. There was something less than convivial lurking not far beneath the oily surface.

A beige-jacketed young waiter clumped down platters of scrambled eggs, sausage, and toast.

Horger beamed. "Of course, my regular guests would detest me for these eggs and sausage, but consider the whole-wheat toast a concession. Coffee?" He hoisted the silver pot.

She left him there with Horger and returned upstairs to pack. After an awkward silence, Don said, "There must be paperwork, a bill . . ."

"All taken care of by your good wife. Quite a remarkable woman. Tell me, has your memory improved at all since we talked yesterday?"

"I'm not sure. Lori has filled me in so completely that I sometimes think I've remembered some fact or incident, then I realize it's something she told me."

"Well, we've done our best. R and R will have to tell the story now. Rest and relaxation, sir. Don't hesitate to indulge in plenty of both. With that fine-looking woman of yours, that shouldn't be difficult."

Now do I get the conspiratorial elbow in the ribs, Don wondered?

The doctor checked his watch. "Ah, duty calls. No need for you to rush. I'll simply be on my way." He stood ponderously and thrust down a meaty hand. "Best of luck, Mr. Franklin." His grip was warm and moist.

The car was at the foot of the broad entrance steps, a metallic-blue Buick.

"Dr. Horger arranged for it, dear," she said into his questioning look. "We are just to leave it at the airport. I'd better drive. You're still a little shaky."

The plane from Albany was a USAir DC-9, smooth enough except for a riffle of sudden turbulence near Toledo. O'Hare was its usual jet-fuel-scented madhouse of people flow. He'd been here before? Somehow the main terminal with its kiosks and central bank of shops looked familiar. At the end of the long trot down the passenger boarding ramp, they entered the sudden calm of first class.

He was impressed by the 747's big first-class section with its open center aisle flanked by the generously spaced rows of twin seats. Smack up front, with the pilots two stories above and behind. First class got there first.

They took off into the purplish industrial haze of early afternoon, extending the day by flying with the sun. She had been right. A vacation was what he needed. He felt a hell of a lot better already. Over the Rockies, he laid his in-flight magazine face down in his lap and closed his eyes.

Thirty-eight thousand feet above the California coast, his eyes snapped open.

"You want to know something?"

She looked up from the paperback she'd picked up at O'Hare.

"My whole life now is entirely what you've told me. If I didn't have you, I wouldn't have anything."

He'd meant that as a convoluted tenderness, but her reaction was surprising. Her expression of bemusement didn't change, but her pupils dilated noticeably.

Then she said, "How about some coffee?"

He shrugged. "Okay."

The tall mahogany-haired flight attendant brought the coffee in china cups with two blue-and-yellow packets of macadamia nuts that were the very devil to open. He finally used his teeth. Lori dropped hers, and he had to bend way down to extricate it from the tangled straps of the tote bag the woman behind him had stowed beneath his seat.

Less than an hour later, he found himself enveloped in comfortable lassitude. He fingered the "seat back" button, reclined several degrees and closed his eyes again. How long had they been married? Eleven years? He was no more than a remnant of what he must have been before that damned truck, yet she had never once lost patience with him. Never once had she considered her own needs before his.

The languor drained him of concentration. He surrendered to sleep, but not before one last filmy thought: With a woman like this hanging in there for me, how lucky can I be?

They emerged from the United ramp into the confusion of Honolulu International's John Rodgers Terminal concourse. Their four bags spewed onto the rotating belt in the terminal's lower level. She picked up two of them.

"Hertz," she said. The counter was nearby. "Come with me." She was still handling everything. The way he felt, as if comfortable warm sludge oozed through his arteries, he didn't care. He hoisted the remaining bags and followed.

The car, a bronze Ford, was across the dual-laned service road, in a vast garage. They dumped in the bags, she finally showing some signs of fatigue herself, he thought. It had been a long flight.

She didn't offer to drive; she got in behind the wheel, and that was that. They swung left on the exit road, then hard right into the eastbound lanes of Nimitz Highway. The setting sun filtered a coppery cast over the industrial section they passed through in light traffic. There was a softness in the air, a contrast to the leaden feeling in Don's legs. It had been a long flight, all right. He glanced at his watch. Still on Eastern time. Past midnight back there. What time was it here? He felt a slippage of reality.

They rolled into the business district on Ala Moana Boulevard. He watched the Kewalo Basin glide past, the masts of its moored yachts dead vertical in the evening's darkening calm. At the confusing intersection with Kalakaua Avenue, she turned into the gaudy tourist stretch behind Waikiki.

The crowd was a mélange of races and nationalities, most of the men in bright Hawaiian shirts, many of the women in color-splashed muumuus, all garishly lighted by neons and fluorescents of the tightly ranked storefronts. The air was rich with the tang of oriental cooking, popcorn, and fried potatoes.

Then they were beyond the traffic snarl, rolling toward a beachside park. The tourist crush thinned, then faded altogether, as Lori guided the rented Ford toward a looming purple crag he realized must be Diamond Head. The avenue was darker here, edged on the right by the low hulk of the Honolulu Aquarium. Beyond, at an isolated cluster of high buildings near the foot of the mountain, she turned into an ascending drive and stopped beneath a secluded hotel portico.

He sat exhausted. The hours in the air, the strain of travel so soon after his emergency hospitalization must have drained him more than he'd thought.

"Don? We're here, darling."

He stumbled through the glazed blue-and-white-tiled portico, conscious of the doorman's reflex thrust of a maroon-clad arm to catch him. He was tottering like an old man.

"Welcome to the Diamond Surf." The nattily jacketed desk clerk spun the registration pad around. Don stared at it, unmoving. The clerk's eyebrows lifted. He glanced at Lori. She picked up the slim gold pen and filled in the registration form.

On the tenth floor, they followed the stumpy, middle-aged bellman along a corridor that was open on one side, dropping abruptly to a waist-high parapet. The unobstructed, open-air view of night-lighted Honolulu was incredible, a carpet of gold-and-white luminescence that reached long fingers up the Koolau Mountains behind the city.

The room was huge: a suite with kitchenette, conversation area, a panoramic picture window thirty feet across the entire front, mammoth twin beds, and two lazily turning ceiling fans.

"No air conditioning?" she asked.

"No need, ma'am. Just open the window wide."

"There are no screens."

"You'll have no bugs up here. This is Hawaii."

She tipped him. She was managing all of this, and Don found himself willing to let her.

"Can we afford it?" He had to force the words against exhaustion.

"No problem, darling. We're loaded."

He could barely drag himself through a shower, and he fell into bed while she was in the bathroom. Glad this isn't a honeymoon, he thought vaguely. Then he was asleep with the lights still blazing.

In the morning, he was a different story, as she had known he would be. The Pyremisine had worn off. The gorgeous view of Diamond Head, brilliantly backlighted by the early sun, stirred her, though she had thought she was immune to such reactions. If the breathstopping view did this to her, it would inevitably do the same to him.

Room service was prompt, and she awakened him with a cup of rich Kona.

"What . . . time is it?"

"A little after eight. We have one day here. You don't want to sleep it away."

She was right about the impact of the glorious mountainscape just beyond their tenth-floor sanctuary. He stared. "My God, that's incredible!" Impulsively, he pulled her close. Then he tilted her face upward, kissed her. "It's still early . . ."

She considered. What would be natural? Above all, every detail had to appear fitting. "Shave first, darling. I love your shaving lotion." She should. She had selected it herself, as she had selected everything else he had with him, primarily to make sure the outer clothing had Baltimore labels.

She freshened his bed, plumped the pillows, then slipped off her silk robe. She waited beneath the cool sheet and light blanket in her white tricot nightgown. No precautions necessary. She'd had a tubal ligation four years ago for career purposes.

He emerged in his pastel pajama bottoms. He was spiced with the Halston Z14. He stood between her and the huge panoramic window, silhouetted against the climbing sun that flooded the room in a golden wash. He pulled the drawstring, kicked free and slid into bed beside her.

She let him make the moves. He held her in a long, side-by-side embrace. Then he slipped her nightgown to her hips and gently pressed her back. She relaxed and accepted. The spiced lotion did help.

His cheek touched hers. She felt the rasp of the scar. Then she could feel him begin to slide into the Pyremisine's grip. There was a slackening of muscle tone, an encroaching inertness. His body pressed down as the drug infiltrated brain cells, inhibited perception, and loosened muscles.

According to Horger, he should have now reached the threshold of mild euphoria. Maybe that would contribute. She experienced an unexpected but only superficial flutter of response. She needed more than this. He needed not much at all. He started to say something. His voice caught, and she felt his abrupt release.

"Sorry," he murmured. "Apparently, it's been a while. Sorry . . ."

"Wait, darling," she whispered. "Don't—" She thrust upward, gasped. "Oh, that was nice," she breathed.

Convincing? After all, this was supposed to be an eleven-year marriage.

An hour later, they left the Ford in the cool ground-floor level of the three-block-long Royal Hawaiian Center on Kalakaua. She had talked him into looking for a pair of bathing trunks, a ploy to use up part of this day in Honolulu.

The rest of it, they spent working their way west—plodding through the huge Ala Moana Shopping Center, then the unusual Ward's Warehouse with its odd in-mall parking. There she bought him a Hawaiian shirt with a pattern of tan vines.

When she'd tired of his languid compliance with her shopping spree (they'd made the small tactical error of giving her carte blanche on the credit cards), she asked him what he'd like to do. He was pretty well worn down, he admitted. Maybe they'd tour Pearl Harbor on the return trip, but now he just wanted to go back to their room and take it easy.

They had dinner in the hotel's Outrigger Room and stayed not quite an hour afterward, listening to the whangy music of a hybrid combo: an electric guitar, electric piano, and a drum array. Quite early, his face took on the gray pallor of exhaustion. She hustled him back to their tenth-floor extravaganza. He was eager to call it a day. The Pyremisine might have been enough, but she had also kept him on the move and filled his deadened mind with the splash and clamor of central Honolulu. She wanted to keep him off balance to head off rational analysis. She felt she had succeeded beautifully so far.

The Big Island could be another matter entirely.

The less-than-two-hundred-mile flight from Honolulu International's Inter-Island Terminal took not much more than an hour, even with Hawaiian Air's intermediate stop at Maui's Kahului Airport. From there, the DC-9 was off again in twelve minutes, angling steeply past the towering crest of Haleakala, Maui's dormant volcano to the east. Then the rough coast fell away. They climbed over the gunmetal blue of the open Pacific.

She had administered the Pyremisine at eight-thirty, when room service delivered their continental breakfasts. She never failed to be impressed by the drug's efficacy. In less than the time to dress, it visibly wilted his initiative and produced a near-abject receptiveness to suggestion.

How long could she get away with this? Long enough, she hoped, or the whole intricate structure could come crashing down, with her hopelessly caught in its wreckage.

The rumble and shake of descending landing gear told her they were starting down. She had been to Oahu and Maui before. The Big Island would be a new experience.

It wasn't like the other two islands at all. The Keahole Airport buildings themselves were a jolt; low, thatched structures resembling the administrative huts of some isolated jungle village. Then, for unremitting miles, there stretched the rubbly carpet of congealed lava, dead black except for occasional silver gray or dun-colored intercessions of older cascades down the long slope of now-dormant Hualalai, its 8,300-foot crown shrouded in clouds ten miles to the east.

This time, they had drawn a Toyota. Again she drove without offering him the option. The roadside was flanked with peculiarly Hawaiian graffiti, not disfiguring spray paint but neatly placed white stones on the stark lava to spell out teenaged love couplings. Nearer town, the graffiti celebrations increased, interspersed among bougainvillea plantings.

Kailua-Kona was eleven miles from the airport, first a couple of tight turns through a commercial section that could have been the outskirts of many small towns on the Mainland. Then they descended to Alii Drive along the attractive waterfront. Kailua was beautifully isolated, a little enclave mostly of tourist shops and restaurants that served clientele from the big resorts further along Alii Drive.

Beyond the town, the blacktop wound along the coastline between scattered houses and ascending tropical vegetation to their left and the lava-fingered shore opposite. The few beaches here were squeezed into coves among the encroaching lava. The sea threw itself against the black outcrops in thunderous cadence.

Next, their little white Toyota wound through the resort section, past unusual, even some magnificent, hotels, gleaming white on their lava outcrops. Then Alii Drive swung inland and climbed a long grade past startlingly green fairways. Just past the unexpected golf course, far downslope at the water's edge, sprawled what had to be their destination: the Kona Imperial.

The sparkling white seven-story resort ranged over several acres of lava, twenty feet above the thrashing surf, its stepped setbacks oddly Mayan. They descended the long drive. She rolled the Toyota up the concrete ramp to the second-floor lobby, surprisingly open, and left it in the care of the buff-jacketed bell captain.

The breezy lobby surrounded a tropical miniforest that rose from a lower level, through the open center of the elevated lobby, toward the sky above. She handled the check-in while Don stood by passively.

"The Sunset Wing, sir."

"What?"

The slender Hawaiian bellman smiled. "Your room is in the Sunset Wing, sir. An ocean view."

"Go along, Don," she prompted. "I'll be up in just a minute." She watched him follow the bellman and his luggage carrier. Don walked like a slightly drunken man trying not to show it.

When the elevator door across the lobby rolled shut, she turned to the desk clerk. "I need an outside line."

"The phones are just beyond the helicopter charter desk, ma'am." The muumuu-clad registration clerk flashed tiny teeth. A Filipina, perhaps. "Just give the operator your room number, Five-oh-seven. Enjoy your stay with us, Mrs. Franklin."

When she got the line, she dialed a 202 area code.

"Yes?" The voice was male, impersonal, but she recognized it from the single crisp syllable. That wasn't difficult; the number was for Vandenhoff's red phone.

She huddled into the hooded wall phone, though no one was anywhere nearby. "Code Franklin," she said.

"Understood."

Her mouth went suddenly dry. She swallowed, darted her tongue along her lips.

"We're here."

—7—

Richard Vandenhoff—never called Dick or Van or even Richard by anyone on his staff of fourteen—sat in a remote corner of The Greenhouse, the informal cafe in Loew's L'Enfant Plaza Hotel in downtown Washington. His back was to the wall. He always sat in a public place with his back to the wall. "Old Chicago custom," he would mutter to others in his party as he jockeyed them around so he would end up in a back-to-the-wall chair. He was indeed an ex-Chicagoan, and someone had once told him that "always sit with your back to the wall" had been a catch phrase during the Capone days. "Old Chicago custom" was as close to humor as Vandenhoff allowed himself to edge. He was a nearly humorless man.

He looked humorless behind his steel-rimmed glasses. His pale-ginger-ale eyes failed to synchronize with the rare smile of his unusually small mouth. Vandenhoff had a prissy look, the aloof gaze of an antiques expert eyeing a blatant fake. The only potentially humanizing feature of his round little head, with its slicked-back, ash-colored strands, was its propensity to cock a few degrees off vertical in conversation. But instead of lending this dedicated little man a disarming air, the head cock made him look all the more dubious of anything constructive coming from any other parts of the conversation.

This morning, Vandenhoff cocked his head over grapefruit juice, a toasted English muffin, and espresso and fixed his pale stare on the left eye of Larry LaBranche. To maintain a truly disconcerting stare, he knew, you concentrated on only one eye of your conversational partner. He chose LaBranche's left eye because the damned thumbprint-sized birthmark just below the corner of the man's other eye tended to draw the gaze and break concentration.

". . . too complicated," LaBranche was saying in that equivocal tone of his. "This whole damned project is too complicated, too expensive, and too risky."

Vandenhoff raised his espresso to pursed bloodless lips, without breaking eye contact. He sipped, then set the cup down dead center in its saucer, still holding LaBranche's not-so-steady stare. "Would you care to elucidate?" There was a degree of warning in his words, but LaBranche, typically, plunged ahead.

"It's complicated by its intricacy, for God's sake. You've already gotten half-a-dozen people directly involved, plus a lot more than that indirectly. The expense is obvious. Horger's payoff, the woman, all the damned travel, the credit card accounts, all that cover. And the risk is substantial. To us, I mean. The thing has the potential to blow the whole damned Section sky high."

"Is that it?"

"What do you mean, is that it?" LaBranche's eyes wavered. Damned if the man didn't look like Errol Flynn. It had to be the mustache.

"Any additional objections?"

"Aren't those enough?"

"No." Vandenhoff broke off his expressionless stare and carefully spread tangerine marmalade on his English muffin. If you weren't a senator's son, he thought sourly, I'm not so sure you'd be indispensable, Mr. Larry LaBranche. You might think about that when dad runs for reelection.

"You are a good tactical man," he said, "but leave the strategy to me. One, the complications themselves are protection."

"Protection?"

"Certainly. Only the woman has had an A to Z briefing. Only you and I have In-Section Need-to-Know Clearance on Code Franklin. Everyone else involved has no more than a bit or a piece." He nibbled the muffin, chewed, swallowed, while enjoying LaBranche's subconscious little fidgets. The quick touch of the mustache. The recrossing of legs beneath the flowered tablecloth.

"Point two," Vandenhoff continued, in his lecturing mode, "the potential benefit far more than justifies the risk and the expense. If you haven't lost sight of our objective, you should realize that the Section's budget is up this year, not down like that of most D.C. agencies and departments. I'm not inept when it comes to appropriations."

"I've always admired that, Vandenhoff."

"As long as our friendly Department of Justice paper shufflers continue to consider us no more than their in-house procedures analysis team, the Internal Management Section has no longevity problem." Vandenhoff finished the muffin, swallowed.

"Your third point, LaBranche. Refer to my comments on point one. The real risk is the man himself. We're counting on a technique that is still experimental."

"I thought controlled testing had—"

"Surely. Laboratory conditions, not field conditions. Chemohypnotic Displacement—"chemohypnosis"—is a technique as yet unproven in the field. That's the risk."

Vandenhoff glanced around the green-and-white dining area. The breakfast rush had dissipated to a scatter of diners. A handful of out-of-town company reps, no doubt, waiting for their target agencies to get through early morning coffee and down to federal business. He leaned closer, involuntarily. Vandenhoff didn't do many things involuntarily.

"Let's get with it, LaBranche. How did the situation up there look to you?"

"I'd say the man is sold. He accepted me as 'Jellicoe,' and from all appearances, he's accepted the rest of it as well."

"You're certain?"

"I found absolutely nothing to make me think otherwise."

"About her. How did she seem to be holding up?"

"You're worried about her, Vandenhoff?"

The cold little man cocked his head. "I didn't say that. But the assignment does present her with a considerable strain. Tension without remission can lead to premature fracture."

"You think she'll fall apart on this assignment?" La-Branche toyed with a spoon. He'd had only milk and unbuttered white toast. Vandenhoff waited. LaBranche looked up, realized he wasn't going to get a response. "I'll tell you what I think. I think I'd hate to have her as an enemy. Does that answer your question?"

He glanced at his watch. "My Boston flight leaves National in a little less than an hour, I'm afraid. You need me on this project any further?"

"Not if it progresses as designed." Vandenhoff signaled the waitress and mouthed his need for the check.

LaBranche stood abruptly, looked down at his superior, then sat again, neatly hiking his pants legs to preserve their knife-blade creases. He hunched forward.

"Damn it, Vandenhoff!"

The small man held up a warning finger, then reached up for the check.

"Have a nice day, sir." The overweight waitress retreated, working an errant blond strand back into her already loosening upsweep.

"You were saying?" Vandenhoff prompted.

"Is it worth it? Is all this worth it? My goddamned gut is on fire, and I just got *off* the project. How in hell do you stand it?"

"You'd better get on to Boston, LaBranche. That's a less critical one up there."

Vandenhoff rose. The taller man got up with him this time, waited in the lobby just outside The Greenhouse's entrance while Vandenhoff paid the check. They walked in silence around the chairs of the adjacent cocktail area and skirted the plump banquettes of a conversation module. Their steps echoed on the beige marble near the sliding entrance doors. The lobby was sparsely populated this morning, too quiet and reverberatory for classified conversation.

They passed beneath the huge central chandelier—

concentric circles of glass tubes recessed in a ceiling rectangle, surrounded by draped state flags—and skirted the Castrillo bronze on its intrusive pedestal. At the entrance, Vandenhoff said, "Just do your work, LaBranche. I'll handle the worry."

The automatic doors slid open with a subdued rumble. LaBranche, wearing an uncertain little grin, strode outside to the cab line.

One immaculate and nervous son of a bitch, Vandenhoff observed. It had been a good move to reassign him to less demanding Code Hatfield in Boston. LaBranche's part in Code Franklin had been no more than short-term peripheral reinforcement, but look at the reaction. The man was back on milk. If anyone in Internal Management Section should be sweating this, Vandenhoff knew, it should be himself.

He stepped a few paces to his right and thumbed the DOWN button of the small elevator near the entrance. He was glad he had sent LaBranche out of town so soon again. The man's manner made him nervous. No, that wasn't entirely accurate. The man's very nearness unnerved him; La-Branche's damned good looks and his height. Specifically his height. Vandenhoff disliked standing with or even near tall men. He particularly detested walking with tall men. He was a distressing four inches shorter than LaBranche.

The elevator door slid aside. He pushed the button labeled SHOPS & GARAGE. The car sank.

Was all this worth it, LaBranche had asked. My God, what a question! Code Franklin would clinch the greatest opportunity to penetrate a major criminal organization, to destroy it, since Valachi had turned government witness in 1963. What Joseph Valachi had done to Cosa Nostra, Frank Murtha would do to El Fabricante and his Sindicato Sud. In spades. Only, however, if Murtha lived long enough to testify.

It is worth it, LaBranche. We're talking about a tidal wave of cocaine that has already engulfed the DEA and everybody else who has tried to do anything major about it. So far, we've only dried up a rivulet here and there. But Murtha can pull the plug on the whole flood. He can let us shrivel up the Sindicato itself, LaBranche. That one man can blow sky high El Fabricante and his associated bastards who have already corrupted too much of this nation—those greedy money suckers with their cobra consciences. It's a war, LaBranche. You haven't quite grasped that, have you?

The elevator stopped. Vandenhoff stepped into the busy below-street-level shopping promenade, strode rapidly past the bright boutiques and food shops. The noisy concourse smelled of doughnuts and coffee. He skirted the kiosk at the juncture of the main concourses and swung down the broad side corridor that led to Comsat's lower-level entrance past a cluster of little-noticed office suites beneath the Comsat Building that dominated the south perimeter of L'Enfant Plaza's parklike open space.

Code Franklin called for the loss of their programmed subject. Sorry about that, he thought, as he pushed open the frosted-glass door discreetly labeled INTERNAL MANAGEMENT SECTION in small block letters. In a war, LaBranche, you can't afford an ulcer over casualties. You accept casualties. The tradeoff in this instance was worth the loss. One man, relatively unimportant in the scheme of the nation's welfare, in exchange for countless American men, women, and especially children, who would not rot their brains with the insidious flood El Fabricante would no longer be able to provide, now that Murtha was in Justice Department hands. That, LaBranche, is the kind of war I can put my whole damned soul into.

Vandenhoff nodded at his receptionist—a graying woman of indeterminate age—crossed the small carpeted IMS lobby, and nodded just as curtly to his secretary in her cubicle outside his office. Eleanor had a young face framed by old hair, gray and lifeless. "Give me a couple of minutes, Eleanor, then send in Stan Surjin."

He shut his office door. He wanted Surjin to knock and wait. He walked past the framed photos on the cherry paneling, low-budget plywood behind its apparent mellow richness, straightened the shot of a smiling Richard Kleindienst shaking the hand of a young Richard Vandenhoff, green out of the Commerce Department with a briefcase of dreams. That had been before real life had set in, before they'd had to close the Ellipse and the east approach to the

White House, build concrete vehicle barriers and make a bunker of 1600 Pennsylvania Avenue. Before the world turned sour and the white plague of cocaine flowed so easily past the cumbersome roadblocks the government had belatedly put in place.

Vandenhoff plopped into his tall, black executive's swivel. He had tried living with the legalistic mumbo jumbo they called justice. Then he had been converted promptly enough, the day the Department had lost Delgado. Protective custody hadn't been worth a rat's ass that day. Sindicato Sud had sent in a piecework gun, and he'd taken out two Department heavies, Señor Alberto Delgado, and half the motel wall behind them. An Ingram Model 10 could do that in an eye-blink with its gush of thirty .45-caliber slugs.

When that information had come over his phone, Vandenhoff had boiled through rage, frustration, a deep burn in the gut, then had incurred a permanent determination to fight just as dirty as the crummiest of Colombian runners. To do that, he needed the flexibility of his own near-autonomous section.

When the budget cutters hit Washington, he heard opportunity hammering on his personal door. He proposed an office dedicated to departmental efficiency. The watchdog's watchdog, not overt, not in the grim Justice Department that hulked on Constitution between Ninth and Tenth, but a small unit unobtrusively established out of the federal mainstream. Out of sight, maybe out of the minds, of the inefficient, right? You don't nail a waster by camping in his doorway. Maybe put this little saddle burr of a section in one of those obscure catacombs under, say, L'Enfant Plaza.

Where? some newcomer had asked.

Across Independence from the Smithsonian Castle, fella. Up there past the Forrestal Building. All that shows beyond that is another office building, then the hotel at the east end, the Postal Service across the way to the west and Comsat across the open square to the south.

You mean there's stuff underneath?

A shopping arcade, theater, garage, and offices. Frosted doors with names nobody notices.

How about that!

Budget me just a couple, three mil. And I'll pare the Department's overall budget down to where it'll look bare bones, but you won't even feel a nip, sir.

That hadn't been hard. What was far trickier was the accomplishment of what he'd really had in mind: the kind of war the Department could never fight above ground. That took real juggling. And it took specific kinds of people. Such as Fannon and Estrella, guerilla lawyers who did what they were told, whenever they were told. Such as Scott, who could infiltrate the President's bathroom if he had to. Not particularly, though, the likes of LaBranche, who had come with the allocation, but Vandenhoff got at least reasonable service even out of him.

And such as Stanley Surjin, who was presently tapping on Vandenhoff's office door. Chief Accountant Surjin was originally hired to handle the ostensible purpose of the Section. He could have improved the efficiency of a one-man band if that had been his assignment. He provided the Section's cover. The periodic fiscal reports that crossed the Attorney General's desk were Stan Surjin's work.

Surjin provided another service to the Section. He was a leaker. Code Franklin now called for precisely that kind of specialist.

Without punching a button, Vandenhoff picked up his phone and called, "Come!"

Stanley Surjin opened the door partway and eased through the narrow aperture he'd left himself. He liked to think of himself as unobtrusive, not an easy illusion to pull off when you were five-ten, weighed one-ninety-four, and knew you looked like a middle-aged, pink-cheeked president of Kiwanis.

But he was a C.P.A., graduate of Columbia and alumnus of Price Waterhouse. His selection by Vandenhoff to become IMS's fiscal chief had been precisely the kind of break he had been waiting for as he bumped along in Justice: a sensitive position of trust that provided him with a flow of information that had dollar value. IMS Chief Accountant Stanley Surjin was a purveyor of information for a price. He enjoyed a tax-free income that sometimes exceeded his legitimate salary. And he enjoyed another fringe benefit—the secret pleasure he took in the naïveté of his fellow staffers; in particular, the density of Little Napoleon himself, Richard Meergen Vandenhoff.

The little man was on the phone. As Surjin neared his desk he instinctively stood to forestall Surjin's towering over him and motioned his fiscal chief to wait. The gesture rankled, but Surjin kept his cool. He was good at that.

"Fine," Vandenhoff said into the phone after a lengthy silence. "See you Tuesday, then." He replaced the handset, scrabbled in a file folder, then kept staring down at it as he leaned on splayed fingers. All this was done in irritating slow motion.

"You wanted to see me?" Surjin prompted.

"Sit, Surjin."

Obedience school? Whatever turned Vandenhoff on. He took one of the chairs facing the big desk. The chairs were purposely low-slung to position the interviewee some inches lower than Vandenhoff in his looming high-backed executive chair, a psychological refinement hardly necessary since Surjin had never seen Vandenhoff sit during a meeting. Everyone else was commanded to sit. Vandenhoff stood. He stood now.

"The quarterly report?"

"On schedule." Can't get me with that one, pal. Surjin insisted on day-to-day expense reports.

"Good, very good." Vandenhoff's eyes returned to the open file folder. In spite of himself, Surjin shuffled his feet. Was he dismissed?

Vandenhoff looked up, seeming almost surprised that Surjin was still in place. "Oh, while you're here. You'll be seeing some billings from Hawaii on Code Franklin. Donald Franklin."

A little tremor rippled along Surjin's back. A vapid smile might do well here. "I hope we're not blowing the roll in a place like the Halekulani." Ha, ha. Would Vandenhoff take that flimsy bait?

"Kona Coast, Surjin. The Big Island. No slip-ups on those billings, you hear? And they're eyes-only accounts. Understood?"

"Certainly."

"That will be all, Surjin." Vandenhoff looked back down at his damned file.

In his own much smaller and carpetless office, Stanley Surjin began to sweat, not from nerves but from anticipation. He already had known what Code Franklin was set up to accomplish. What he hadn't known was the subject's alias first name and where he was to be sequestered. Surjin, in his position as fiscal officer, would have learned those essentials some weeks hence when credit card billings began to arrive, but by then the information could be of diminished value. Or no value at all. But Vandenhoff had just inadvertently handed it to him. The little idiot had to be the world's worst security risk. With him at the Section's Big Desk, the Department shouldn't let IMS handle anything larger than the ballpoint-pen inventory. Wouldn't they drop blue bricks if they learned what their little tucked-away efficiency department was really up to! But Surjin was no whistle-blower. There was nothing lower than that in this city. And there wasn't any money in it. Not a dime.

On Code Franklin, in fact, there wasn't any whistle to blow that wouldn't rack up Surjin, too.

What Stan Surjin had going on Code Franklin, though, was quite another story, and there was money in it, all right. In fact, Vandenhoff had just handed him a cool . . . what? Could be worth as much as twenty-five Gs, he guessed. Above his monthly retainer. Suddenly, he had to swallow. He was salivating.

He made the call during his lunch hour. Surjin believed in buffers. No call like this one from an IMS phone, though he doubted that self-assured little Vandenhoff had the convoluted guile to bug his own people. Surjin avoided making calls from anywhere in L'Enfant Plaza. Who knew who might be watching?

He had walked briskly down the long promenade beneath the office bridge that connected the flanking wings of the Forrestal Building, out into the tourist-clogged sidewalk of Independence Avenue, then three short blocks to cross that wide avenue and stroll up the steps of the Air and Space Museum. His careful casualness belied the anticipation that warmed his gut this bright April high noon. He also enjoyed a comforting level of self-satisfaction. He had long professed a fascination with aviation history, thus his occasional lunchtime visits here were in character, even if observed.

He made the call from a pay booth on the block-long, visitor-crammed first floor. A local call.

"White, Murtha, Honeycutt and White. Good afternoon." Eastern finishing school. A bright preppie whose father had the contacts for her summer job in downtown Washington.

"Mr. Farnum White, please." He'd be there. For his lunch, Farnum White nibbled fastidiously on fruit and nuts in his office, followed by twenty precise minutes of desk aerobics.

"May I say who is calling, sir?"

Sweet-kid voice. Wonder if she knows who certain WMH&W clients are?

"His doctor." They'd arrived at the cover phrase with a degree of satisfaction that he had later thought was a touch sophomoric. The business they transacted was anything but. In a moment, he heard another phone picked up.

"Farnum?"

"Yes." Noncommittal, even guarded.

"Clear line?"

"Yes." Even that single syllable conveyed White's tenseness, a matter of constriction in the throat, brought on by apprehension.

"He's in Hawaii. Kona Coast. Under the name 'Franklin.' Donald Franklin.

Silence.

"I want twenty-five for this, Farnum."

"From one Judas to another."

That certainly wasn't necessary, but he ate it. "I know you will have no problem getting them to cover that amount."

He was aware that Farnum White was concerned with a lot more than money amounts at this stage. He had to be sweating about the basics, about family, about Rutgers son and Vassar daughter and Georgetown-oriented wife. And his own well-tailored ass. When one of your partners offers to turn federal informer against a client—particularly such a demonstrably lethal client as El Fabricante—you had to worry about everything.

Surjin enjoyed Farnum White's helpless silence. He leaned against the wall beside the little phone carrel and gazed upward at the suspended *Spirit of St. Louis*.

"Twenty-five," White said.

"Thank you, sir!" Surjin replaced the handset with a tight smile. He walked around the information desk to the front entrance. The cash would arrive via USPS in a Woodward & Lothrop carton, which he would tell Myra in advance was a surprise present. Tens, twenties, and fifties. Used money. Untraceable. Surjin's thirty-six-year-old sister, interrupted from her work-at-home nationally syndicated gardening column, wouldn't know what she had signed for. He'd have to pick up some knickknack at Woodie's later this week to give her in a fit of brotherly appreciation. That would complete the cover.

Outside, he bought a hot dog from a street vendor at the curb of the wide sidewalk. Stanley Surjin was a frugal man. No need for a celebratory splurge. That would come in a few short years when he would resign, then quietly evaporate. At the moment, he favored Mexico, but the idea of more exotic placement—perhaps Fiji—had become intriguing of late. The only problem would be the conversion of all that accumulating safe-deposit cash into a more convenient medium. Given the well-publicized laundering activities of certain nationally respected brokerage houses, even that might not be a large problem.

But first things first. He wiped a dollop of mustard from his chin, dropped the wadded paper napkin in a nearby municipal trash bin and strolled westward, back toward L'Enfant Plaza. Beautiful out here today. Warm, sunny. Not a cloud in the open, blue sky.

By the time he had walked back the three blocks to cross Independence at the light in front of the baroque red-stone Smithsonian Castle, the key words he'd given Farnum White had traveled more than two thousand miles, almost due south.

• • •

The man was not particularly tall, but he projected an impression of height that made those around him believe he was. He also projected, without making an overt effort to do it, power—the same kind of marrow-congealing power one must have felt in the presence of a Mussolini or a Franco; the kind of paranoid omnipotence that can be directed at a personal target as intensely as at a business activity.

For a man edging sixty, he was remarkably trim at the beltline and smooth of face. The white-belted waist was flat because he had a digestion problem. "Everything goes straight through," he had told a succession of ineffective doctors. None of them had been able to correct that problem permanently, because he refused to believe it was his body's response to his bow-string-taut lifestyle. The condition wasn't going to kill him, but at times it was damned inconvenient.

The face was drum-tight as a result of a well-executed lift four years ago in New York City. It wasn't the surgeon's fault that the gather-and-tuck had not only erased any sign of facial looseness but had at the same time unfortunately accentuated the mouth. The wide, bloodless lips appeared to be stretched over teeth that did not fit. The teeth were his own, though they seemed false: too white, too even. His frequent but fleeting smiles produced a bared-fangs effect. It gave those around him the chills. The eyes, deep-set, black agate chips, never smiled but glared nearly unblinking from that taut, yellowish mask. Most of his people thought the facial tint was a light suntan, but the jaundicelike tinge was the legacy of malaria he had contracted decades ago, when he'd been a lowly "mule," running coke out of Bogotá and Caracas in 35mm-film canisters, chocolate candies with replaced centers or even—twice—sewn into the abdominal cavity of a corpse purported to be his sister on a return home to Cuba for family burial. Those had been gut-frosting early years but nonetheless small bananas.

Now he was big bananas. He owned the Bogotá and Caracas mules and those who worked out of La Paz, too. He owned, at distant ends of paper trails only the craftiest of lawyers could follow, tracts of coca trees in Colombia's Magdalena Valley and along the San Miguel in central

Bolivia. Anyone other than his people approached those guarded holdings at peril to life. He owned the intricate supply routes out of Bogotá and La Paz by air and out of Barranquillia, Maracaibo, and an obscure operation in Puerto La Cruz by boat. And he owned seven processing plants in Bolivia and Cuba, where raw yield was refined into snortable and injectible snow-pure cocaine. Thus he grew, harvested, refined, and transported this marvel of a product that created its own desire for more without the outlay of a single advertising dollar.

He was El Fabricante, "The Manufacturer." Only his mother, four close Sindicato Sud associates, and a thus-far benign God knew his true identity. One of the four business associates was Frank Murtha.

El Fabricante leaned forward in the wicker chair, elbows on his knees, and peered ten floors down into Avenida Jorge E. Gaitan. In the rarefied Andean air, the Avenida's traffic noises reached up here as clearly as if he were at street level. He liked street sounds, the putter of engines, the blare of horns, the cries of sidewalk vendors, the almost surflike rush of traffic. The people, many of them down there wearing traditional, brightly colored poncholike ruanas over Norte Americano-style suits, went about their business of making money—of which Sindicato Sud would inevitably acquire a share. Local money was as lucrative as export income.

He liked the impersonality of the mingled street noises. El Fabricante did not enjoy being noticed. He worked out of modest Miami offices, had a comfortable but not opulent apartment on Key Biscayne, and on his occasional trips to review operations down here, he took a suite in the gleaming new high-rise Bogotá Presidente, but not one of the penthouses.

He did insist on top-quality women. Adolfo Bellota, his half-German, half-Paraguayan Chaco human Doberman, who was now close by in the suite's smaller bedroom, arranged that sort of thing. El Fabricante liked a beautiful woman at hand on these brief inspection visits, providing she knew her place, exhibited much skill, and lacked curiosity.

He sat back, crossed pink-gabardine-clad legs and turned to admire Susana openly. In red and white candy-striped shorts and a frilled, white sleeveless blouse, she could have been the polished daughter of a local major business executive. Perhaps she was. Her black hair gleamed in the sun. Her dark eyes held the reserve of a cultured woman. She spoke well. Strangely, a modulated female voice of culture was more erotic to him than a curve of thigh or moon-shadowed breasts. Last night, he had encouraged her to continue talking in her fascinating low-pitched timbre while he set the pace. She responded in supple, unhurried cadence, murmuring in his ear the while, matching her release to his, then softly praised his lovemaking as they lay spent in each other's arms. A rare gem, this one.

Now reclining on the balcony's cushioned settee, her sun-bronzed arms crossed beneath young-girl breasts, she met his gaze. The full lips softened into a brief acknowledging smile. Then she closed her eyes against the sun. Tonight, after seafood at the elegant La Fragata, with its nineteenth-century sailing-ship decor, he would enjoy her again. Perhaps, if he could make this post-breakfast serenity last, perhaps even during siesta.

God knew he badly needed whatever moments of peace he could steal, now that they had Murtha. He'd been a fool to trust that man with his crooked nose and scarred cheek. What kind of procurado inteligente could allow himself to become scarred like a common Sindicator soldato? Murtha had told him it had happened long before he had become an attorney, but even so, a street-smart muchacho should have been better able to take care of himself.

Damned Irishman! Damned South Boston gringo! He should have known better than to put faith in him. Even Adolfo had seen through the man, but Adolfo thought he saw through everyone. When the news arrived that Murtha had walked through the big entrance of the United States Department of Justice six weeks ago, Adolfo had only snorted. El Fabricante had felt that he'd been struck by a bolt of lightning straight up his spine. His chest compressed his thundering heart. His left arm throbbed. Sweat glistened on his smooth saffron forehead. He thought he was dying.

But that had been only the initial reaction to Frank Murtha's astounding treason. It passed in five anguished seconds, displaced by deep-seated anguish at the betrayal, and overlaid with an urgency that had since made El Fabricante's fingers sometimes shake. It was necessary to silence the man, to remove him before serious damage was done to Sindicato Sud and to El Fabricante personally.

The cursed Justice Department worked both rapidly and slowly. With the potential weapon for catastrophic damage right in their hands, they had whisked Murtha out of reach like a puff of smoke dissolving in a breeze. That had been the fast reaction. The slow aspect served the Sindicato: the clogged gears of American federal justice could arrange official hearings no sooner than early summer. That had given the resources of Sindicato Sud some eighty days to correct the problem. But El Fabricante's most appropriately placed people, the three at Justice, had proved useless despite their generous retainers. Murtha seemed to have evaporated from the face of the planet. El Fabricante knew he would not appear again to the public eye until the cumbersome wheels of American bureaucracy materialized him before a Senate committee not much more than three weeks hence.

Murtha was a time bomb ticking in some remote Midwestern hotel or New England fishing cabin or on a federal cabin cruiser in a San Diego marina. The crooked-nose bastardo could be anywhere. Anywhere. Small wonder that in moments of physical delight with such confections as Susana here, his brain could not totally shake the fury at the defection of his trusted procurador or the menace of the man's act.

"Señor Montero?" The sudden lilt of her voice surprised him, musically cajoling. Montero was the name he used for this trip; Enrique Montero. But he never encouraged the women to address him by his alias's first name, not even in the most intimate of moments.

"Sí, Susana favorita?"

"You looked so grim, Señor Montero. Is this not your holiday?"

"You are right, Perdone, perdone, favorita. Perhaps

today we should visit the—" He turned away from her to the tapping on the balcony's closed glass door. Adolfo used the nail of a forefinger. His sharp-featured face wore a compelling set. El Fabricante nodded.

Adolfo handled routine housekeeping calls. El Fabricante was to be disturbed here only in matters of urgency.

"Perdone, enamorada," the head of Sindicato Sud said gently to his hired companion. "Unlike time with a beautiful woman, business does not grow more to be desired by postponements."

When they had shut the balcony door behind them and stood in the suite's large sitting area, Adolfo said quietly, "It is Washington. Señor White."

El Fabricante's lips drew back on clenched teeth. Farnum White. The man had the gall to contact him after his accursed partner had betrayed them all?

He snatched the handset and cradle from Adolfo's offering hand, turned his back to the balcony, and walked to the limit of the wall cord. Adolfo made a gesture toward his bedroom. El Fabricante shook his head. No need.

"Yes?" he said quietly.

"I called your home office," White said circumspectly. He'd called Miami. "I was given this number." Hugo Salazar, the Sindicato's Miami presidente segundo, was one of the four men who knew El Fabricante's true identity. He was also the only person in the Miami office who knew where El Fabricante was at this moment. If Hugo thought White's call was important enough to clear him through, then it must indeed be. He waited.

"My former partner . . ." White accentuated the middle word, then cleared his throat. Distancing, the Norte Americanos called it. The man was justifiably nervous and was distancing himself from the accursed Murtha. "My former partner is in Hawaii. I thought you would want to know that." Now the voice was better controlled.

Blood pounded in El Fabricante's temples. A new moisture, this of animal excitement, beaded his forehead and upper lip. He drew a long breath to steady his own voice.

"Hawaii has many islands. If I wanted to . . . contact him, where would I—"

"Kona," White blurted. "The Kona Coast. Ask for 'Donald Franklin.'"

"The hotel?"

"That's all I have, sir. And you will remember where this information came from?" There was a plaintiveness in White's voice. El Fabricante hung up.

He handed the phone to Adolfo. "To eliminate a cockroach, Adolfo, one needs an exterminator."

"At your disposal, señor." He spoke in Spanish, but Adolfo Bellota sounded German when he said that.

"My good friend, that is much appreciated. But what would I do without you at my side?"

Adolfo's blue eyes, odd in his Indian-sienna face, held his. "If not me, señor, then Prettykin."

El Fabricante nodded. "Excellente. For Señor Prettykin: the Kona Coast of Hawaii. Donald Franklin. Prioridad. Relay through Miami, Adolfo."

El Fabricante gripped the handle of the balcony door, then turned back. "Prioridad! Comprendes?"

Adolfo nodded, one dip of the chin. He was already dialing.

—8—

He had taken early supper at the famous Café Sacher behind the Staatsoper, Vienna's huge opera house. Now he stood across the rain-glistened expanse of the Opernring portion of the Ringstrasse that girdled the old Inner City.

His narrow raincoat collar was turned up ineffectually against the penetrating drizzle. His short-cropped, curly blond hair was bared to its soaking. Droplets ran down the sides of his large black briefcase. To passersby, he could have been a youthful businessman stoically waiting for a taxi. He worked to create that impression while he never took his peculiarly lifeless metallic eyes off the straggle of cars that had begun to discharge their passengers beneath the long portico of the Opera House. His surveillance was interrupted only by the irregular passing of the Ringstrasse's red-and-yellow streetcars, hopelessly quaint in his view.

A bitch of a night. He pulled his hand from his coat pocket and wiped moisture from his forehead and pale eyebrows. Objectively, he found the rain helpful. It closed people in on themselves, cast their eyes downward at sloppy footing. Rain made people less wary of what went on around them. That was all to the blond man's benefit. The only negatives on this gloomy, wet Austrian evening were the discomfort, which he barely felt, and the added difficulty of spotting Hermann Bruckner's Mercedes 500, though silver Model 500s were not that common.

The man observing the huge Renaissance-styled State

Opera House from across the street could have easily passed for a native of the region, perhaps even a youthful apprentice at the Winter Riding School four blocks north. He had the classic sculpted look of a future Lipizzaner expert, the litheness of body, the quickness of reflex. But he lacked the performer's flair. Had any of the hurrying pedestrians taken the trouble of a careful second look at the slim man at the corner of the Opernring and Kartnerstrasse, such peering eyes would have been rebuffed by the man's gaze, cold and lifeless as glacial ice.

He could have passed as a Karl or Johann. Two hours earlier, he had checked out of the nearby Astoria as Erich Milch. He carried an American passport, credit cards, and an Arizona driver's license in that name. All these credentials were forged. The slender young man with the black briefcase who stood so stiffly erect in the early evening drizzle was American. His name was Arthur Prettykin. He was in Vienna on assignment; a *negocio*, the Sindicato Sud people insisted on calling it—a negocio that would net him ten thousand American dollars.

As the evening's last light faded, the colonnaded facade of the Opera House fell into deeper shadow. From across the Opernring, its two tiers of five deep arches made ten black holes in the front of the looming stone structure. The flanking wing along the Operagasse, he knew from yesterday's observation, though he could not see it from here, was now in even deeper shadow beyond its half-block of open courtyard and big circular fountain.

Now lights began to bring the block-wide building to life. The brownish stone suddenly seemed weddingcake fresh. The railroad-stationlike superstructure of the Opera House's central roof appeared to float against the lowering sky. The giant mounted figures that surmounted the corner capitals of the front elevation seemed almost able to prance off into the scudding clouds.

The growing stream of automobiles began to congest the entrance far below. In black tie, even some in white-tie regalia and sweeping evening gowns, the elite of Vienna and affluent tourists fortunate enough to have booked well in advance streamed up the broad steps into the magnificent interior.

By now the man who carried the passport of Erich Milch had descended into the brightly lighted Opernpassage to cross beneath the rain-slick, congested, 185-foot pavement of the Opernring. When he had emerged again into the evening chill, he took up a new position in shadow at the corner of the looming Opera House that abutted the open space around the west fountain.

Mingled in the traffic stream that nosed through the front portico during the next fifteen minutes, three silver Mercedeses disgorged their formally dressed passengers. None were the object of Prettykin's intent observation. More cars arrived, let out their operagoers, departed to be parked.

Then a fourth silver limousine turned in to the colonnaded entrance. This one, at last, was Herr Bruckner's. The tall financier emerged in a crouch, then straightened to his full six-feet-two. A strong retention of military bearing there, Prettykin noted, and a strong suggestion of residual military arrogance, too.

Bruckner did not enter the building. Instead, he walked toward Prettykin, his hatless head reflecting silver in the portico's lighting. Prettykin turned to stride along the shadowed wall behind the fountain, followed the building's ell to the smaller portico of the jutting wing; this one, a half-block back from the Opernring, unlit and deserted. He took a position behind one of the portico's supporting columns.

In not quite a full minute, he heard Bruckner's patent leather dress pumps crunch loose gravel at the portico entrance. The suddenly cautious footsteps halted. Prettykin now heard another pattern of hesitant footfalls, faint but distinct from the distant sounds of the Opernring. Bruckner was being followed. Then the fainter footfalls halted as well.

He heard an uncertain scrape of Bruckner's shoe. Perhaps the edge of the sole had caught on the drive's paved surface as the financier turned to check behind him. The sound seemed loud to Prettykin concealed in the shadows of the arched portico.

The tension sharpened his senses. The odor of wet stone,

a dank, earthy smell, hovered here. An eddy of raw night air chilled his cheek. Leather scuffed the courtyard's surface again, fainter this time but eloquently expressing Bruckner's apprehension. Prettykin edged the right side of his face past the column's shielding stone.

The financier stood just short of the portico opening, his head cocked forward as his aging eyes tried to penetrate the interior gloom. His long shadow, cast by the distant lights of the Opernring, arrowed toward the portico like a probing finger. Prettykin looked past him.

Fifty feet behind the tall Austrian stood an equally immobile figure, not as tall, much wider. An obvious bodyguard. "Come alone," Prettykin had told Bruckner, but the cagey SS veteran had ignored that. His caution was late-blooming. He'd been a reckless old bastard when he'd taken Sindicato money—a lot of it—ostensibly to establish a Bavarian foothold for El Fabricante's European interests. Bruckner had taken the money, then had gone over to competition much closer to home: Salvatore Renata's Compagnia Venezia.

That much, Prettykin had been briefed on, though his personal need to know certainly did not extend that far. He was a singularly incurious man. All he needed to know was the identity of his target. In this instance, the more-than-adequate briefing did serve a purpose. He had been able to use it to fabricate a plausible reason for Bruckner to meet him in this public, yet remote, place.

"Herr Nagel?" Bruckner's soft call was hoarse with apprehension. Nagel was the name Prettykin had given him.

"Yes." Prettykin kept his voice equally low.

"You do have the papers?" Bruckner's English was better than passable. On the phone, Prettykin had told him that "Rollo Nagel" was the American-born son of Austrian émigrés who had refused to speak German from the date of the Anschluss.

"Yes," Prettykin said again.

"Come out where I can see you."

"Sorry, Mr. Bruckner. I can't afford to be seen with you. You understand."

The furtiveness, the "papers"—a code word for a

purported second installment of Sindicato funding—all this was Prettykin's fabrication to accomplish just one small goal: to get Bruckner in a secluded place for no more than thirty seconds. Prettykin had followed the corrupt old ex-colonel-general for much of this week and discovered the man had a flair for avoiding lonely byways. Was it purposeful? Had Bruckner instinctively kept to public places because he sensed Prettykin's surveillance? No matter now. The lure of a quarter-million American dollars in well-worn Austrian schilling notes had taken the sharp edge off the man's caution.

"Tell your man to stay where he is," Prettykin said quietly, "or you'll find nothing in here but air."

Arms at his sides, Bruckner made rearward motions with his hands. Then he walked slowly forward. The bodyguard stayed in place. The old soldier entered the portico's shadow, then stopped again.

"Over here, Mr. Bruckner." Prettykin slid a West German Heckler & Koch P7 automatic out of his coat pocket. The sharp rear edge of the front sight caught on the pocket's opening. Prettykin turned his body to shield the motion of twisting it loose.

This had to be a close shot, because he hadn't had a chance to test fire the weapon. He had picked it up, as instructed, at a cluttered and musty antiques shop on Kettenbruckenstrasse the day after he'd arrived. The muttered exchange of code phrases the Sindicato loved so had yielded the paper-bagged weapon from beneath a counter in the rear of the shop. But there had been no opportunity to test fire it. There seldom was.

He held the P7 close to his body, arm straight down. Who knew the extent of the old man's nighttime visual acuity?

Apparently, he hadn't noticed Prettykin's difficulty in drawing the weapon. He was twenty feet distant now. He stopped.

"The papers, Herr Nagel. If you would be kind enough to toss them out to me."

Twenty feet to a target in darkness, silhouetted only by distant street lighting was far from a sure shot.

"I'll bring them to you, sir."

"No, you will not. You will remain where you are, and you will throw the package here. I am armed, you understand?"

Bruckner accompanied that announcement with an arm motion that silhouetted his pistol. A Luger or Walther. Hard to tell in this gloom.

"I understand, sir. Just a minute."

Hell of a shot from here, and a dangerous departure from Prettykin's plan. He had intended to press the muzzle of his P7 deep into Bruckner's gut to mask the flash and muffle the explosion. That wasn't possible now.

"I am waiting, Herr Nagel."

Prettykin held the P7 with both hands, steadied his locked grip against the edge of the column, and did his best to center the muzzle on Bruckner's chest.

The blast, amplified by the portico's confines, deafened him. Its flash painted the Opera House's side entrance yellow-white, as if Prettykin had popped a massive flash bulb.

In that eye wink of brilliant light, he had seen Bruckner slam backward, his mouth making a black O in his long, white face. When darkness closed into momentary blindness, Prettykin aimed at the image seared into his retinas. He fired a second time. The repeat flash and crash added another smaller O to Bruckner's stricken face, this one just below the right edge of the receding hairline.

Prettykin didn't wait for him to fall. The bodyguard had leaped forward at the first flash and explosion. He was a heavy man, but he covered a full four yards before the portico flared again.

Prettykin's plan to walk almost casually back to the Opernring had dissolved when he'd realized Bruckner had brought a bodyguard. But he had improvised rapidly. He dashed from the portico's cover to the adjacent side street, shielded from the onrushing bodyguard's vision by the line of portico columns.

A young couple strolling arm in arm stared at Prettykin as he rushed toward them. He flailed his arms. "Help!" he shouted, half turning to point back at the Opera House wing. "Get help!"

Whether they understood him didn't matter. He had diverted their attention from him to an unimaginable emergency in the dark portico. He raced to the next cross street, swung behind the looming Opera House, then forced himself to slow to a brisk walk.

He had rammed the automatic back in his coat pocket. He'd been assured that it was untraceable, but he wasn't a trusting man. He crossed the Kartnerstrasse where it became a pedestrian shopping mall and glanced behind him.

Damn! Bruckner's bulldog stood a block away, his big head swiveling.

Prettykin strode rapidly eastward along Walfischgasse, seeking to blend into the sparse sidewalk traffic. At Akademie, he stole another rearward squint. The man was on him, all right, now less than a block behind.

Prettykin increased his pace through what had become a steady downpour. He rounded the corner of more heavily populated Schwarzenburgstrasse. A distant, foreign *beeboo* howl of a police siren grew louder. Blue lights flared briefly two blocks ahead as the car raced through the big intersection at Schwarzenburgplatz and the Ringstrasse. He realized he was headed right back to the Ringstrasse, only a couple blocks east of the Opera House. Behind him, Bruckner's man rounded the Walfischgasse corner.

Not good. Prettykin rushed across Mahlerstrasse and plowed through the crowd that jammed the sidewalk of the short block at the north end of the broad Schwarzenburgplatz. Now he ran. The passage he forced as surprised pedestrians fell back made pursuit that much easier for the onrushing man behind him.

Then he saw the taxi. He burst out of the sidewalk crush and raced for it, flouting the strict Viennese jaywalking prohibition. The driver spotted him, screeched his brakes. Prettykin wrenched open the door. Fingers locked on his arm.

"Schwein!"

The hoarse voice exploded in his ear. He could smell the man's yeasty breath. He looked down, raised his left knee high, then crashed the heel of his shoe into the arch of the man's foot.

Beer breath erupted in a gust of pain. The fingers dropped away. Prettykin twisted into the taxi's rear seat and slammed the door.

"Go!" he yelled. "*Raus!* Or whatever the hell it is!"

The blunt-faced middle-aged driver jumped the little taxi out of Schwarzenburgplatz, then said over his shoulder, *"Wohin gehen Sie?"*

"What?"

"Wohin—Where?"

What in hell was the name of the place he'd scouted yesterday? Aspirin. That was his thought-association key. Aspern, that was it.

"Aspernplatz," he said.

They went straight up the east side of the Ringstrasse. The driver let him out near the Donau Kanal. The rain had diminished to a light drizzle. Prettykin strolled along the canal near the Aspern Bridge until he was alone. He slipped the P7 into the dark, still water.

Then he walked back to Aspernplatz and hailed a second taxi. This one he directed to Schwechat Airport. Halfway there, in Vienna's rain-gloomed suburbs, he had a case of the sweats. He didn't change expressions. The ball-bearing eyes did not vary their flat stare through the windshield wipers' arcs. His fingers didn't tighten their grip on his briefcase's handle. But quite suddenly his face took on the hard sheen of a man who had just thought of something life-threatening.

It was the bottom line of a thought sequence that had begun with the reflex notion that Bruckner's clumsy bodyguard had wasted little time watching Prettykin's taxi disappear into Ringstrasse traffic. He had to have taken one of two alternative actions: grabbed a taxi of his own in pursuit or rushed to the nearest phone to notify Vienna's police. But the man had not appeared at Aspernplatz. It was obvious that the first driver had inadvertently lost him, or Bruckner's man had taken alternative two.

At this moment, were squads of police infiltrating railway and bus stations? Setting up highway roadblocks? Were plainclothes officers mingling with the crowd at Schwechat Airport while he headed straight into them? All this was a possibility, to be sure. But it was not the one that brought to Prettykin's face the moisture that glinted as the taxi bounded past occasional street lamps.

Almost as quickly as he had built his scenario of an activated police net, he had dismissed it. Bruckner was not the model Viennese whom the public had been led to respect. That veneer would crack and strip away quickly under the cold light of a murder investigation. Bruckner's man would want no part of that.

No, surely the big bodyguard had made a phone call, but not to the police. He would have called Bruckner's people. And that was the realization that now gripped Prettykin.

He forced himself to think, to analyze. The man could describe Bruckner's assassin down to the last detail. Prettykin could still feel the grip of his fingers. Medium height, the man would report, slim with curly blond hair. Prettykin could change the hair. He had an hour and twelve minutes until plane time.

A dye job? Too dangerous to ask the driver to—What? Even if he could get his hands on the stuff, using it would be messy, complicated.

The taxi rolled on through the light rain. Time and miles ticked away. A barbershop. Were any open this late? He wouldn't bother with dye. He'd have his head shaved, darken his eyebrows and lashes with shoe polish—if he could find that. Wear a tam if a clothing store . . .

Again, too complex.

He took one hand off the briefcase handle, pulled out a handkerchief, mopped his face. He could see the airport lights haloed in the mist ahead.

Another possibility struck him, more of a rationalization to let him step from the taxi into the terminal with a lessened fear that he would hear the *phut* of a silenced automatic and feel the slam of a hollow-nosed slug into his heart; the bodyguard may have called no one at all. He had failed in his assignment. Bruckner was surely dead. Bruckner's people could want the inept guard's blood as badly as they must want Prettykin's. Yes, that was it. The man had called no one at all. He had his own problems.

"Der Flugplatz . . . Airport," the driver announced

unnecessarily. Prettykin paid him, probably overpaid him with the unfamiliar schilling notes, and did his best to melt into the concourse crowd.

His best was very good. He walked in the near company of the tallest people he could find, unobtrusively keeping them between himself and whoever looked like authority. At ticket check-in, he felt a crawl of apprehension. If anyone searched for him here by name, that name would be the nonexistent "Rollo Nagel," he hoped, not the name "Erich Milch" that was computer-printed on his ticket forms.

He had a bad moment at the security-check station when the magnetic field beeped in his ear. The damned groschen and schilling coins. He had acquired a pocketful. He dumped them in the guard's basket, went back through and retrieved them with slippery palms. In his business, it didn't do to have the sweats, did not do at all. But he had them often.

He didn't feel really secure until he was settled in the British Airways Airbus. Even then his stomach was sour. He bought a scotch from the chestnut-haired flight attendant. "No, no water or soda. Just rocks." The stuff hit his roiling stomach hard, then spread out its warmth. He settled back.

Was he getting too old for this? Too old at thirty-four? Twenty-seven had made him an old man at Malibu, where he had parlayed a boy surfer's good looks and ruthless ambition into a beach bum's deceptively lucrative career as supplier to the stars. Some far cry, as they say, from the private day school in New Orleans, then three rocky edge-of-dismissal years at an Alabama version of an east-of-the-Hudson prep.

He had been a purveyor of illicit goods: cigarettes, beer—stronger if a classmate wanted to pay the price. A faculty inkling of that, not his grades, came close to dumping him out of there. His grades saved him and even got him into Tulane, much to the relief of his annuity-wholesaling father and women's-club-presidential-timbre mother.

All that had been before his parents had disowned him.

They did that when he dropped out of Tulane halfway through his freshman year and thumbed west.

In four months he was retailing horse and snow, siderailing into Acapulco Gold if a leggy soap queen wanted to get started slow. Discreet to-your-door delivery up and down the beach built his rep. When an occasional female customer, driven into lonely longing by the sea's relentless empty rhythm, wanted him to stay a while, that built his rep, too.

Then he discovered that instead of getting rich slowly by killing his customers slowly, he could get rich quickly by killing them fast. His first hit had been a pathetic little Mexican, or Colombian, who had begun his own operation on Malibu's north end. Coke. Good stuff, too, from some South American source Prettykin hadn't heard of. He iced the guy with two shots in the chest from a silenced Iver Johnson .38. He was going to put a couple in the greaser's knee caps, after the fact, to give the L.A.P.D. the idea that the Mafia had a hand in it. But sudden footsteps at one end of the Elysian Park pathway had rushed him out the other.

The little runner had turned out to be a Sindicato Sud retailer. That should have earned Prettykin a fast ticket to a one-way evening dive off Catalina. But the guy had been "skimming," peeling off more than twice his legit take. The West Coast office of Sindicato Sud owed Prettykin thanks for doing what they should have done themselves. The local presidente segundo interviewed him in a once A-1, now class-C, restaurant on Sunset. At high noon. The guy had worn an off-white three-piece suit, no less. Prettykin got a position, though he hadn't asked for one. The hours were a hell of a lot better. So was the money. And in the long run, the risk was lower.

They set him up in a Studio City apartment as a "producer." There were more than six hundred producers listed in local directories. No one knew how many more professional drifters called themselves TV or movie producers. Most of them produced very little. Prettykin produced whenever word came from Miami via the tucked-away office in downtown L.A. with the block IMPORT-EXPORT lettering on the frosted glass of its narrow door.

In a year, he was given the whole western territory. He was efficient and remarkably free of the law. Except for one brush with the Utah State Police, a DWI charge. He wasn't drunk. He was bone tired during a nonstop drive from L.A. to Salt Lake City. Fortunately, he was to pick up his piece in Provo, so he was clean at the time of arrest. He hadn't been able to make any headway against the charge until after he'd been booked and fingerprinted by an overzealous rookie. Then the night court judge listened. So much for that. He drove on to Provo, picked up the clean gun, continued to Salt Lake City, and made the hit.

Shortly after that, he graduated to specialized assignments worldwide. His cover now was more exotic. As product demand made its way into the heavy-money strata of Silicon Valley and other high-tech markets, heavy competition created an increase in Prettykin's contractual opportunities. He acquired a remotely sited ranch near Scottsdale, Arizona, halfway up the north side of Mummy Mountain. It overlooked a lot of desert and offered the solitude he'd found he needed more and more after each increasingly complex assignment.

If anyone talked about him at all—and he'd taken pains to be civil but uncommunicative with the infrequent half-mile-distant neighbors he had unavoidably come across—he hoped such gossip was restricted to "that young fella up there in the old Harsch place, he's some kind of urban-renewal consultant. Always off to Mexico or Europe or someplace."

Waiting for his plane change at Heathrow, Prettykin spent some of the time in the cocktail lounge, nursing another scotch, the rest of it drifting through the airport's shops. He bought a dark-blue tam, feeling that his blond hair was more of a badge here than in the Teutonic crowd at Schwechat. The tam was something of a badge, too, combining oddly with his banker's gray. He put it in the briefcase twenty minutes later, acutely aware that his indecision was a sign of lingering unease.

But nobody touched him. The huge Lockheed 1011 roared steeply out of London's western reaches like a giant flying barn, then settled into its hissing throb. He slept for a while, read *Newsweek*, ate the utilitarian food from its utilitarian tray, slept again. Then the big barn slid down through muggy darkness into Kennedy.

He didn't pick up his little metallic-blue Porsche at Sky Harbor until late in the afternoon, though he had flown with the sun all day. He felt gritty and dragged out when he swung from the airport exit into Twenty-fourth Street.

Too old for this. Six traffic-congested miles north, he followed the street's suddenly rural bend into eastbound Lincoln Drive. Between Mummy Mountain and Camelback, the lowering sun was red-orange and huge in his rearview mirror. At the light at Scottsdale Road, he turned hard left, then after two miles, swung left again to complete the U around the mountain.

The road skirted the mountain's flank through increasingly sparse residential development, then he turned off the public road to climb a private lane up the craggy north slope. He passed only a few entrance drives, all leading sharply downward to sprawling one-story ranchers on perches carved out of the reddish mountain's rock. Only their tiled, or graveled, roofs were visible from the road above.

His own house was on the lane's upslope side, with a driveway only an idiot would build had this been snow country. The driveway swept upward in a semicircle so steep that it forced gasps from first-time users. There weren't many; an occasional repairman. His twice-a-week Mexican housekeeper was used to the precipitous slope by now and took it handily in her four-wheel-drive Bronco. Sindicato Sud sent no one, ever. All contact was by scrambler phone. His answering machine had a built-in decoder and the security of a six-digit activation panel. The machine recorded in silence, and he alone knew the number sequence that activated the playback.

He tossed his rumpled raincoat on a chair and laid his oversized briefcase on the table in the Spanish-tiled entryway. The soiled shirts, underwear, and socks could go in the laundry hamper later. A small accumulation of mail, neatly stacked by Mrs. Garcia, held nothing of immediate importance except for a nine-by-twelve envelope emblazoned with the USPS overnight delivery eagle. Damn!

He set it aside for the moment and walked through the wide living room. He noted the glow of the answering device's little red eye. That too could wait. What he needed now was an icy margarita in one of his broad, tall-stemmed glasses rimmed with salt. Jet lag had begun to hit him.

On the open patio off the living room, he settled in a cushioned Salterini chair and sipped the tart drink. The tequila's tang began to make him feel semihuman again. The execution of a negocio was exhilarating with its sudden adrenalin surge and grab at the heart. The damned travel, though, the rush to make connections, the multiple identities, the hours cramped in a narrow tube that hurtled through thin air thirty or forty thousand feet up had drained him.

He watched the shadow of the mountain creep across silent Paradise Valley. From up here, he could see almost to Carefree. Lights began to wink along the valley floor. He finished his drink, glanced at the answering machine's red gleam as he returned to the kitchen. Not yet.

He microwaved a pair of enchiladas, peeled an avocado, split it, poured on a dash of oil and vinegar, made a second big margarita and took it and his plate back to the darkening patio. He ate slowly as dusk deepened into night, warm as Southern California day. The patio's stonework breathed back stored heat.

He sat there an hour to let space, silence, and solitude begin to rebuild the sharpness and desire that had been dulled by too much travel under too much tension. He would need more than an hour of this. More than a couple of days. He would need Francine, the elegant Vietnamese who was worth every cent of her thousand-dollar weekend fee.

On his return to the kitchen, he finally fingered the answering device's control panel.

"Priority." The flat voice sounded metallic. The odd tone was not the result of the quality of the machine, which in fact had an excellent speaker. The disagreeable tone was in the voice itself. That was the voice in which purchases—negocios—came from the Miami customer.

"Donald Franklin. Kona Coast, Hawaii. Photo to arrive USPS overnight. Your supplier will be A. K. Bennett, Kona Inn Shopping Village, Kailua-Kona. More detail in USPS package. Operative phrase is 'This sure beats Apalachicola.'"

How these people loved their cornball cloak-and-dagger approach.

"Pay-level four," the voice rasped.

Forty Gs! Cloak and dagger would be just fine.

He erased the answering machine's tape and took the big eagle-emblazoned envelope from the hall table.

—9—

Don Franklin sprawled in a comfortable rattan chaise on their fifth floor lanai and sipped his second cup of rich Kona coffee.

"Grown right here on the island, just a few miles down the coast," the heavily tanned, gaunt-cheeked waiter had told him. "The clouds come down off Mauna Loa like clockwork around midday and shield the coffee plants from the real heat of the day. That's why coffee grows so good here."

The man, probably in his mid-twenties, spoke with a native's pride, but he'd turned out to be from Akron. From the look of him, Don had speculated, he'd probably come to Hawaii for a cure from God-knew-what habit.

That had been during breakfast, during what Don had begun to recognize as the part of the day when his mind was relatively clear and, well, stable.

"Seems I'm a morning person," he had told Lori. "After that, I'm not worth much of a damn."

"Reaction to shock is unpredictable, Don." He wished she would not sound so persistently clinical.

"This can't be much fun for you, all my energy draining away after I've been up and around for only a couple of hours."

"We're here for your sake, Don. Don't worry about me. I'm perfectly happy at poolside or doing a little shopping.

There are some perfectly wonderful shops right here in the hotel."

"I'm sorry to be such a damned lump."

On their second morning, she had come to him early; woke him, in fact. Freshly showered, sandalwood-scented now, murmuring soft insistence. She was adept. Good word for it, he thought beneath her pleasant weight. ("No, let me," she'd insisted. "My treat.")

No fire here, though. But would there be after eleven years? She was neat and efficient, but despite his not wanting to, he detected a nagging little undercurrent of insincerity. Like that of a dedicated therapist who jollied him through her routine all the while timing it carefully for maximum efficiency.

Was that how she regarded this early morning passionless nestling as she reached daintily for Kleenex? Therapy?

He finished his coffee, set the cup and saucer on the lanai table's glass top and let his gaze drift along the sharply defined rim of the sea. Surely no one would complain about this room—big, airy, in yellows, greens, and white, glass-walled at the ocean end, its wide sliding door opening on the secluded lanai two steps down. The view was infinite to the sea's gunmetal edge, etched along robin's-egg sky. Footing the five-story drop was the resort's tropical garden, its emerald foliage, bursts of brilliant hibiscus and bougain-villea and its rustling palms seen from above as green starbursts, all were nearly too lush for his dulled eyes.

Beyond this verdant buffer crouched a wide stretch of black lava that fell beyond into sheer cliffs twenty feet down to the sea. Incoming slate-colored rollers swelled lime green and threw themselves against the obstinate lava escarpment in rhythmic thunder. An occasional outsized comber burst against the cliffs with a force that exploded spume high over the lava's ragged lip. Don felt the vibration of such impacts against his shoe soles on the lanai's cement floor.

He opened the Ken Follett novel she had bought him downstairs, but the effort of concentration through only a few pages numbed him into inattention. Here came that damned clockwork lassitude again. Three weeks of this? He'd be rested, all right. He lay back, closed his eyes. The surf seemed to have taken on a more regular rhythm. The paperback lay face down in his lap.

". . . *Don Franklin. Don Franklin. Don Franklin. You understand? You will say it.*" Squinted eyes behind half-lenses were close to his.

"Don Franklin . . ." Don muttered, and that woke him up.

He glanced around. He was on their empty lanai. A waking dream that real? Or had he been truly asleep?

The glass door slid open behind him. "Lunchtime, darling." Lunchtime? He *had* been asleep. "Do you feel well enough to go down to the dining room?" Her smile was sweetly solicitous. A therapist's indulgent smile?

He forced himself on legs of lead. He had to *do* something, not just sit here and stare at the ocean, drop off to sleep after five pages of Follett, and dream of insistent voices.

Lunch in the lobby-level dining room with its brightly flowered decor should have helped pull him out of this depressing languor. It didn't. The sounds of serving and diners' chatter blended into a constant drone after they had ordered. He sat numbly, then when his pineapple salad arrived, forced himself to eat. He couldn't have faced anything heavier.

"It's damned odd, Lori. I wake up feeling fine, then all that goes down the drain after an hour or so." He had to grope for the words.

She glanced up from her corn chowder. "Maybe we shouldn't have been so . . . adventurous this morning, darling." Her eyes failed to reflect the coyness in her voice. He noticed that through the cloying mist in his brain that urged him to overlook such insignificant detail.

Something wasn't right here. He had no idea how a man should feel this many days after a severe cranial jolt. But this regularly occurring state of torpor and the persistent memory loss—don't forget your memory loss, Franklin. Ha, ha. Not right. Just not right.

"Funny thing this morning." Should he go ahead with this? Why was he hesitating?

She had put down her spoon. "What happened, Don?"

Was that an anxious edge in her voice? Well, why not? It must be just terrific for her here with a husband who's got the mental acuity of an ox and the memory of an erased videotape.

"I thought I heard someone saying . . ." He stopped. *I heard voices, Doc. Sure you did, Don. Nurse, the hypo, please.*

"Saying what?"

Not the condescension he'd expected. More a tone of— what the hell was it? Tenseness?

"Someone was saying my name over and over. Someone wearing those dumb little half-lenses. Ah, this is stupid. It was a dream. I fell asleep out there on the lanai, and I dreamed it."

"I'm sure that's what it was, Don." She went back to her chowder, but he caught an upward flick of her eyes a few seconds later. She didn't look all that convinced, and he found that unsettling.

The third day, she began to run him around in public again, as he thought of it. They toured Kailua's waterfront shops, most of the time with him sitting on a bench on the wide walkway behind the shopping promenade. She seemed unusually tense, he thought, manifested by her smoking more than her occasional slim, brown cigarette.

Yet who wouldn't be uptight with her husband hunched in the sun like a tired old man? Babbling of hearing voices, for God's sake. What was the matter with him? He resolved to keep his mental aberrations to himself. She had enough problems.

The voice came a second time in the early morning.

"Don Franklin. Don Franklin. You understand?" said the looming man with the half-lenses. He appeared as a nearly focused head against an out-of-focus bright blur that threw the uncomfortably close face into shadow. Don could make out a bristly iron-gray mustache.

"That's your name. You will not remember any other name. Any other name is now excised from your memory, Don Franklin. You will forget—"

He snapped awake in the dark room. God Almighty! Sweat soaked his back between his bunched pajama top and the rumpled sheet. Gray first light barely filtered around the edges of the drapes across the glass wall to the lanai. He heard Lori's rhythmic breathing in the adjacent bed. He smelled the faint linger of her sandalwood scent. He felt a quickness in his nerves as a man recovering from a drug must feel.

A little knot of ice spiraled through his chest. Like a man who had been drugged . . . Was it possible? His ebullience upon awakening, then the suddenness of its fade, would be less baffling if he had leaped out of bed to tear through a set of tennis or eighteen brisk holes. But in the mornings he did nothing. Except yesterday when she had slipped insistently into his bed. That could account for yesterday's near stupor, he supposed. But what about the other mornings?

He tossed angrily from his back to his side. What in hell was he thinking! She had done everything for him; put up with that insipid ass, Horger; handled every detail of this trip; done all the driving; checking in and out; taking him for diversions. All of it.

But there persisted an overriding strangeness to all of this. A feeling of unreality. Her never showing doubt or uncertainty. How about that?

She's a totally organized woman, that's what about that, Franklin. And she has stuck by you through what has to have been hell for her. What in God's name are you thinking here in the warm gray light of a Hawaiian dawn? If you're so suspicious, just ask her.

He didn't. She woke an hour later, showered, then dressed in light-blue slacks and a flowered yellow blouse. She called room service, ordered their breakfast. He feigned sleep through it all, not wanting to face her with his suspicion, with his growing kernel of guilt. Getting up was inevitable, though.

"Ah, you're already dressed."

"And breakfast is on the way, darling."

He rolled out of bed and opened the drapes. Sunlight streamed in, painfully bright.

"I thought we might drive into Kailua again. It's only a

couple of miles. Wouldn't you like to get out of here for the day?"

"If you want to." He showered, shaved, and dressed, thinking all the while that he was an ass, an idiot. When he emerged from the little ell of the dressing area, she already had breakfast set up on the lanai's glass table.

He walked down the two steps and stood with his arms spread along the parapet's rounded top. The early sun had already warmed the smooth, white-painted concrete. A little iridescent green bird rose from the top of a coconut palm three floors below and streaked past them to perch on the eave of the hotel roof two floors above. Halfway to the horizon, a blue-and-white inter-island cruise ship, a two-stacker, silently drew a dark line across the glittering sea. Then a thunderous wave slammed into the lava cliffs. Its spume flew high above the black escarpment, then fell inward with a noisy splatter. The lanai shook underfoot as he sat down.

"Coffee, darling." She had already poured it, as she had other mornings. He took the cup and its saucer, added cream and sugar.

"It's so peaceful, Don. So perfect."

In the new sun, her exquisite facial structure, vivid emerald eyes, and her satin mouth surely made her one of the most beautiful women on this whole damned island. He was an ungrateful son of a bitch, a true blue bastard for doubting her.

The rich Kona was the best coffee he'd ever tasted. And you couldn't beat fresh Hawaiian pineapple served in Hawaii and croissants so light they almost floated off the plate. Maybe today was going to be different.

It wasn't. Too soon, the sluggish lassitude began to seep irresistibly through his muscles. He knew that it would deaden his thought processes until he welcomed her thinking for him. With today's depressing relapse, though, came a recurrence of his early morning ruminations—and this time, for the first time, a determination to act for himself. That determination came hard, like walking up a steep slope of loose sand.

Was he truly an idiot? How much easier it would be just

to drift along with her. Was there any sense in resisting? He could be wrong. Surely he had to be wrong. He was going to feel like a fool.

Or was he already a fool for such easy acceptance? He forced himself to realize how incredibly difficult it was to think coherently, an almost physical wrenching that came close to nauseating him.

But he said, "I'm afraid I'm not going to be much company this mornng. Didn't you say you wanted to take a look at the shops in Kailua? Maybe this morning would be a good time for you to do that by yourself, without me to drag along. I'll be fine here."

Her look was a curious combination of concern and satisfaction. "You do look tired, Don."

"Woke up too early, then had to struggle to get back to sleep. That does me in. Maybe I'll go back to bed for a while. I'm sorry to be such a damned drag."

She bent over his chaise, kissed him. "That's all right, darling. You're still recovering. I'll be back in time for lunch, all right?"

"Fine. Don't worry about me." Deceitful bastard, Don thought, still fighting hard against a nearly overpowering impulse to tag along and leave the thinking to her.

No. What he had determined to do had to be done. Something was wrong with him. She was glossing over it. Why she was doing that, he couldn't imagine. Or could he? If whatever drained his strength and initiative so dramatically day after day was . . . mortal, then yes, he could understand. She was protecting him. Yet she constantly assured him that he would soon be right and well. Was she that good a liar? Did that explain her out-of-context glances and her now-obvious manipulation? Was he dying, for God's sake, of some hideous illness she couldn't bear to tell him about?

He had to find out. He had determined to do it today. Fifteen minutes after she had left, he called the desk.

"This is Mr. Franklin in Five-oh-seven. Have you a house doctor avaib— available?" He struggled for coherence. A house physician could be good or not so good. But in his hazy retrospect, any physician would be better than Elmo Horger.

"Is this an emergency, sir?" The woman's voice was musically calm, but he caught her undertone of concern. Hotel staffers no doubt were instinctively apprehensive about guests' illnesses.

"No, not an emergency. I think I need a . . . general practitioner. A physical exam." The right words came hard. His struggle for rationality was exhausting.

"There's a clinic in Kailua—"

"Not a hospital. A doctor."

"We do have a Dr. Fukada on call. His office is up on Alii Drive. His driveway is to the left just after you leave the hotel entrance. It's about a quarter mile. Do you have a car?"

"I'll walk."

"I can get you a taxi."

"Walk might do some good."

"I'll be glad to make an appointment for you, sir."

Damn. He hadn't considered the possibility of a doctor's crammed schedule.

"Tell him as soon as possible, will you?"

Whatever she told the doctor, it worked. Or the guy had a slack morning. The desk clerk rang him back promptly. "Dr. Fukada will see you in fifteen minutes, sir. I've arranged for one of our bellmen to run you up there in an electric maintenance cart. I hope that will be all right, Mr. Franklin."

"It's not necessary."

"No problem, sir."

In the descending elevator, the oppressive torpor took a deeper hold. A numbing of toes and fingertips. An involuntary release of muscle tension. A further deadening of mental sharpness as if a cap of gelatin had been lowered over his brain.

He swayed out of the elevator into the lobby, then forced his legs to coordinate. He found he could fight this thing briefly, succeed, then it would creep relentlessly back over him.

The bellman waited beside the registration desk, a stumpy, small-featured oriental.

"Mr. Franklin? I have the cart just outside."

You don't *sound* like a—whatever. Wasn't that the punchline to an old joke? Maybe he should turn around, get back in the elevator, and sleep this off.

No, damn it! He'd come this far. This was the only thing he had done on his own initiative since he . . . since he could remember.

"Fine." He forced a weary sort of jauntiness. "Let's go."

The little green cart rolled down the sloped entrance apron in near silence. Its electric motor whined as they glided through the hotel's big landscaped parking area in blinding sunshine.

"Beautiful day, sir."

Don nodded. The bellman made no further effort at conversation. They passed between the squat lava pillars that flanked the hotel's entrance, turned right, onto the blacktop road that rose steeply toward Alii Drive on the mountainside above them. Partway up the hill, the bellman guided the cart into a small driveway that climbed even more steeply. Don wasn't sure he would have made it on foot.

The drive leveled into a small parking area between a sprawling white stucco house and a stand of Norfolk Island pines. They screened a steep drop back down the hillside that overlooked the ornate obtrusiveness of the Kona Imperial near the ocean's edge.

"If you'll have the doc call when you're ready, sir, I'll be glad to come back for you." Not a trace of an accent.

Don nodded, tipped the man.

"That door, sir." The bellman angled his thumb toward a birch-paneled door halfway along the rear wall of the house. The discreet black metal shingle at eye level read HIRO FUKADA, M.D., in machine-cut aluminum lettering. The cart made a tight turn and rolled away down the drive.

The door opened inward on a small waiting room paneled in rough bleached plywood and smelling faintly of antiseptic. A similarly paneled waist-high counter ran partway along the room on the left. It screened a desk, chair, and a clicking electric typewriter. The typist, a young oriental woman with tiny crow's-feet beginning to pucker her smooth flat face, said without looking up, "Mr. Franklin?"

"Right."

She rolled whatever she was typing out of the platen and inserted a large file card, all without looking at him. She took name and address. He had to refer to his wallet for the address.

"Cash or charge?"

"Charge?"

"Credit card, Mr. Franklin."

"American Express?"

"Fine. Your problem?"

"What?" A wave of weakness came close to sickening him. He leaned against the counter.

Now she did look up. "Your symptoms?"

"I'm not sure. I feel—" He hesitated. What he'd been about to say would have sounded like the opening of a Geritol commercial. Geritol? Where had that thought come from?

She squinted up at him, lengthening the crow's-feet. "I think you'd better go right in. That door." She pointed diagonally across the room.

He opened the second birch-paneled door. The office was surprisingly spare. Same rough, pale paneling as the waiting room. Two Japanese bird prints on rice paper on the far wall. They flanked a framed diploma. He peered at the diploma.

"Not Grenada, Mr. Franklin. University of Pennsylvania. Interned at Hahnemann in Philadelphia."

"I didn't mean to—"

"Ask for that kind of information? Why not? My receptionist surely asked how you would pay. That's quite personal. I'm about to have a personal look at you. Why not ask whether I know my business?"

The loquacious Dr. Fukada rose from his black plastic chair behind his black-enameled steel desk. He didn't rise very high, barely five feet. He was a brown barrel, his neck as wide as his bald head. A narrow U of startlingly black hair enclosed the back and side of his furrowed skull. His forehead sloped back in a ladderlike series of creases. The eyes were close-set above a large, flat nose and wide mouth. The man had the face of a stand-up comedian, not one that transmitted instant reliability. He wore pale-orange slacks and an open, white, short-sleeved polo shirt. Sports clothes. That wasn't so reassuring, either.

"Come, Mr. Franklin. Sit down. Tell me your troubles. You have troubles or you would not have called, right?" He opened a plastic-bound folder, picked up a ballpoint pen, and poised it over a form.

"I feel tired all the time. Dragged out." That sounded dumb as hell.

"All the time?"

"Well, not right after I wake up. I seem to be okay then. But in an hour or so, it's like I've been hit with a brick."

"A brick," Dr. Fukada echoed thoughtfully. "And this brick effect lasts throughout the day?"

"Yes."

"How long has this been going on?" Fukada grinned. "Sorry. I don't usually speak in song titles."

A joking doctor. Not exactly a confidence builder, this guy.

"Ever since I can remember."

Hiro Fukada's heavy eyebrows climbed partway up the ladder of his forehead. "All your life?"

Don hesitated. Then, because Fukada did have an unexpectedly engaging personality, because Don hadn't felt able to confide in anyone at all since . . . since he could remember, but most of all because Fukada was a total stranger, he began at the beginning. Which was not many days ago.

Eight minutes later, his outpouring stopped. He gulped water from a paper cup Fukada had filled from a carafe on a small table behind him. The little Nisei physician folded his blunt fingers on the desk blotter, peered up at Don, and said, "Remarkable."

"You don't believe me."

"I don't know what your motivation would be to take the trouble to come up here and lie. You say you think your wife is hiding facts of your condition from you? Interesting."

Abruptly, he stood. "Interesting," he repeated to himself. "Let's have a look at you. Next room, please, then remove your clothes down to your shorts."

The adjacent examining room was unremittingly white with a black-cushioned examination table and glass-fronted utilitarian cabinets. It was cold, its air conditioning set on the low side.

Fukada, in his golf-course attire, weighed him, sent him into a tiny bathroom to produce a specimen, then rapidly checked eyes, ears, nose, throat; took blood pressure; laid him down to finger lymph glands and more personal areas, check sensory perceptions and reflexes; listened long and hard through his stethoscope's cold disc; wheeled out an EKG machine and put him through that; pulled on a plastic glove and checked prostate possibilities, muttering that a "procto" was not practical because it required certain preliminaries; took blood with a reassuringly sharp needle, pointing out that lab results might not be perfect because Don had indulged in breakfast. Then he left him alone to dress.

He joined Fukada back in his barren little office.

"Good news and bad, Mr. Franklin. The good news is that I didn't find anything. Oh, a little up on the blood pressure, but I shouldn't wonder. It's still within limits. Coordination and reflexes seem slightly off, but you say you are tired. So, pending lab results, you appear quite healthy."

"The bad news?"

"The bad news is also that I didn't find anything. You came in here with a problem. I haven't helped it. I find only an ostensibly healthy man who has had a recent rhytidectomy and rhinoplasty."

What was the man talking about?

"A face lift, Mr. Franklin, and to use the vernacular, a nose job. Those scars at the hairline and in the nose."

"I told you, I was in that accident."

"That may account for the nose and the scar on the cheek, although the work in the nasal area suggests cosmetic surgery. The hairline incisions and suturing are the typical cicatrixes of rhytidectomy, executed, by the way, by a very deft surgeon."

"He told me he had tightened up the forehead when he repaired the damage up there."

Fukada jutted out his lower lip and frowned. "But there is no evidence of damage in that area. Did you say the same man did the repair on your cheek? That scar doesn't seem to be the result of the same skill."

"All of it is Dr. Horger's work. Maybe he had a rough day."

The creases in Fukada's brow deepened. "Somehow I feel I'm taking your money without having done much for you. I could prescribe a stimulant, I suppose. You say you are not taking any medication?"

"Nothing."

"Interesting. Let's wait until we get a look at the lab results. I'll send the samples to Honolulu by air this afternoon and push them a bit over there. Can you call me tomorrow around eleven?" He handed Don a card from a little plastic receptacle on the desk.

Then he stood, opened the door to the waiting room and followed Don to the outside door. "It's possible your wife is right, Mr. Franklin. You told me she thinks you are still recovering from severe shock."

"How possible, Doctor?"

Fukada looked down at his white net golf shoes, then up again. "Barely possible. Do you want my daughter to call the hotel for the man with the electric cart?"

The willowy receptionist was his daughter? This plug of a man had sired her?

"I'll walk. It's all downhill from here."

Fukada smiled. "Be an optimist, Mr. Franklin."

Damned good thing it was downhill, Don realized when he'd reached the hotel's entrance pillars. Fukada's probing and pricking had drained him of more than a few ccs of blood. He leaned against one of the rough lava columns until dizziness diminished. Fortunately, the dependable late-morning cloud layer had drifted down Mauna Loa's long slope to shield the Kona Coast from the tropical sun. Now there was even a light breeze.

He pushed himself erect and concentrated on traversing the hotel's big parking lot, one step, then the next, like an exhausted soldier straggling back to the barracks. He desperately hoped Lori wouldn't suddenly appear. Would she believe he had just been taking a stroll around the grounds? Luck held. Their Toyota was nowhere to be seen.

What good had the clandestine trip to Fukada done? The doctor hadn't found a damned thing of consequence. He supposed he should be happy about that, but what he felt was frustration. He was back in the room, asleep on his bed in his clothes when she returned. The rattle of shopping bags awakened him.

"Sorry, Don. But it's lunchtime, anyway. You shouldn't stay cooped up in here all day. I thought we could have a salad or sandwich downstairs, then drive out to the Painted Church or the City of Refuge."

When they had first arrived, she'd urged him to rest. Now she was pushing him to be up and around. He sat up and grimaced. He was raw from Fukada's poking.

She caught it. "You all right, darling?"

"Just stiff." That was the truth. Stiff in the leg muscles from the walk back. He stood clumsily, suddenly ashamed of his furtive visit up the hill. But he was determined for vague reasons, but strong instinct, not to reveal his morning to her.

She wouldn't relent and let him return to the room after lunch, so he opted for the Painted Church. For all its publicity, it was smaller than he'd expected, a tiny frame chapel perched on the side of a steep hill above the twists of elaborately landscaped Route 160. He sprawled in one of the pews while she studied the primitive paintings that covered the interior. Then she took him through the adjacent cemetery, moving more rapidly than he among the old markers. He hadn't the energy to close the distance between them.

They had supper in a little Mexican restaurant along an otherwise deserted stretch of Kuakini Highway several miles above the Kona Imperial. Then she guided the Toyota down the connecting road to Alii Drive, around the tight bend above Keauhou Bay and down the long hill to the hotel's entrance. He was in bed and glad of it by nine-thirty.

In the morning, he experienced the same stupid pattern. Were it not so traumatizing, he could have written a song about it. Up in the morning, bright as the sunshine, ready to lick the day . . . But along about ten, my ass drags again, ta-dah-dah, ta-dah-dah, can't play. Or something like that.

After their now traditional room service breakfast, she wanted to drag him to the City of Refuge. Sounded appropriate. Easier to go along with the idea than to work out a way to make the eleven o'clock phone call to Dr. Fukada.

For a long couple of minutes, he almost gave in. Yesterday's plotting had been ridiculous. The stumpy Japanese doc hadn't found a damned thing. Don was ashamed of his sneakiness. It had been a slam against her. God knew she had been with him through every dismal phase of this hard road back. To hell with Fukada.

Did he mean that? The stubble blurring his jawline sent a stronger message.

"Don?" She stood at the door, dressed to travel. Pastel yellow slacks and a light-blue blouse with yellow-and-white daisies. A knockout with that polished-anthracite hair. The time was ten fifty-one. He'd thought she'd never get herself together.

He rubbed his jaw. "For Pete's sake! I forgot to shave. It's almost lunchtime. Why don't you go down and order me one of . . . one of . . ." This was taking a lot of effort by a rapidly numbing brain. "One of those pineapple salad boats. I'll be down in a couple of minutes. Then it's whatever you say."

"I'll wait for you."

Hold yourself together, Franklin. Get her out of here.

"No," he said as evenly as he could manage. "Go on ahead. I'll be right down."

Would she go for it?

She did. She shut the door behind her and left him alone. His carefully worked-out subterfuge told him he didn't trust her. Or was this more of a case of not wanting to appear a jerk in front of her?

He took Fukada's card from his wallet and dialed for an outside line.

"Ah, Mr. Franklin. My enigmatic Mr. Franklin."

He didn't get it.

"You told me you were taking no drugs, sir."

"That's right."

"But you are."

A hot burst between his shoulder blades quickly turned icy cold. Fukada took his silence for admission.

"The Pyremisine, sir. Not easy to isolate and identify. Not at all easy, they told me. The charge will include more than the standard lab fee, I'm afraid. Why would you go to the trouble—"

"I'm not on that—What did you call it?"

"Pyremisine, Mr. Franklin," Fukada paused. "You're not taking it?"

"No. Absolutely not."

"Then somebody is giving it to you."

God Almighty! There was only one possibility.

"What is the stuff?" His voice sounded sick.

"A relaxant, something of a sedative. A hypnotic. To generalize, it impairs one's will power. Quite new, uncommon. Not in general use, as a matter of fact. That's what gave the lab people a challenge."

"No mistake about this?"

"None, sir. Not those fellows in Honolulu." Fukada paused again. He was obviously feeling his way through what he had recognized as a touchy situation. Then he said, "Are we edging up on a—well—a matter for the police, Mr. Franklin?"

"I hope not." He'd sound like a fool if he tried to detail the whole sequence of the past couple of weeks to some doubting Hawaiian detective. Watching Fukada's expression had been rough enough, and Fukada was a doctor, presumably inured to wild babblings.

Fukada was silent.

"No, not a police matter, Doctor. But you've been a real help."

"I hope so, sir. Your problem turns out to be quite simple. Stop the ingestion of Pyremisine."

Carefully phrased, doc. You still don't quite believe I'm not doing myself in.

"Good advice," Don agreed. "I thank you." He hung up with cold fingers. Your problem is quite simple, Mr. Franklin? The hell you say, Dr. Hiro Fukada.

He sat on the edge of the bed and stared at the phone. The shock of the incredible finding of the Honolulu lab slowly lost its initial impact. The Pyremisine, of course. He was grogged on it, almost a goddamned zombie. No wonder she'd been able to manage him so efficiently. It had to be Lori. He didn't want to believe that, but there was no alternative.

He rested his chin on his hand, felt the stubble. Shave. He would have to shave, then try to behave normally. Abnormally. A holding action to let her suspect nothing had changed. When the stuff was out of his system, then he would be able to think more constructively.

Covering his emotional tangle was easier than he'd thought it would be, thanks to the very drug she was apparently using on him. The Pyremisine let him draw back into its comfortable, slightly uncoordinated daze. He greeted her in the dining room with a glassy-eyed nod, ate his salad in silence, then slumped on the passenger side through the drive down Kuakini Highway through the settlement sprawls of Honalo, Kealakekua, and Captain Cook, then through six miles of silence to the sharp right turn, and down the mountainside on 160 again. They passed the entrance to the Painted Church this time, swung through tight, impeccably landscaped switchbacks, then into the level parking area of the City of Refuge National Park.

In old Hawaii, said the folder given them at the entrance, the City of Refuge was a haven for the lawbreaker who managed to scurry here up the hard south trail or to swim across Honaunau Bay from the north. Those who made it were purified by the priest in the bayside temple. Where, Don thought suddenly, is the priest when I need him? The place was a reconstruction now, without life.

Along the rebuilt Great Wall past the replica huts and among the palm-shaded thatched temples and looming carved wooden idols on the lava finger that jutted into the sea, he felt again that she was distancing herself from him—as she had at the church yesterday. They had begun walking together, but soon she had drawn well ahead. Was she impatient with his languid pace? The encroaching dullness of mind and body did slow him down. He couldn't deny that.

He slipped on the loose gavel that skirted the fenced temple. She looked back, then past him. Jumpy. Had she somehow learned of his visit to Fukada? He'd thought he had carried that off quite competently, considering his drug-impaired condition. Yet she could have run into the desk clerk or the little bellman who had ridden him up there. "Was the doctor able to help your husband, Mrs. Franklin?" That's all it would have taken. Just a friendly throwaway line.

Had her attitude toward him subtly changed? Or was that perception an inevitable assumption on his part, following Fukada's startling find?

Twenty minutes later, they returned to the Toyota. She opted for a perfectly abominable little road through sugar cane fields along the coastline flats between the City of Refuge and Kealakekua Bay, four shattering miles of it. It was on this deserted road that he became aware of how often she glanced up at the rearview mirror.

She seemed to have a penchant for out-of-the-way travel. At a scruffy little bayside village, the road swung abruptly up the hillside, a snake of narrow pavement that mounted with breathtaking rapidity. Either she drove well or the Pyremisine made him not care. Both, he decided through the comfortable fuzz of the drug.

At the top of the winding climb, she turned north again on Kuakini to the Keauhou Bay access back to the Kona Imperial. He knew he should be incensed at her sneaked medication, then her dragging him up and down the coast at will. Her will. But such was the insidious power of the drug that he felt only languid bemusement. Tomorrow, he determined, would be another story.

Prettykin flew United, tourist class. With twenty-five-hundred dollars in twenties and fifties clipped inside his shirt and five hundred more in twenties in his wallet, he could have afforded the comfort and pampering of first class. But he wanted near-anonymity for "Edward Leonard," the name he'd used when he paid cash for his ticket. His driver's license, selected from his file of excellent forgeries, also featured Mr. Leonard on a laminated-plastic Florida card bearing Prettykin's own photo in not-so-glorious color.

The blind-alley license, and each of the several others he purchased annually from a certain gentleman in an obscure Tempe print shop, cost him three hundred dollars. Steep but essential overhead. Renting a car for cash was more difficult than using a credit card, but an oversized deposit and agreement to pay the rental company's inflated fee for collision coverage invariably brought negotiations to an amicable settlement.

The flight, coming so quickly after his return from Vienna, seemed endless. From Phoenix to L.A., he was on the aisle next to a near eighth of a ton of ebullient Detroit motherhood with great pendulous breasts that vibrated on takeoff, beneath a screaming-green knit pullover. She had literally settled into the narrow seat by perching on both armrests, then applying full weight to force her pillowy buttocks to conform to available space.

She wanted to talk.

He put a quick end to that. "I'm flying to L.A. to visit my brother. He's in Q."

"What's Q?"

"San Quentin. He's in for aggravated rape."

That finished it. On the 747 out of Los Angeles International, he got a window seat. The adjacent seat was empty. The aisle space was occupied by an elderly man in rumpled tan polyester.

"Staying on Oahu, sir?"

Prettykin-Leonard tapped his ear and shook his head. The white-haired seatmate-but-one nodded and did not try again.

He arrived at Honolulu International early enough to take the wiki-wiki bus to the Inter-Island Terminal, catch a Hawaiian Air DC-9 and arrive at Keahole Airport in daylight. He rented a caramel-colored Chevy Camaro redolent of stale cigarettes, drove it with the front windows wide open and the A/C on MAX down the desolate stretch of Queen Kaahumanu Highway, Route 19, as the dying sun threw a final brassy sheen across black, umber, and gray lava flats, then slipped behind purple clouds that rimmed the sea. Now the lava field was flat black from the highway up the rising flank of the mountain to his left and across the mile-wide flat on the right, burned out and black to the distant furrowed lead of the sea. Unexpectedly, the sun emerged through a purple rift. It tinted the crests of the chop blood red.

He pulled into the Hotel King Kamehameha, where the highway essed into north Kailua-Kona to follow the waterfront. This was a busy tourist hotel, right in the mainstream. He'd called in his reservation just thirty hours ago, after a discussion with a Phoenix travel agency. He hadn't given the agency his name. He told the eager female voice he was doing some checking for a possible trip later in the summer, then made his own reservations. The scantier the paper trail, the safer.

He checked in, bought a detailed big-scale map of the island, took a selection of tourist guides from the lobby rack, followed the bellman to the third-floor room, took a shower, had Chicken Polynesian and a huge mai tai sent up. Then he sat in his shorts, feet propped on a second chair with the air conditioning rippling his near-white chest hair, and a Raleigh in the corner of his mouth. He began systematically to call area hotels for Donald Franklin.

By ten-fifty, he had contacted eleven, working right down the coast with a thick guide titled *This Week* and the local phone book. It struck him that calling the major hotels first might have been more efficient. He studied the brochure's Kona Coast map and called the biggest ones remaining. Two calls later—he was becoming damned tired of this—he struck pay dirt.

"Yes, sir. We have a Donald Franklin registered. Mr. and Mrs. Shall I connect you?"

"No," he told the girl. "It's late. I'll be in touch with them tomorrow."

The Kona Imperial. He pinpointed it on his island map. Not quite four miles out of Kailua to the south.

Mr. and Mrs.? The assignment had said nothing about a woman. He stood, stiff from cramped travel and an hour's worth of air conditioning while he'd sat without moving anything but his arms. In the middle of the large room, he forced himself through a routine of thirty pushups, fifty situps with his fingers locked behind his head and forty waist bends, placing his palms flat each time. No deep-knee bends. He used to include thirty of those until he read that the military had dropped them because that particular exercise could ultimately cause knee injury.

He flopped on one of the twin queens and took another look at the photo the Postal Service had delivered in the big eagle-emblazoned envelope. He'd memorized it by now, but it never hurt to be one-hundred-percent certain.

Then he snapped on the TV set. Flipping the dial, he came across an old MGM Al Capone flick with Rod Steiger. Until the final scenes, the cops did all the scut work. Capone's boys had it good. Wasn't it always that way in the movies? You never saw Frank Nitti dialing fifteen hotels to find some clown with a bent nose and a scar on his cheek.

At twelve-thirty, he turned out the bedside lamp. Funny how hard it was to sleep when you were on an assignment, even when you were dragged out thin as a thread by all the travel.

He'd left a call for seven, but he was up instead at six, jolted awake by a flash of wildly out-of-context dream. Sausage fingers grabbed his arm as he yanked a taxi door open. Then the fingers were around his neck. His eyes snapped open. He was soaked. Not like the movies at all.

He showered, dressed in off-white slacks, tan sports shirt, white belt, and net shoes. In the already crowded hotel coffee shop, he indulged himself with two scrambled eggs, French toast, a side order of bacon and two cups of Kona.

At seven-ten, he walked along the little seaport's waterfront. The road that edged the harbor was full of joggers—mostly scrawny ones, burned brown, wearing baseball caps, and so wiry it was hard to tell the guys from the broads until you saw the dancing T-shirts. There were some chubbies, too, hitting middle age, their Adidases slapping the pavement to jolt the impact of a hundred-eighty pounds straight up those varicosed legs to the flabby gut. He didn't jog. He walked. The body was built for the stretch and flex of walking, not banging up and down on its heels.

He covered the quarter-mile to the Kona Inn Shopping Village in ten minutes, then ambled along the open-boardwalked arcade to the arched passage through the old inn to the restaurant and lawn and the sea beyond.

He stood in the archway's mouth, appreciating the light sea breeze. Across sun-flecked Kailua Bay, back at the public pier near the hotel, a crew of three brown men in flowered trunks readied a pseudo-Polynesian glass-bottomed boat for its first morning trip. A larger two-masted version swayed gently at anchor nearby, this one Captain Beam's earth-toned dinner cruiser, according to the pamphlets he'd studied last night.

At eight-ten, Prettykin tired of his time-killing stroll along the strip of shops that made up the Village. He found a seat in a coffee shop that afforded him a view of the wide pedestrian walkway between the shop fronts and the street, bought a local paper, and nursed two cups of coffee for an hour.

No one seemed to find anything unusual about his haunting presence. The town had begun to fill up with strollers and browsers, people who had a long time to spend not doing much of anything. Tourists.

At nine-fifteen, a stocky man, well into his fifties, Prettykin judged, trudged to a kiosk on the board promenade, a display space made up of four-by-eight pegboard panels set on end. The man wore faded gray denims hacked off high above nubby knees and a ragged, paint-spattered blue shirt, tails out, sleeves rolled. And beach sandals. He put down his armload of canvasses, walked back to his battered VW van at curbside, hoisted another dozen canvasses out its side door, then left the stack unattended while he pulled the van into a nearby side street.

He was back in a couple of minutes, now toting an easel and a box of what Prettykin assumed to be oils. After he had hung most of his seascapes from clips on the pegboard, he set up the easel, opened his paint box, placed an unfinished moonrise-over-lava on the wooden tripod then—and only then—did he hang his shingle above the display. It was a two-foot-long piece of driftwood. The name . . . Prettykin leaned across his little table and squinted against the morning sun's dazzle.

Van Buskirk.

Well, shit. Prettykin ambled out anyway, stood to watch the artist fill in his ragged night sky in blue-blacks with deft gray-and-white highlighting. When the intense little man glanced his way, Prettykin nodded.

"Morning."

The artist nodded back.

"Mr. Bennett around? A. K. Bennett?"

"Comes and goes. Mostly here by ten. Sets up on the other side here."

Another half hour. This was driving Prettykin nuts. He crossed the now heavily traveled main street adjacent to the closely ranked shops on the landward side. A dark-gray Mustang cruised past. Prettykin noticed with a little twist in his gut that the Polynesian face wore a cop's uniform cap. Unmarked prowl? Impossible that it was for him. Then he remembered reading last night that in some Hawaiian jurisdictions, the police routinely used their own cars.

Time dragged like a lead sled. He walked back toward the hotel, blending, he hoped, with the tourist flow. When he returned to the block opposite the Kona Village center, a second artist had begun to set up his outdoor shop. This one was a tall guy with a beard scruff, maybe three-days' worth, a garish Hawaiian shirt of red-and-yellow splashes on shiny black, and paint-spattered black pants.

Prettykin crossed the street. The guy had set up a display of unframed paintings on black velvet. Clowns and fat Hawaiian women. Bad stuff compared to Van Buskirk's seascapes, around the other side of the pegboard kiosk. No name. I wouldn't put mine up, either, Prettykin decided. The guy wasn't much for atmosphere. No easel. No paints. Just a big brown plastic shopping bag between his feet as he sank to a low backless bench near his display.

"Mr. Bennett? A. K. Bennett?"

The slim man looked up from between hunched shoulders. He nodded without interest. Prettykin sat down near him, stretched out his legs, and leaned back on bracing arms. He hated this dumb code crap.

"Hot here, but the breeze helps." He paused. Then he said, "But this sure beats Apalachicola."

Bennett stroked his unshaven chin, then looked over at him. Prettykin met his gaze without expression. Then the slim man reached down into his plastic bag. He pulled out a smaller blue bag emblazoned in white with the name of a nearby souvenir shop.

Right in the open, for God's sake! Prettykin's eyes swung along the street. The Mustang was out of sight. The guy could be handing him a bag of Maui Zowie or Hong Kong hash. The confident openness of it shook him. These bastards were too damned sure of themselves.

The bag weighed a lot more than it looked it would. No Taiwan fist-buster, this. Back in his room, he discovered he had been supplied with a sweet-actioned Bernardelli Model 80, seven .38s in the clip. Checkered plastic stocks with a deeply indented thumb rest. Nice balance, not too heavy, not too light. Italian-made. He wondered how much the overt "A. K. Bennett" had been paid to supply this little gem.

—10—

Don Franklin thought he hadn't slept all night. But now the light around the closed drapes was bright. Only a moment ago, it seemed, the room had been dark as a mine.

She had to be doing it at breakfast. In the coffee. If the stuff had any taste to it, the heavy-bodied Kona would be the ideal mask. Fruit juice didn't have the flavor density or flexibility. If it wasn't the coffee, though, the fruit juice was his second choice.

He turned on his side to watch Lori's rhythmic breathing. She lay on her back, one arm crooked above her head, her hair flat black over the ivory forearam. In sleep, she looked young-girl vulnerable. Appealing. He felt a hard jolt of guilt. She had stuck by him all the way, hadn't she? Not a single complaint. Handled the travel details, financial arrangements, even packed his stuff for him. Slept with him and was patient about his problems with that. Never a word of irritation.

And every morning she slipped him a stiff dose of some damned chemical that turned him into human putty.

Or so logic persisted in telling him. It had been one hell of a night. One: there was the between-the-eyes matter of Dr. Fukada's lab report. No mistake, the fire-plug M.D. had assured him. Two: his physical and mental relapse was on a clockwork daily schedule. Shortly after breakfast, he was poleaxed. Three: she had insisted on daily room service for that breakfast. That certainly wasn't an incriminating action, but it was circumstantially contributory. Okay, a weak three.

But a strong four: in retrospect, and circumstances gave his concentration a fine edge this early morning, he could not recall a single morning when she had not had, or herself created, an opportunity to be unobserved with the breakfast tray for at least a few seconds since they'd left Horger's clinic. She had asked him to get her a sweater from the closet in Oahu. Here in Kona she had sent him for a Kleenex to wipe her dark glasses; had already poured the coffee when he emerged on the lanai.

Well, not such a strong case after all. What about yesterday? And how about the day they'd left the clinic?

Concentrate, Franklin, and you'll recall that your plug hadn't been pulled that day until you were high over the bright blue sea. What about those two not-so-little inconsistencies in your quaky hypothesis?

Her slumbering profile seemed to mock him. He rolled on his back and stared at the pebbled ceiling. Yesterday? Ah, so, as Dr. Fukada had never said once. The cruise ship. He'd stood at the lanai parapet for a couple of minutes admiring the inter-island cruise ship. She'd had time enough to mix a daiquiri behind him.

Just the one flaw now. She and Horger and he had all enjoyed coffee from the same pot the day they had checked out of the clinic. No opportunity there. He'd felt relatively fine until his pronounced ebb over the Pacific. How could she have managed that? The flight attendant had brought their meals. He'd never taken his eyes off his, had he? Something must have happened. Something had to have happened, else his whole hypothesis was smoke, and Fukada's finding was a mile into left field.

All right, Franklin. They'd had lunch shortly after taking off from Chicago. You unwrapped the silverware, noticing how cold it was. Spread out your napkin. A cloth napkin in first class. For three-times tourist, you got a cloth napkin. And you uncovered the little china compote. You got real china, too. And you ate. Pretty damned uneventful, that. Where had been her opportunity during that placid meal? There hadn't been one, had there?

So much for the . . . Wait a minute. Over the California coast she had—Yes, she had suggested coffee. And when it came, she'd dropped her little packet of macadamia nuts. He'd had to scrabble around under his seat to find it for her. Had that given her time?

That had given her time.

He clamped his eyes shut, suddenly nauseous. It all locked in place, but it all was mechanics. What's missing, my dear Fukada, is the motive.

"Don?" Her voice was soft with sleep. "It's so early. What woke you up?"

"I don't know. Some noise outside, I guess." What had awakened *her?* Was it possible to transmit this sickening clutch of puzzlement, alarm . . . and guilt over suspecting her?

She raised her head on her elbow and smiled. "It's so early," she repeated. "And quiet and peaceful." An invitation. The satin mouth, the almost oriental cast of the facial structure, the eyes of emerald fire, all promised nirvana. And delivered mechanics.

"I think I'll get up and have a quick breakfast down in the dining room. Maybe take a dip. We haven't even been near the pools yet." This is a little test, my dear.

"Oh, the dining room is so utilitarian, darling." She moved back to make room for him and patted the open space. "We have some time to make up for, Don. You came so close to . . . So close. I want to hold you. Please?"

There was no way around it. She wanted to hold him and hold him here. They held each other, and he felt like a deceiving bastard. Then there was no plausible way not to progress. He found himself playing the role of the satisfying, then satisfied, husband. Good mechanics, Lori, baby. Neat and effective. All the right moves. Two actors without an audience.

She slipped out of bed and pulled down her nightgown. "I'll just call room service, darling. I don't want to lose this wonderful glow in a public dining room."

The waiter delivered while Don shaved. So much for observation opportunities. He pulled on gray slacks and a yellow sports shirt. She wore her yellow robe splashed with green, black hair brushed to a satin sheen. She had taken breakfast off the tray and arranged the glasses of pineapple juice, the sweet rolls, and their coffee on the lanai's table between them. The coffee was already poured.

Her flawless lips had a touch of iridescence. Her eyes held him. Surely she was one of the most beautiful women on these islands of beautiful women.

And he was a true-blue son of a bitch for doubting her.

But he stretched out his legs.

"Oh, for God's sake, Lori. My damned socks don't match. One charcoal, one navy. I must be getting color blind. How about giving an old man a hand?" He kicked off his sandals, stripped off both socks and handed them to her. "Would you match up the gray?"

She took the mismatched socks, gave him a curious look, and stepped back into their room. Shielded by the bunched drapes, he emptied his cup over the parapet. Its stream broke into droplets two floors below and pattered among the palm fronds. He sat down hurriedly and raised the cup to his lips as she reappeared. Then he set it back on its saucer.

"More?" She gestured toward the ceramic pot as she handed him the gray socks.

"No, thanks." He halved a sweet roll. Now it was a matter of waiting.

She finished her breakfast leisurely, rose, stretched. Sighed. "I'll dress, then we'll decide what to do with the rest of the lovely day."

She took her time about that. Waiting for him to sink into narcotic half-life? How long had it taken all these mornings? Less than an hour. A Honolulu paper had accompanied the breakfast tray. He picked it up, but it couldn't hold his attention.

He stared out to sea. The morning was warm, and the breeze up here on the fifth floor was softly cool. Far out on the dark water, a tiny sail caught his eye briefly. But only briefly. He was becoming drowsy.

Damn!

But he hadn't slept well, had he? Wouldn't anyone feel a shade tuckered after a night like that one?

"Don Franklin. Remember that. You are a slate, a blank slate. We will do the writing."

God! The droning voice, half-glasses, bristly mustache . . . And now . . . Now reddish hair, parted carefully above one ear, pulled across the skull but not completely hiding its glisten under blinding lights.

Like a quick cut on TV. How long had it lasted? Ten seconds? Five? Not even a second?

He was wide awake now. He mopped his forehead with his handkerchief.

Confront her or fake it? He dreaded the idea of confrontation. If he was wrong about all this, faking it could be hard to explain. Tough road either way.

He decided that consistency was the course of a prudent victim. He dropped the newspaper across his chest and sank back in the chaise, eyes closed.

"Don?" She touched his arm.

He looked up from beneath drooped lids.

"I've heard that you can sometimes find lava with olivine in it. Right along the road." She unfolded a map she'd picked up somewhere during the past few days. "We'll drive out Route One-eighty to the Hawaii Belt Road."

Flat statement. She didn't wait for his concurrence. An order? He got up, taking care to do it cumbersomely, and followed.

She drove, as always. Route 180 climbed and wound interminably through scrub that had managed a toehold on the ascending lava slope. Several miles off to their left, he could see the Pacific, its roiling reduced by distance to a rough, glittering texture. They passed an orchard of low leathery-leaved trees that he realized was a coffee plantation. Five miles further north, they turned into the wider Belt Road to Waimea.

The highway, nearly deserted, undulated along the lower slopes of Hawaii's westernmost mountain, Hualalai. Not as lofty as Mauna Kea to the east or Mauna Loa, now to the south, its distant crest was nevertheless haloed by late-morning clouds against the higher sky's flawless azure.

She had her rearview mirror fixation again today. After a few miles, she pulled wordlessly to the shoulder, got out, and began to inspect clods of loose lava near the highway's edge.

He stepped from the Toyota, purposely tottering a bit. That wasn't hard. The footing on the crushed lava shoulder was uneven. He wandered off after her.

"You check that way, Don. I'll go up here a way."

He found a little ingress into the black lava field, a secluded parking niche with many tire tracks in the grit underfoot. Maybe teenage lovers from Kailua came up here in the Hualalai foothills.

Damned if there weren't occasional pinheads of glassy green in the lava boulders. He found a loose baseball-size piece of lava embedded with an olivine the size of a lentil. Maybe a hell of a find. When he returned to roadside with it, he heard a car approaching.

And two hundred feet distant along the shoulder, Lori did a curious thing. Her attention was riveted on the car, a light-green Datsun. It slowed. She appeared to freeze, one hand at waist level holding a piece of lava. She didn't know he was watching. She looked as if she were expecting the car to do something, though she just stood there and stared at it.

Then the Datsun rushed past, a man at the wheel, a woman beside him. It disappeared up the highway toward Waimea.

He got back in the Toyota, his olivine-bearing lava forgotten at road edge. Without the air conditioning on, the seat was hot to the touch. He rolled down the window.

You check that way.

He thought about the Painted Church. And the City of Refuge. She had separated from him there, too. Once they'd reached where she was taking him, she was big on distancing herself from him. That, he realized with undiminished sharpness, was not the way a husband and wife usually visited points of interest.

She returned to the driver's side, got in, and lit one of her brown Casinos before she turned the key. Now she seemed to have lost all interest in her olivine hunt. A hard tension had replaced it, as if she'd been waiting for something to happen that hadn't. He was a different man today, his mind clear, though the memory loss persisted. The physical logginess that he had come to accept as a chronic condition was gone. So was the dullness of mind that had served as something of a shield.

His brain was active now, seizing on facts and incidents and processing them rapidly. Fukada's lab report and Don's avoidance of this morning's coffee told it all. He knew now that she had been systematically drugging him, robbing him of mental acuity and physical stamina.

Told it all? As she swung the Toyota off the Belt Road and gunned it down Waikoloa Road toward Queen Kaahumanu Highway along the coast, he realized he had managed to unlock only one small part of what had to be a much larger puzzle.

They flew through the intersection with the Waikoloa Village access road. Something disturbed her, ate at her. Her driving told him that. But she was silent. Of course she was. To her, he was peacefully subdued, not capable of complex thought through the fog of this morning's Pyremisine.

Now what? Was there anything to be gained from perpetuating his charade? From feigning the influence of the drug while she drove him up and down the Kona Coast like a retarded child?

The Waikoloa Road dipped downslope for another mile to a T intersection with the coastal highway. Here she turned south. They passed the Royal Waikoloa Hotel and its golf course, a near-fantasy of brilliant fairways and greens and sugar-frosted buildings that defied the surrounding desert of congealed lava. This highway back to Kailua reminded him of some mined-out Pennsylvania strippings in its desolation, but the vast reaches of lava that had solidified in midflow decades ago did have a unique stark beauty.

Pennsylvania strip mines? Was that a valid memory? Could the medication have acted as a recall suppressant along with its insidious mind-and-body relaxant properties? He tried to expand his slim impression of Pennsylvania. He failed, as one fails when trying too hard to recall a slipped name.

As they passed the scenic overlook near Kiholo Bay, he made a decision. That in itself was something of a mental milestone. The blacktop, unvaried in its gentle undulations across the old seaward-bound lava flows, was empty of traffic. They drove alone across a black desert, the afternoon heat creating silver shimmers in oncoming pavement dips.

"Why?" he said abruptly. "Why the secret medication?"

Her face, the blank mask of the distance driver, didn't change. The emerald eyes held the highway. The lips didn't tighten. The facial muscles showed no sudden tension.

But the Toyota's arrow-perfect course wavered. There was a barely discernible deviation in scant inches. Or had he imagined that?

"Medication, Don?" A stall? Was she fishing to learn how much he might know?

"Pyremisine, Lori. Why are you slipping me that stuff every morning?"

Her eyes stared forward unblinking, but her mouth now showed a tight little hairline at the corner.

"Doctor Horger advised . . . He thought it would be more productive if you weren't under the mental pressure of knowing you needed daily medication."

She had hesitated too long before delivering that mumbo jumbo.

"No good, Lori. I want the truth. I want it *now*."

"When we get back to the hotel."

The half hour back to the Kona Imperial would give her time to collect herself. He had her off balance. For the first time, he had a degree of advantage.

"Now, Lori!" He seized the ignition key, turned it. "Now. Right here."

"Bastard!" The power steering faded. Her fingers whitened on the wheel. The Toyota swerved to the graveled shoulder. She braked hard to override the failed power assist. She jolted back in her seat, and the green eyes flared.

"All right, all right! After all, every bit of this has been done for your own good!"

On the way back to his room, Prettykin had stopped at a lobby shop to buy a brown Hawaiian shirt figured with white sailboats. He took off his Mainland sports shirt, slipped the Bernardelli under the waistband of his slacks and pulled on the loose-fitting Hawaiian shirt. Worn outside the trousers, it concealed the pistol and its slight bulge.

He took a pair of small, beautifully crafted Zeiss 8X binoculars from his big briefcase and slid them in a pants pocket, stuffed the oil-stained cloth that had wrapped the pistol back in the souvenir-shop bag and rode the elevator down to street level. He dropped the bag in a receptacle at the edge of the guest parking area behind the hotel.

The Camaro was an oven. He turned the air conditioning to MAX, fan speed on HI, and drove, with his windows open, through the first few blocks of downtown Kailua. Then he rolled up the windows and headed south on Alii Drive.

Twelve minutes later, he parked beneath a feathery acacia tree in the Kona Imperial's big parking area. He entered the building through a lower-level public entrance and followed a long, uncarpeted concrete hallway to the lobby stairs. He passed a scatter of people in beachwear. Apparently, they were bound for a pool that was accessed from the corridor's opposite end.

In the lobby, he idled around the perimeter of the open tropical planting to covertly eye passing guests. After twenty minutes of this, be bought a *Wall Street Journal* in a shop off the lobby, chose a secluded, pink-upholstered, white wicker chair with a clear view of much of the broad lobby, and settled in for another half hour.

After that, he walked to the open-sided cocktail lounge at the north end of the lobby level. It was in sparse use this early afternoon. He took a table that overlooked the sea, ordered a chicken sandwich and beer, and watched—and felt—the waves crash against the face of the lava cliff directly below.

Beyond the lounge was a second swimming pool, a small one with a curved slide off a platform above the edge of the cliff. He called for his check, then ambled out to a chair at the edge of the pool's perimeter paving. He spent a few minutes there, long enough to earn an interested glance from a slender brown girl in a black bikini. He didn't respond. Another time, baby. He returned to the lobby.

He didn't expect to find Franklin this way. There was the

off-chance possibility, sure, but Prettykin didn't believe in chance. He was a planner. Now he had the feel of the place and a good sense of its interior layout.

He stopped briefly at a little writing desk, folded a blank piece of hotel stationery, sealed it in a Kona Imperial envelope, wrote D. FRANKLIN on it, and took it to the desk.

"Will you see that Mr. Franklin gets this, please?"

The muumuu-draped, pleasant-faced Hawaiian desk clerk smiled, nodded, took the envelope. Prettykin drifted away, eyes alert. She reached up, slid the envelope in the slot numbered 507.

He took one of the wood-paneled elevators to the fifth floor. The corridor's cream walls and coral carpeting were brightly lighted with fluorescent ceiling inserts. Room 507 was on the ocean side, the second room from a sharp bend in the deserted hallway. He stopped outside the door, listened. No murmur of voices in there. They were probably out sightseeing. Or on the room's balcony.

He returned to the lower level, followed the concrete parking-and-pool access corridor to its south end and stepped outside into a much larger pool area than the one he had checked at the other end of the hotel. He skirted a group of middle-aged women on poolside chaises, their leathery skins already nut brown. Regulars, no doubt, following the seasons to Hawaii, Scottsdale, Palm Beach. He wondered what their husbands did.

Past the noisy pool area, Prettykin strolled up narrow steps cut in the oceanside lava shelf to emerge in the extensive tropical landscaping that flanked the entire building front. Midway, he left the meandering pathway, through carefully manicured bougainvillea, crotons, plumeria, hibiscus, and gracefully arching palms, to walk out on the naked lava shelf that overlooked the sea. Now only an occasional comber bulged its blue-green swell to gain inbound momentum, then slam the cliff face beneath his feet. He could feel those impacts through the soles of his soft tan Guccis.

When he returned to the garden pathway, he glanced upward without raising his head. The fifth floor corridor layout was photo clear in his mind. There was Franklin's balcony, directly above him. Empty. And two floors above that, on the building's seaward ell, was a small, open observation deck. No doubt it was accessible from the seventh floor corridor. The deck jutted above an Aztec-like decorative frieze between the sixth and seventh floors. It offered a superb view of the ocean. And of Franklin's balcony.

The straight-line distance from the observation deck to the balcony, Prettykin judged, was not more than eighty feet. A giveaway shot with even the most inaccurate of rifles. But with a three-and-a-half-inch-barreled Bernardelli, even if the piece were new, with its precision parts unworn, such a shot at the steep, downward angle would be less than sure.

It would have to be done when Franklin was on his balcony, of course. Add to that the possibility of being spotted up there by other balcony sitters, even of the chance appearance of someone on the deck itself. An unfortunate glance upward at the wrong moment by a stroller down here . . . If Franklin's wife were on the balcony with him, she'd be a prime witness. Prettykin would have the added need to take her out along with Franklin.

Messy. Too messy. And damned risky, even if he'd been provided with a silencer that the Bernardelli most certainly lacked.

A full circuit of the building was blocked by the elevated cliff-edge construction of the north swimming pool. He returned to the registration desk through an entrance off the garden and used his wide-eyed college boy routine.

"Ma'am, I left a message for Mr. Franklin. But I've had to change my plans. I wonder if you might return the envelope, please? I see he hasn't picked it up."

She had a sweet smile.

"Much obliged, ma'am." On his way out, he tore up the envelope and its blank insert and dropped the shreds in a lower-level receptacle.

The car was stinking hot again. He adjusted the A/C vents to blow full in his face as he backed out of the space, then guided the Camaro to the hotel access road and up the rise to Alii Drive. Hell of an assignment. He'd been given a name, a general location, and a short-range weapon. He'd found the guy's hotel, his room, had checked out potential lines of fire.

Didn't know Franklin's car, though, or even if he had one. Didn't know the guy's habits: what time he got up, whether he spent most of the day with his wife or was more of a loner or spent time with friends he might have here. Didn't know what Franklin did for a living. Sindicato Sud's geniuses might think that was beside the point, but if your negocio was a pasty-faced accountant type, that was one thing. If he was a top-condition undercover cop on vacation, that was plenty other. He'd take out either one, but ease of handling would sure vary.

What made Franklin worth forty Gs?

When he'd left the King Kamehameha this morning, Prettykin had debated the advisability of checking out in order to move into the Kona Imperial. But he decided to follow his practice of not registering in the same hotel with a target. A lived-in room could offer leads. Better to cope with the inconvenience of a commute than to worry about a maid's noticing a shirt described by an unexpected witness or to sweat hotel security watching checkouts for the tiniest excuse to detain and question. He would stay where he was.

He drove back to Kailua at an easy speed, welcoming the time to think. A shot downward from the observation deck was not top choice, but it was a possibility. Sindicato Sud wanted this guy exed fast, but that was all the instructions had covered in that area.

If Mr. and Mrs. Donald Franklin had rented a car, and chances were they had, that offered additional possibilities. Opportunities that could prove less risky to Prettykin than a balcony ambush. This was something of a tourist byway, this southwest coast of the Big Island. Miles of isolated roadway connected primary points of interest. That created potentially usable vehicular exposure. He might not have to use the Bernardelli at all.

Tomorrow morning early, he would return, somehow devise a way to survey the parking area until the Franklins emerged, then he would improvise. If they elected to stay at the resort, or if they had taken an overnight trip somewhere else, he would face another kind of problem.

On the shoulder of the deserted Queen Kaahumanu Highway, two miles above the exit for Keahole Airport, the white Toyota stood motionless in a frozen black sea. Its stalled engine pinged as it cooled.

She reached in her purse, pulled out the pack of Casinos, and lit one with her silver butane lighter. She inhaled deeply, exhaled in a long, shaking breath. Had he noticed that?

She rolled her window down slowly. She needed time to collect herself. He wasn't as helplessly tractable as she had assumed. She had begun to accept the effects of the medication as true personality traits. But apparently the stuff had a much briefer residual effect than Horger had informed her. Possibly during their pre-breakfast snuggle, her charge had managed to do some thinking on his own.

Alarmed at his seemingly increasing acuity during the early morning hours in the past couple of days, she had increased the dosage to a tablet and a half. That had been a mistake. The stuff had made him barely able to walk a straight line. Yesterday he'd just wanted to stay in the room. That wouldn't do at all. She had gone back to the regular dosage this morning, not that it mattered after yesterday's colossal blunder.

Obviously, she never should have left him alone. Somehow he had discovered something. But she had been going quietly crazy tied to this drug-numbed, brain-scrambled subject. And Vandenhoff had supplied the temptation: the open-end charge card accounts. God, Lorraine, how deplorably feminine!

The long fumble for the cigarette, the leisurely use of the dash lighter, the slow roll-down of the window, all were stalls, ways to give her tumbling fears time to sort themselves out. When he'd actually said, "Pyremisine," only her training and experience had covered her astonishment. So much for her conviction that she had been handed the control strings of a six-foot Elmer Fudd.

"What was that stuff you mentioned?" Answer an unanswerable question with a question of your own.

"Come off it, Lori—or whatever your name really is."

"Don!"

He shook his head. He wasn't having any. "Pyremisine, according to a Honolulu lab analysis."

My God! How had he managed that? She had the tablets concealed in a lipstick tube she had kept with her. And she knew the tablet count. The controlled reduction of their number had not varied.

"I want answers. Now. Or we both go to the police."

"The local police? That would be an unfortunate move."

"I'm sure it would."

"Not for me. For you."

His righteous anger backed down a notch. "For me? You've got to be kidding, lady. I haven't done a damned thing that I'm aware of. I imagine the Big Island police would be very interested in the victim of involuntary medication that robs him of the ability to think straight."

"It would be a disaster, darling." She put a sarcastic emphasis on the endearment and forced a confident smile. "Believe me, you don't have the remotest idea what kind of scorpion can you would be popping open."

A dusty black van materialized far down the road behind them. They both were silent as it raced closer, then yowled past, and disappeared beyond a slight rise ahead.

"Tell me."

She had him off balance. But only a little. "*If he blows,*" Vandenhoff had briefed her, "*you can let him in partway.*" Then the little man had detailed for her the "fallback."

She dragged on her brown cigarette. Its glowing end quivered despite her control. She held the smoke deep, then let it out slowly. She hadn't thought it would come to this. He had seemed so utterly controllable.

"You're better off not knowing." She didn't want to give it to him too easily.

"What, damn it? Knowing what?"

"You're right about the name. It's not Don Franklin. There isn't a Donald Roberts Franklin."

His steel eyes bored into her. He was quite a different

person. Hard bone now, with the induced flab stripped away.

"Then who?" His voice was as cold as winter wind.

She took another deep drag, let it seep out slowly between nearly closed lips. "Murtha. Frank Murtha." She waited.

"That doesn't mean one goddamned thing to me."

"That's because of the accident . . . Frank. The accident was real. 'Don Franklin' has been a protective cover. You're in the Federal Witness Protection Program."

That shook him nicely.

"Who the hell is Frank Murtha?" The words were aggressive, but some of the iciness had given way.

"You really don't remember, do you? You were the Procurador, the lawyer, for Sindicato Sud. Ring a bell?" A trickle of perspiration tickled her left side just below her armpit.

"Nothing."

"Sindicato Sud, the major source of South American cocaine, means nothing to you?"

"I was part of that?"

"Up to your eyeballs, Mr. Murtha. But now you're trying to redeem yourself by turning—"

"Informer." He was clearly shaken now. "Federal witness protection equals informer."

"Probably the first decent thing you've done in your whole damned life, Frank."

Just who the hell *are* you, 'Lori Franklin'?"

"I'm your bodyguard, Mr. Murtha. Working out of the Justice Department."

"You're kidding."

"I'm not kidding."

"You got proof? An ID card, maybe?"

"In my purse. You want to see that?"

"Yes."

She shrugged, zipped open the linen purse beside her, and extracted a plastic card complete with color Polaroid and a bronze shield.

She let them do the talking.

He handed them back, an uncertain frown pulling his

eyebrows together. "So how in hell are you supposed to protect me?"

"It's a departmental operation. We were doing fine, I thought. When I was driving you to the Albany Airport from Syracuse, we did hit that damned truck. You came out of Horger's surgery with a blanked-out memory. Temporary, maybe, but a consulting psychiatrist advised us that it would be much easier on you if we were to convince you that you really were the alias we'd set up for you."

He was silent, no doubt trying to absorb all this left-field info she was throwing at him. Then he said, "Syracuse? Why Syracuse?"

"You tell me. That's where you wanted to surrender. From there, we were going directly to the Albany Airport, then here. We're here to wait out the weeks until the Senate Drug Control Committee Hearing. The accident threw us a hell of a curve, but we worked it in. The big question mark, of course, is whether that screwed-up memory of yours will snap back into place so you can testify and justify all this TLC we're giving you. So far, I'd say the results are zero on any scale you want to use. You've really got us worried, Murtha."

A loosely spaced trio of cars droned past, northbound. Maybe airport rentals taking new arrivals to the Royal Waikoloa or Mauna Lani, those green oases they'd passed ten miles back.

"Abner Jellicoe," he said abruptly. "How'd you work that little con?"

"No problem. He was a department man."

"Then it was on to Hawaii. Okay, if you're my bodyguard, what have you got to protect me with?"

"Distance. The cover you are so intent on blowing. Plus a Smith and Wesson Model Four-sixty-nine Mini-Gun. It's a cut-down Model Four-fifty-nine but carries the same fourteen-shot nine-millimeter clip."

"Where's that stashed?"

"In my purse."

"How do you get it past airport security?"

"Prearrangement. Easy when you're a fed, Mr. Murtha."

He pondered. "Why the secret doping?"

"That what?"

"The goddamned Pyremisine."

"Just a mild relaxant. You were in a hell of a shape mentally, Murtha. It was to calm the inner turmoil, help you get it together. You realize you're no damned help to us if you can't get your recall back. What good is a witness without a memory?"

Now he looked at her with a most curious expression. "My God," he almost whispered. "This is damned hard to believe."

"From your viewpoint, I can understand that." She reached for the ignition key. "May I start the car now, 'Don,' darling?"

As she pulled back on the pavement a fragment of a folksong parody came to her from nowhere. Pat Paulsen in an old album she had bought at a Georgetown flea market, playing a woebegone native spinning an ancient tale: *"My people believe this . . . because they are stupid."* Pause. *"I believe it, too."*

She almost did.

—11—

He stood at the closed glass door to the lanai and stared through it far out to sea. Everything had changed. With her clever manipulation, he had truly begun to feel as if he were indeed an architect with a temporary impairment. Now he was adjusting again, with sick reluctance, to the fact that he wasn't at all what he had been led to believe.

A criminal lawyer. In the literal sense. For a ruthless drug syndicate! He felt prickles of new fear across his chest. His mind was a kaleidoscope of conflict. Then out of the reeling confusion came a question with an edge as sharp as hollow-ground steel.

He said it aloud. "What if my memory never comes back?"

She had taken off her slacks and blouse and stood in pastel-blue bra and bikini panties.

"That's the gamble, friend. We're banking on this little rest cure to restore all those wonderful recollections you promised us. It's set up as a trade. Immunity for full disclosure, remember? Oh, I'm sorry. You don't." Her jade eyes held his. "Or do you?"

"You think I'm holding out? You think this is an act, for God's sake?"

"I'm not sure what I think now. You told me you snuck up the hill to that doctor. What kind of trust did that demonstrate?"

"In you?"

"Yes, in me, Don."

"Forget the 'Don' stuff, damn it."

"No, it's still intact cover. Recuperating Don Franklin and his dutiful wife, Lorraine. You'll stick to that role, Mr. Murtha." She reached behind her, unhooked the bra, and slid it off her arms.

"You are remarkable, Ms. Burch."

She scowled, then understood. "Oh, come on. You're expecting sudden modesty because now you know we're not who you thought we were?"

"You don't think it's different now?"

"Not to me, Procurador. I must have done one hell of a job on you."

"You're good, Ms. Burch." He gave that a sarcastic twist.

"You seemed to appreciate it."

"I mean as a role player. You're only passable in bed." He felt deceived, foolish, and he wanted to sting.

"I don't believe a man with a memory like yours is in a position to make comparisons." In an odd gesture, a lot like defiance, she hooked her thumbs under the bikini's elastic and slid it off.

He sank into a chair near the lanai door and gazed at her challenging creamy nakedness. "For God and country?"

"I do consider myself something of a soldier, Murtha."

"Just call me Don, sweet stuff, and stay the hell in your own bed." He didn't trust her. Not now. Not after she had so unabashedly detailed her intricate deception. Not when he thought how willingly she had let him have her, had even initiated some of their supposedly conjugal couplings. All part of her Justice Department job. He'd been one of the world's prize marks in an elaborate con. She had used the hell out of him.

"What if the memory doesn't come back?" he asked again.

She stuck her head out of the bathroom. "Then, darling, you will be hospitalized until it does."

That, delivered in her matter-of-fact flat style, brought out the sweat again. He knew she meant it. He was in federal hands. If he didn't deliver, he could disappear forever in the labyrinth of institutional public health.

She could still strip naked in front of him, but he couldn't do that with her watching. Stupid, since she'd already stripped him of nearly everything—pride, if he'd ever had any; faith in himself; probably manhood, too. He didn't want to test that. She could stay away from him now. He took his pajamas into the bathroom; changed in there.

In the room's darkness, he tried to put it all neatly together. Murtha. The name meant nothing to him. Nothing at all. A mob turncoat, for God's sake. He'd thought he'd had troubles before, but as pathetic Don Franklin, he'd had it made compared to what he knew now. Nobody loved an informer.

What had she called it? The Sindicato Sud? It *had* to be after his butt. And he could sense her disdain, now that her dutiful-wife act was blown.

On one side, the threat was heavy enough for the Justice Department to smuggle him way the hell and gone out to this remote Hawaiian coast. And on the other? Suppose his damned brain stayed half-dead, and he couldn't come up with the information he'd promised? Was she telling him the truth about the hospitalization alternative? Or would the feds simply put him out on Pennsylvania Avenue for Sindicato Sud's disposal of an embarrassment? Either way, he was a bum bet for a bright future.

He had a hell of a time getting to sleep. Something nagged at him, something back there in what she'd told him.

Then when the rhythmic thud of waves against the lava cliffs did at last lull him to the fuzzy edge of sleep, he heard the damned voice.

"Don Franklin. You will remember that." Beyond the looming face with its stiff gray mustache, squinting eyes, and those strange half-lenses, he saw white-painted walls. Not smooth plaster, but stone whose edges had been blunted by many coats. Old stone. The overhead fluorescents were bright in his light-sensitive eyes.

"You are . . . ?" the half-lenses demanded.

Don said nothing, not to this insistent voice, almost unctuous but with an undertone of hard control.

"Your name, sir!"

He couldn't remember, but he was not going to give this insistent stranger the satisfaction of his parroting "Don Franklin." He didn't like the son of a bitch.

The big head turned away. "The recall blanking seems to have been highly effective. But he's fighting the replacement input. I've done all I can, and I'm due back in Cambridge by morning. You will have to handle the balance of the input here. Are you up to that?"

Something pricked his left upper arm. He forced his strangely unresponsive eyes downward. Pudgy fingers withdrew a syringe.

"Yes, Dr. Krupas. I can handle that." The voice, a woman's voice, projected a familiar confidence. Don inched his leaden head upward against the chair's padded headrest. The mustached doctor rose from the stool on which he had been hunched between Don's splayed knees. When he moved aside, Don saw the woman with the confident voice. Hair smooth and black and shining in the basement's stark brilliance. Eyes green and cold as January ice. Lori.

Don's leg muscles clenched, jerking him awake. And abruptly he realized she had lied to him. Just a relaxant, she had told him so smoothly. But Fukada's information had not been so benign. "Impairs one's will power," the little doctor had reported.

The surreptitious dosing? They'd wanted to be certain he was drugged on schedule; didn't want to depend on his fogged brain for the essential daily administration; didn't want him to connect the dosage with his chronically passive state. They hadn't wanted him to do exactly what he had done: tie in the regularity of the stuff's effect with its cause. And he hadn't. Until Fukada discovered he was being medicated.

Something still did not add up. He realized that as he drifted toward sleep again. Something definitely did not add up.

If anyone with art training came across the hotel parking lot and looked closely at what Prettykin was up to, that could blow it right here. But one man's daubing was another's masterpiece, right? Prettykin didn't know anything about art. He didn't even know what the public liked. He had noted, though, that amateur artists were as much a part of the Kona Coast's landscape as the congealed folds of lava. He had seen them dabbing at canvasses on Kailua's waterfront, along Alii Drive, out on the lava promontories overlooking the sea. He had invested some of his cash wad in a cheap easel, a sixteen-by-twenty canvas stretched on a wood frame, a beginner's box of oils, a plywood palette, and the brushes the cheerful little brown woman clerk had suggested.

He had parked the Camaro just outside the Kona Imperial's lava-columned entrance, left the hatch open and set up his easel before six A.M. He positioned himself where he could check every emerging vehicle without seeming to take his attention off the gentle rise of Mauna Loa's western slope that began its slow rise from sea level here to climb twenty-five miles to its still-active crater, more than two miles high. The crest of the world's largest mountain was invisible to Prettykin beyond the swell of its foothill slope, but he wasn't here to admire the view. In fact, the upslope vista wasn't one of the greatest for a painting subject. Even he could see that. But whoever questioned a hack artist about subject choices?

By seven-thirty, if anyone had stood thirty feet away and squinted hard, he or she might have discerned crude beginnings of a representation of the road ascending to Alii Drive, the scar Alii itself made higher up, and a roughed-in skyline. Prettykin had surprised himself.

He had also carefully checked all eleven cars that had thus far rolled out the hotel entrance, none of the occupants of which resembled his memorized photograph of D. Franklin.

By nine, his fruitless scanning of a dozen more emerging vehicles had been no more productive. The painting had progressed too fast. Now it looked like a child's exercise. He stood back a few steps. No, not that bad, as a matter of fact.

He took off his aviator sunglasses and wiped them with the tail of his Hawaiian shirt. He was glad he'd passed up liquids at breakfast. This was turning into a long pull out here. The sun had worked him over pretty good before the scatter of clouds had begun to provide occasional shade.

A Bronco jounced past with four bronzed teenagers aboard. Probably heading up the mountain. A pale blue Datsun followed close behind, with two white-haired women up front, nobody in the back. Then there was no more exiting traffic for ten, maybe fifteen, minutes.

Now a white Toyota rolled out of the parking area. Two people, man and woman. The guy at the wheel, Prettykin noted as they passed, had an odd angle to his nose. And yes, a scar on his left cheek!

The Toyota began the climb up to Alii Drive. Prettykin slammed shut his box of oils, wrapped an arm around the easel, grabbed the canvas, threw it all in the Camaro's open rear hatch. He had dropped the little palette face down in the drive. It was crusted with black grit. He scooped it up, tossed it in after the rest of his gear, and slammed shut the hatch. He scrambled behind the wheel and gunned the Camaro up the hill in time to see the Toyota's brake lights flash as the little car swung left on Alii Drive. They had headed toward Kailua. A shopping trip? How in hell could he get at Franklin in the middle of Kailua?

Then the Toyota turned off Alii and began to climb a steep connecting stretch to the Hawaiian Belt Road, higher on Mauna Loa's flank. There was no way to tail them up the almost straight mile and a half of the connecting blacktop without being obvious. He had to hang too damned close to see which way they would turn at the top.

They turned south, down the long empty state road chiseled into the mountainside high above the coastline.

For a main artery, the Belt Road was narrow by Mainland standards. It had been carved out of flint-hard lava, and it followed the undulating contours of old lava flows. She should have insisted on driving, but there was no convincing way to get herself behind the wheel now that he so obviously felt a male need to assert himself.

"A long ride," she had urged, "to help us sort things out."

She wasn't sure that had sounded at all convincing, but

she had to make him more accessible than he was in the hotel. And it had to be done promptly. The project was beginning to fray at its edges. She was already on fallback, and there wasn't anywhere to go from here.

When Vandenhoff had detailed all this, he had made it sound as foolproof as a geometry theorem. Angle A plus Angle B would produce the obvious result. His major concern had been her ability to hold together under the unique pressure. "This won't be like Code Hatfield."

"*You* took me off Code Hatfield," she threw back at him.

"That's correct, Burch. To free you for Code Franklin. Hatfield's on hold until I give it to LaBranche."

"After what I've done with it, you're turning that project over to him?"

The little round-headed man's washed-out eyes hardened. "I'll worry about LaBranche. And I'll worry about you. You worry about your ability to handle this complex a scenario."

"Trust me." She suppressed a flippant smile. She had seen Ollie Trent dropkicked twenty-five yards into Biscayne Bay by a shovel-nosed Corvette in Miami. In New York, Sid Gurney's femoral artery had been razored through while he stood against her in a subway crush. He hadn't fallen until the train pulled in and the crowd surged forward to let him drop. She had made it past both of those breaks in IMS's daily routine without visible scars.

But Vandenhoff had a point. Ollie and Sid had been IMS people. She hadn't lived with them nearly a month, slept with them as she had with "Don Franklin." Was that going to make a difference? Galloway had gone under after the O'Hara bombing incident. She wouldn't forget the clucking sound of his out-of-context laughter in staff debriefing as it turned to weeping, and the call from Vandenhoff at one-thirty the next morning.

"Galloway just phoned. Threatens to eat his thirty-eight. Get over there and talk to him."

Vandenhoff wouldn't go himself? She'd been less than a minute late; heard the flat detonation as she stepped off the elevator. God, that had been such a mess. But she hadn't lived or slept with Galloway, either.

"Okay," the man they had named Don Franklin had said at breakfast this morning when she'd suggested this drive south. He had insisted on the dining room. No more room service. Well, the Pyremisine wasn't a factor now, anyway. She was dealing with a wide-awake man who thought he was no longer confused. Some of the details had changed, but the big picture was still in its frame.

She had first noticed the tan Camaro when they had turned off the access road into Alii Drive. Not so easy to check behind you when you weren't driving and didn't want to be caught checking.

At the sharp right off the connecting road into the Belt Road, she glanced to her right and saw it again. Its driver was alone. A mile later, she decided to put her big purse on the back seat and thus manage another glimpse of the low-slung tan car. It matched their speed a half mile behind.

It was still there when she reached back for a tissue. Her chest tightened. Normal enough for the abnormal situation you are in, she thought wryly. Then she had another thought. What if this son of a bitch had no compunction to be neat? She felt sudden moisture between her breasts, first hot, then ice cube cold.

Tropical brush had gotten toeholds along the roadside here. Beyond the green fringe, the oceanward side dropped away so steeply as to be invisible from the car, until it flattened maybe a mile below to run another mile, in sugar cane and coffee trees, to the lip of a second escarpment at the sea's edge.

A hard jolt against the left rear or a quick pass with the cut-in too soon, and the Toyota would rip through the thin roadside hedgerow of brightly flowered shrubs and feathery ferns to plunge hundreds of feet straight down onto the flint-hard lava that formed the brief plain below.

That she wasn't willing to face.

"Let's pull over for a minute. There's such a lovely view from here."

Had he not heard her? She could no longer be certain of controlling his actions. Their relationship as Franklin and wife had been bizarre. Now that the Pyremisine was out of the picture, and she'd had to tell him he was Murtha, the problem was even more volatile.

Then the Toyota slowed on a steepening downgrade. She had made an effort to appear tractable this morning, an essentially decent woman stuck with a rough job. She wondered, though, what he felt after accepting her as his wife, then learning she had been massively deceiving him? Could there still be a subconscious remnant of the dutiful husband in his jumbled thought processes?

Then he stopped the car and shut off the ignition.

"I think the view is better up ahead," she said.

"I'll move up."

But she was already getting out. He stayed behind the wheel. She hesitated. At her suggestion, he had stopped—apparently without thinking about it too thoroughly. Could she get away with urging him to step out of the car?

She glanced back down the highway. The tan car had slowed to a crawl. She felt a curious tingle break across her shoulders. Had to be. At long last. Vandenhoff, you slick bastard. You're right again.

Now she had to get her subject out here and properly set up. Away from her. She trotted ahead. This would look strange, but how long could the Chevy dawdle back there before the confused Mr. Franklin-Murtha began to assemble some pieces?

A hundred feet beyond the Toyota, she stumbled, gasped, hopped on one foot to grab the other. There was almost no shoulder here. Would unimaginative Franklin-now-Murtha pull the car ahead to reach her or would he rush to her on foot?

The driver's door opened. Very helpful, sir. And incredibly stupid.

Behind him, she saw the tan car accelerate. He trotted toward her. The Chevy grew larger. Then he heard its onrushing howl. He sidestepped off the pavement to the narrow shoulder, less than a foot wide, between blacktop and encroaching scrub.

The Chevy whistled past the Toyota, veered sharply to its right. Don—she thought of him as Don in this final fraction of a second—whirled toward the tire squeal. He stared straight into the onrushing radiator grille.

Then he sprang sideways.

The Camaro fishtailed wildly. A fan of gravel flew over the hedgerow and sailed into space. The car screeched back on the pavement. She could see the driver fight for control. Then the car's snout, now growing huge, centered on *her*.

She froze. This wasn't supposed to happen. The engine howled. The driver swerved the right wheel off the pavement again to the narrow strip of shoulder. The front fender plowed through weeds, brush, and fern fronds. He'd left her no margin for escape. No margin at all.

The white-faced blond driver seemed to loom over her, hunched above the wheel, fighting the pull of the heavy scrub.

One slim chance. The onrushing Chevy was just feet away, its engine revved to a banshee howl. She faced it, legs spread wide.

She feinted to her left. Then with all her strength, she lunged the opposite way.

The speeding car's inboard fender slapped the toe of her left shoe as she sprawled across the highway's centerline. Her shoulder slammed the rockhard blacktop. She skidded along the abrasive pavement on her side, arms and legs drawn tight.

She heard the Camaro's roar and squeal fade. She sat up, sprawled in the middle of the highway. The car rocked on down the grade. Its brakelights flared blood red. Then it disappeared around a descending curve.

She scrambled to her feet. The narrow shoulder where her subject had stood was empty. The incident had happened so fast that she didn't know whether the Chevy had managed to hit him. She ran back to the ugly skid marks and peered over the road's foliage-choked rim.

He pulled himself up, hand over hand, through tangled growth. When he stood beside her, scratched and dusty with a triangular rip above the left knee of his sports slacks, he stared down the road. "That," he said, his voice hoarse, "was too goddamned close!"

"Are you all right?"

He stared at her torn and road-stained slacks and blouse, the abrasions on her hands and arms. "Are you?"

"I'm fine," she lied. The Sindicato Sud driver had been inept. That was the only word for it. He had certainly reinforced the Murtha fallback, but reinforcement hadn't been what she'd needed. And she was stunned to find herself a target. The failed effort couldn't help but make Franklin-Murtha as wary as a shot-at-and-missed quail. Or pigeon. Were they both Vandenhoff's pigeons now?

"This little trip wasn't such a great idea, Burch." He dusted his trousers with hard slaps. "We're going back to the hotel."

As he opened the door of the Toyota he stared at the purse perched on the back seat. Then he looked at her, his eyes hard as fragments of quartz.

She had really blown it. Dear God.

Prettykin was in one hell of a sweat. He'd let the Chevy rush downhill for a half mile, guiding it almost subconsciously, his mind rolling over the colossal botch he'd left up there on the highway behind him. Franklin had most unexpectedly dived over the side. Maybe he was bent a little by that, but he surely wasn't zeroed unless he'd hit his head on a chance rock. Prettykin's quick glance, though, had told him that beyond the shoulder, tangled vines had in all probability made a dandy safety net. No, he hadn't offed Franklin.

And the damned woman! A closeup witness, she'd had to go, too. Only she had turned out to have the smarts and the reflexes of a panther.

He braked hard, slowed, and beat the wheel with his fist. Damn! They'd been set up like a six and a nine pin, and he'd had a bowling ball half a lane wide. How could he have foreseen Franklin's taking off into space like a gazelle? And her! Faking one way, then diving into the center of the road like it was a mattress. Had she actually been smart enough to realize that his wheels in the damned bushes were dragging him to the right? He had badly underestimated these people, both of them.

Prettykin screeched the Camaro across the highway, hit

reverse, spun the wheel the other way, jerked into drive, and gunned the car back upgrade. Blue smoke drifted above the road behind him.

They had gone, of course. What else could he expect? That they would get back in their Toyota and cruise down the hill after him? Maybe, if they'd assumed he was a drunk driver and wanted his tag number.

But they had to know his deliberate swerve toward Franklin, then his nearly hundred-foot slash along the shoulder to get at her, was no morning boozer's sloppy driving. They had enough smarts to escape two tons of roaring steel. They certainly could guess that he was here to take the guy, or both of them, out.

Island tourists, Mr. and Mrs. Donald Franklin? In a pig's butt.

Whoever they really were, they weren't going to wander around on deserted roads in their little white Toyota now. What would he do in their place? Check out pronto and hole up somewhere far, far away. No forwarding address.

Did they already have his tag number? Would they have the balls to report a "tan Camaro driven by a male Caucasian with blond hair and sunglasses"? He thought yes.

Then he thought no. Sindicato Sud didn't bull around contracting out respectable citizens. The chances were better than good that they would want no contact with the local law over this.

He should change cars, anyway, on principle. But there wasn't time for that. As soon as they packed and checked out, they'd race out the Kona Imperial's entrance, burning rubber for the airport.

How long would that take? Twenty more minutes? Twenty minutes left to recover a hell of a fumble and head off a possible Sindicato negocio on himself. Those rock-headed Colombians allowed zero tolerance. He could watch his own tail for a year, two years. Maybe take out a couple of their people. But he couldn't take out their whole army, and what was the quality of a life like that?

The Franklins had to go.

—12—

He let her in the room first, then slammed the door behind them.

"All right, Special Agent Burch! Where in hell was your damned artillery?"

"Keep your voice down, Murtha."

He grabbed her by the arms. "You walked out there a good hundred feet. *Without* your pistol. What in the hell kind of security have I got here?"

"I'm sorry. It was a slip. It won't happen again." She twisted her arms free, tossed the purse on her bed, and went into the bathroom. She closed the door hard.

"I need more answers than that," he called through the white paneling.

Silence. That galled him, too.

"Such as your damned distancing. You got yourself a hundred feet away from me out there today. At the City of Refuge, you managed to put that much space between us. Same arrangement on the Mamalahoa Highway, when you had me looking for olivines. What kind of game is this?"

She came out of the bathroom in her bra and briefs, the torn blouse and slacks over her arm. She had washed the angry abrasions on her hands and arms and a larger raspberry-bright patch on her shoulder. An ugly blue-brown bruise ran almost the length of her right thigh.

"You tell me they're after me, but look at yourself." He

nodded at her assorted damage. "That guy had us both lined up."

"You'd better wash out your own scrapes, then I'll go down for a bottle of Betadine."

"And leave me up here? You're doing it again."

"You'll be behind a locked door."

He couldn't read her. Shock over the near thing they'd both just barely managed to live through? Disgust at having blown her job? Or something else? There was a prickly surrealistic undertone to all of this, something he couldn't put his finger on.

He stripped off his ruined sports shirt, balled it up, and slammed it on the bed.

"Goddamn you! I think you've been setting me up!"

She stared at him without change of expression in that sculptured ice-block face. But he saw what she could not control. Her color drained down like mercury in a suddenly frosted thermometer. A slick of perspiration glazed her shoulders and chest above the bra.

"*Why?* Why in great bloody hell would you set up the guy you're hired to protect?"

She stood by the bathroom door like a twelve-year-old caught naked with a boy and unable to come up with a reasonable explanation.

"The game is over, Lorraine. Check me if I'm wrong. You may be on the Justice Department payroll, but that's not your sole source of income, is it?"

She didn't move, flinch, twitch. Didn't do a damned thing but stand there nearly naked with her ruined clothes over one arm and stare at him.

He paced across the room, swung around, then leaned against the lanai door jamb, arms folded, legs crossed. He felt that he had control now. For the first time.

"Amazing what money can do, right? You've been setting me up all along. Frank Murtha turns himself over to the feds. There's an accident. He comes out of it with his memory off its track. Justice needs him so bad that it hopes a rest cure will jog his memory back in gear. So he's fixed up with a phony name, a cover complete with wife, a bogus visit from a 'business associate,' special credit card accounts and driver's license and business cards. All right so far?''

She still hadn't moved. The sweat slick seeped into the top edges of her bra cups. He crossed his legs the other way. He needed a little time to think.

"But what Justice doesn't know is that you're on the take from the very same bastards you're supposed to protect me from. Neat little game, Agent Burch. No doubt you tipped them where we are staying, then it was just a matter of putting the target out there in the open. First the Painted Church, then the City of Refuge, then the Mamalahoa Highway. But nothing happens. They haven't gotten their guy on site yet, or he's run into complications.

"Then today, on the Belt Road, bingo! There he is. There I am. But surprise! There you are, too. Then a big surprise for him: he misses both of us."

He jammed his hands in his pockets, pushed away from the wall, and abruptly sat down in the chair near the door.

"Damn it, will you say something?"

Her eyes had never left his. Now she carefully laid her slacks and blouse on the bed, then sat beside them, her back to him.

"It's not altogether like that."

"It's a lot like that."

"Yes, it's a lot like that."

"What the hell is it with you? You've used me like a damned puppet for money. You've even used yourself. In bed at the drop of a hint. Didn't that mean anything to you?"

She threw him a cold gaze over her shoulder. "Don't be naive, for God's sake. I didn't hear any complaints."

"You're hearing them now." This must be how a woman feels, he thought, when she's told that all the tenderness, all the whispered endearments, all the warm couplings and shared releases, were just a con.

She twisted around. "Do you want to thrash around with your theories or move on from here?"

"You are one cold bitch, Lorraine. I can see why Justice issued the card. But recent experience tells me I'd be better off without you, maybe even in the hands of the local cops."

She swung her legs over the bed and her whole body faced him, her arms bracing her stiffly on each side. "Are you serious? Go to them as Franklin, and you're a tourist with a wild story. Go to them as Murtha, and you can bet it'll be in the island papers in twenty-four hours—and on the wire services just as fast."

Her hard tone softened abruptly. "Look, we are dealing with one Sindicato trigger. We can handle that. *We*, Murtha. On your own, you wouldn't make it as far as the airport."

"I damned near made it to hell *with* you this morning."

"That changed things for me."

"I would hope so."

"I mean it, Murtha. The problem now is to work our way out of this."

The perspiration sheen had faded.

"I hope you aren't suggesting that I trust you?"

"I'm suggesting that we work together to get away from that murderous son of a bitch out there with his blond hair and attack driving. That's what I'm suggesting."

"But he's one of yours," he said with a hard, satisfying smile.

"Not anymore."

She asked him to have lunch sent up—a salad and iced tea for her. He'd have a roast beef sandwich and coffee. She asked him to do the ordering, insisted that he check the door's security peephole, then admit the waiter, sign the check, tip him. It was important to let him believe he had gained control, taken over.

The project had unraveled but only partly. Pathetic, chemically confused Don Franklin had become aggressive, suspicious Frank Murtha. That made her job tougher but had not aborted it. As putty-brained husband Don, he had been wonderfully cooperative. As Murtha—and off the Pyremisine—he was as wary as a cornered bear.

Yet she still had a handle on him. They still were here, not fleeing to Keahole Airport in a taxi to throw the blond man off the track. She could still fulfill the assignment.

In fact, she realized, she could wrap it in an even neater package: Sindicato Sud's cannon ices Frank Murtha, then she offs the cannon. There would be a royal flap with the Hawaii police and a hell of a story on the press wires. But Justice would prevail. And the publicity would be convincing. The little man with the round head should be pleased as punch.

The waiter had set up their little room service table near the lanai door, but they were five floors up. They left the drapes open. They ate in silence. Fine with her. Gave her a chance to reweave the frayed edges of what had seemed such a slick arrangement when Vandenhoff had detailed it in his ABC = QED staccato.

It was amoral as hell, but when was the last time she'd worried about that? Certainly not since she had become an IMS rep. You didn't pull down six federal figures by being Ms. Nice Guy.

She crossed her legs beneath her robe and daintily sipped her iced tea. She'd had a conscience back in Pittsburgh. She was really from Pittsburgh. Joe Berchoffski's daughter had been a sweet kid once, on the gawky side but with strangely piercing eyes that got her splay-fingered evil-eye signs from some of Joe's Fairless Works buddies. From the Three Eyeties, he called them, not long off the boat from Palermo.

She had been his little green-eyed girl. Until the night one of the buddies got liquored up, got mad at some ethnic joking, and got Joe Berchoffski just below the rib cage, in a McKeesport alley where he bled to death.

Her mother, Lorraine Berchoffski remembered, had shrunk into herself after that, an emotional turtle until she died of indefinite causes a year later. Lorraine, though now a blossoming nineteen, did no such thing. She began her intelligence gathering at Joe's funeral. The gossipy trail soon led to one Figlio Luchese, a saloon braggart who had been on her father's shift. One of the Three Eyeties.

She had no problem being noticed by Luchese. She was a cold beauty now. The men of McKeesport had their tongues hanging out. The women were beginning instinctively to distrust such an unexpected orchid in their southeast Pittsburgh cabbage patch. Luchese, a wiry man with big fists and a mercurial temper, dated her, took her to his boardinghouse one wind-whipped October night, and got two surprises.

The first was her readiness to bare her glorious body and let him climb on top of it. The second was the lightning strike of agony just above his left kidney at his precise moment of triumph. She'd given him a split second of paradise on his way to hell. His convulsive death thrash had given her intense satisfaction. No one had seen her enter the place with him or depart without him, but she left Pittsburgh within a week.

Something about police work fascinated her. She put in a year with store security at Sears in Altoona, then a couple more with Strawbridge & Clothier near Philadelphia. She also took night classes in criminology at Temple. She made it into Philadelphia's finest when brotherly love was not near the top of the qualification requirements.

She was a street cop at twenty-four, with Hard Arnie Bonner for a partner. He taught her a lot before he was shotgunned dead beside her as they leaped out of their unit just as three adventurers with stockings over their heads leaped out of a South Philadelphia discount liquor store. She got one of them square in the chest while he wondered if he should use his double-O shot on that great-looking face. The other two evaporated, one of them leaving Hard Arnie limp and instantly dead on the sidewalk.

That had brought her to federal attention, specifically to the stone-faced interview with Richard Vandenhoff at the airport Holiday Inn. She hadn't been impressed until he hinted at what he was up to and offered her remuneration that made her city stipend look like the ante in a very small poker game.

For Vandenhoff's retainer, plus potential bonuses, she accepted the status of a permanently on-call independent contractor. She would have full credentials and IMS would pay on-the-job expenses but no fringe benefits. She would have to set up her own IRA.

Vandenhoff used her looks, her intelligence, her cold-mindedness to terminate three deserving people with varying degrees of prejudice. Mr. Franklin-Murtha, sitting across from her in this pleasant luxury resort double, grimly chewing his roast beef sandwich, was targeted as number four. The pathetic bastard still didn't know what was going on. If the blond man could get it together, he never would.

The problem was twofold. First, she had to keep Mr. Franklin-Murtha here on Kona. Secondly, she had to make him accessible without undue exposure of herself, such as she had so stupidly provided this morning and the other three times she had tried to set him up. That meant no more open stretches in the Toyota. Not with Sindicato Sud's man now obviously trying to collect them as a matched set.

A puzzlement. She had to let "Don" believe she'd been under the table with the Sindicato. That supplied a plausible motive for her setting him up. Now the challenge was to convince him that this morning's fiasco had turned her, had put her on his side.

Could she manage that? Could she further maneuver this abused, manipulated, mentally brutalized dumb bastard back into line long enough to bring this nearly blown contract to its originally projected termination? She certainly could use more time. There wasn't any more time.

She nibbled daintily on a slice of papaya. Silhouetted against the lanai's glass-rectangled high noon, their rebuilt man stared at her. For a long moment, she tried to read him through those gray eyes, once so moistly vulnerable, now hard as agate. She and Krupas and Horger and the Pyremisine had made him into prime putty. Now that he was off the stuff and watched her every twitch, now that she had gone to fallback and the project was devoid of a second fallback, she wondered if she might be underestimating this man.

Then he said, "Just what happens now?" with a surprisingly blank look on his surgically scarred face.

No, she wasn't underestimating him. But she needed to regain control. She couldn't bring this off without control. When was a man's resistance at its lowest?

Play along, Murtha, he told himself. But watch this woman. She's as trustworthy as a treed tigress. And smart as hell.

An actress, Academy Award caliber. He'd gone for her dutiful-wife routine hook, line, sinker, bait box, and half the pier—in Horger's questionable clinic, in Oahu, when she'd indulged in her shopping sprees (wonder if Justice foots *those* bills?), and here on the Big Island. Until he had dragged himself to Fukada's medical aerie up there in the Mauna Loa foothills, she'd had her hands on all his strings.

This morning, the thing had apparently blown up in her face. She had learned the hard way that he wasn't the only target. But she was gutsy. Hadn't panicked. Hadn't run.

He pushed back from the room service table and peered through the glass of the lanai door.

"I wouldn't go out there, Murtha."

Was that concern part of her act? Wasn't she running a string of inconsistencies? She had set him up four times that he was aware of. Now she had turned protective. If this morning's action out there on the deserted Belt Road really had turned her around though, he realized, then she wasn't inconsistent. He didn't know what to think now.

She stacked the dishes in the center of the wheeled table and dropped its leaves. He pushed it to the door.

"Check first," she said.

He peered through the wide-angle peephole. The corridor was empty. He rolled the room service rig into the carpeted hall and left it along the wall. He stepped back in, grabbed the complimentary copy of *Aloha* magazine from the top of the TV and stretched out on his bed in his shorts and T-shirt. This was more like the traditional witness protection he had seen in movies. In movies? Or had he lived it before? He opened the magazine, but his concentration refused to focus on the four-color, two-page spread of Oahu's Hanauma Bay.

Wasn't it odd that when she had tossed him the name, Frank Murtha, he hadn't felt one damned thing? Shouldn't there have been a "boing" in his brain, a gate swinging at least partway open?

There had been no recognition at all. He'd had to accept her word, just as he had accepted the Don Franklin charade.

Shouldn't that revelation have triggered *some* reaction? A flash of a Sindicato face? A mental frame or two of a clandestine payoff in a dark limo? A quick flash of a law

office? She had said he was the—what was the term?—
Procurador. The Sindicato's procurador. Say something in
courtroom-ese, Counselor Murtha. What does, uh, *nolle
prosequi* mean?

Lying on the bed and reading, after he'd eaten, made him
drowsy. She sat in her yellow robe near the bathroom door
working on her nails. She had turned on the radio built into
the TV set, and Oahu's KCCN fed subdued steel guitars into
the room.

Where did they go from here?

He let the magazine sag onto his belly. His eyes closed.
Had she somehow slipped him the damned dope again? No,
this wasn't that numbing, leaden medicated collapse. This
was logical reaction to getting up early, then playing dodge
'em with two tons of squealing Camaro.

Franklin. Murtha. He didn't know who the hell he was
anymore. Or who she was. Lori Franklin. Lorraine Burch.
How did he get into this astounding mess?

The whine of the guitars faded.

Then he saw an office, clear as a Kodacolor print. Walnut
paneling. Shelves along one side, with a hodgepodge of
mismatched books. On the opposite wall, a framed diploma. Couldn't quite make it out. Around it, a scatter of
framed photos.

You are a blank slate, Mr. Franklin. The voice of the
man with the half-glasses.

The hell I am, Dr. . . . Krupas. Was that his name?
The hell I am now.

A window took up the far wall. A window with plum-
colored drapes. He could visualize a desk. Teak or walnut,
with a . . . What was that? A ledger and a yellow pad
spread open on the uncluttered desk top. Electric calculator
on a side table. A TI with thermal paper runout. How did he
know that?

The executive chair behind the desk was upholstered in
nubbly plum—

She cleared her throat. He snapped awake, trying
desperately to retain the imprinted scene. That had been *his*
office. But the books on the oiled hardwood shelves had not
been law volumes.

• • •

Unless they had somehow slipped past him, Prettykin reasoned, they were still in the hotel. Their Toyota hadn't moved out of its parking slot.

He had backed in the Chevy nearby, out of sight of the doorman at the elevated main entrance. He sat in it now, trying to determine just why they hadn't cut and run. He'd found a space in the shade of one of the lot's acacias, but the Chevy was still plenty hot. He'd rolled the windows down but moisture soaked the collar of his Hawaiian shirt as he ticked off possibilities.

One, they were scared shitless and had holed up in their room not knowing what to do next.

Or, two, they had called the police and were waiting for them to arrive.

Or, three, the guy was a real pro and had realized that running for the airport would give Prettykin fifteen miles of highway to work in. So he and the broad were engineering another way to get out of here.

Or, four, they'd assumed he'd made his pass, blown it, and was at least an island away by now.

Or, five, they had something totally unpredictable planned for him.

A steaming hour passed. No cops showed. Scratch alternative number two.

If the guy was important enough for Sindicato Sud to blow away, then Prettykin could scratch alternative four as well. An important candidate for a hit couldn't be that naive. It would be a combo of one, three, and five. Only he doubted that the guy was all that scared. The woman maybe, but not the guy. They were holed up, nicely alerted, thanks to Prettykin's overconfidence this morning. And they were planning who knew what?

He got out of the car, bought a broad-brimmed planter's hat from a lobby gift shop and strolled around the south pool to the ocean side of the hotel. Sure enough, up there in Room 507 sat the guy, his back to the lanai. Looked like he was eating, for God's sake. The target was calmly having lunch in an air-conditioned sanctuary while the cannon snuck glances from the steaming garden here and listened to his stomach growl between crashes of surf and wore a stupid straw hat to cover the damned yellow hair.

He threw another venomous glance upward. The guy hadn't moved. Hell of a rifle shot, if Prettykin had had a place to fire from. And a rifle. No cover here, and the guy knew it. Which was why he could sit up there in plain view with his back showing like a dare.

The place was a trap. The concrete parapet of the north pool blocked that end. There was no way around to the south without barging past the bigger pool. That left the entrance off the garden into the lobby. Nice arrangement. Minimum of two dozen witnesses, whichever way he routed himself out.

All this was theory, of course, never to be tested. No rifle, no cover, no go. Certainly not in daylight. At night, you could bet your dumb hat, Prettykin, that the guy wouldn't leave those drapes open.

But he had seen something else in that glance upward to Room 507. How had he missed that before?

When he had checked out the seventh-floor observation deck on his first swing out here, he'd been concerned with the firing angle. That was why he had missed the significance of the decorative concrete striping just below the deck. The wide bands of Aztec-styled frieze relieved the blankness of the building face. They also offered more than eye appeal.

Well, Mr. Artful Dodger, you just stay where you are a few hours more, and ol' Arthur P. will bank a cool forty.

Prettykin was so pleased with himself that he walked into the cocktail lounge and ordered a cheeseburger and Coors. But he made sure he took an obscure table in a remote corner near a rear exit. He did not remove the planter's hat.

All in all, he thought, it had been one hell of a day, starting with their joy ride that had escalated into attempted murder. Then they had dashed back here with his gut twisting. Then he had experienced the photo-sharp vision—was that the right word?—when he'd dozed off after lunch. Following that, their uncommunicative afternoon up here had set him on edge all over again. Then they had ordered supper and again carefully checked the corridor before admitting the familiar waiter.

He had tried to watch TV, but his mind wasn't anywhere near it. Something was badly skewed. She was preoccupied now, filing her nails, but no more interested in that than he had been in television. He pushed himself off the bed, showered, pulled on his pajamas, muttered good night and grumpily turned his back to the light. He heard her in the bathroom. A few minutes later, she clicked off the bed lamp.

Two things did not properly fit. If the situation were reversed, if she were the prize witness and he her security, he would have them the hell out of here and headed for safer territory. Damned if he'd sit around waiting for something else to happen.

That was one piece of illogic that nagged him. The other was just as perplexing. Why, if he was Frank Murtha with a lost memory that the feds desperately wanted retrieved, wasn't she pumping him full of Sindicato background and Murtha lore to jump his memory back on track? Surely the J.D. had fat files of that kind of information. She should be working him over like a shrink. Or a shrink should be working him over. In a D.C. office close to the scene of action, not here on a Pacific island.

Why, in fact, the elaborate "Don Franklin" charade in the first place? Her story that they had done that to help him live his cover just didn't wash. None of this washed.

He slept, anyway. His exhausted body gave way, but his mind wouldn't stop. He heard the dull boom of surf, felt the vibration up the cliff face, through five floors of concrete, through the bed. It was soothing in its primal drive. Real. You could understand crashing surf. . . .

Don Franklin . . . You are Don Franklin. You will remember that. The insistent voice was right in his face, its breath smelling of coffee and mint. It had been a long session in Horger's basement. The overhead lights glittered on the half-lenses.

"Don't you mean Murtha?" Damned if he'd just sit here and take this.

Dr. Krupas ignored that. "Think of yourself as a blackboard, Mr. Franklin. Your past was on it, but it has now been erased. It no longer exists. Do you understand that?" The porcupine mustache was inches from his nose, the doctor's squinted eyes intent on his. "I asked you a question, Mr. Franklin. Do you understand?"

The drug haze was paralyzing.

"Forty ccs," Dr. Krupas said to Horger. The stuff was yellowish in the barrel of the syringe. Horger pointed it ceilingward and tapped out the air bubbles.

"He's already had full dosage, of course," the pudgy surgeon pointed out.

"Chemohypnosis is an inexact procedure, Doctor."

What in hell was chemohypnosis? The needle stung, but he didn't feel any different. He was the subject, but he was an observer, too. Was this how it was to die? To be there but looking on at the same time? Was this happening? A dream. A vision. What?

Not happening but had happened. This sleep vision was too consistent to be just the sensory lashup of a screwed-around brain.

"Donald Roberts Franklin, you understand that?"

He didn't answer.

"Your name, sir?"

Damned if he would cooperate.

Krupas shrugged and turned away. "The recall blanking is effective. He's fighting replacement input. You'll have to handle that here. You up to it?"

He'd lived through this before, hadn't he? Now she would say:

"Yes, Doctor. I can handle that." And she was Lorraine, hair lustrous as polished onyx above the collar of the borrowed pastel-green medical smock.

He'd anticipated that. He was controlling this strange sleep vision now.

Wait a minute. Where were the bandages?

He willed the drifting sequence back to the porcine eyes above the half-lenses. No blur of gauze across his nose. No pull of adhesive on forehead or cheek. *No bandages!*

What did *this* mean? He had forced the sequence

backward. Now further back, scene by scene. He concentrated on his own control, not theirs. Further back.

He had come to consciousness on a cot, a hard cot. No, what did they call these? A gurney. He reached out, touched stone, white painted stone. Lots of coats. No revelation here. He was in the basement's clinic.

Before that.

Before that, not much. Glimpse of a ceiling, low over him. Perforated, with a couple of heavy plastic supporting ribs. He heard engine noises. A car roof? No, an ambulance. Prick in the arm, then out.

Further back. Before that.

A restaurant. Off a big, busy lobby. Two people with him. He didn't know either of them, not the big guy with the brown hair in his eyes who didn't say anything or the little round-headed one with the steel-rimmed glasses.

There was something strange about this lunch. He didn't know what he was doing here. Something about the gay-o. What in hell was the gay-o?

Or was it the G.A.O.?

They wanted to talk about something he was doing for whatever G.A.O. meant.

Didn't make a hell of a lot of sense, whatever they wanted to talk about, because he suddenly was sick as a dog. His stomach convulsed. Acid bile erupted in his throat. He swallowed, gagged.

The big guy had stumble-walked him out of there. Acted like he did this all the time. The little guy didn't seem to want to touch him. Gave the bug-eyed waiter a big bill. Think it was a fifty. The big guy wobbled him among the tables. Other diners stared. Drunk at noon. The guy's hands never eased on shoulder and belt.

Elevator. Going down. Then through a long raw corridor. He puked in there. The big man yanked him back up. They went out a door recessed in a curved wall, onto a sidewalk. The pavement climbed out of a garage to meet the avenue above. Familiar as hell. From TV.

Reagan had been shot here. He was on the sidewalk at the service entrance of the Washington Hilton. And here came the car, rushing out of the garage. Not a presidential limo, though. A what? A blue Mercury with white agency-pool lettering on the door.

They bundled him in. The car climbed, turned north on Connecticut.

"What the hell—" He looked down. The needle had gone right through his shirt and undershirt just above his belt. The big man's face showed nothing under all that blow-dried mink hair as the walnut-sized ball of his thumb drove the barrel down. Whatever it was turned off the car noise and blotted out the sun.

Even before that. He had real control now. He could fine-tune. Here were the haphazard bookshelves, the plum drapes, the teak desk. Yep, it was teak. The framed diploma. The nubby exec chair.

The diploma. Back to the diploma. Orange-and-black ribbon on the gold seal. Princeton. The name, the name. He strained his eyes in his sleep, knowing how surreal this was, but he fought to make out the calligraphic name. P-U-T . . .

Something tried to stop him. *"You are Donald Roberts Franklin, sir!"*

To hell with you, Krupas!

He forced himself closer. PUTNAM. WALTER ROD-NEY PUTNAM.

Then a curious thing happened. He couldn't see her, but he knew a woman stood beside him. She didn't wear a stitch of clothing. He was naked, too, but not chilly. He felt soft warm pressure, the unmistakable satin cosiness of nude breasts against his chest. Then an exotically feather-soft fitting of smooth loins to his.

The amorphous female shape nestled into him. He felt himself respond. Then without his sense of their having moved, they lay on the fleecelike office rug. Now he was in his pajamas. She wore nothing. He knew that, though he couldn't see her, could only feel her. This was the most overpoweringly erotic sensation he had ever experienced.

And she took him, still in his PJs, inducing a curious sensation that suddenly amplified his increasing desire into carnal need. And woke him.

Lorraine had crept in beside him, then had actually

managed to get this far while he slept. He knew he couldn't trust her, shouldn't touch her, but he was powerless now to do anything but rush on.

It was over in an explosive instant. Then they lay together, damp and panting. He was aware for the first time that he had locked his arms around her. She nestled in the curve of his neck, her soft hair warming his shoulder.

"Darling—" she began, but he would never know what she was going to say.

He heard the slightest of scratchings at the lanai door beyond the closed drapes. He tensed against her. She had heard it, too. And she began quietly to slide out of the bed.

—13—

The seaward elevation of the Kona Imperial was lighted through the night by carefully placed floodlights hidden among the lush landscaping. Prettykin had noted that the high angle of these lights threw the lanais into deep shadow, but the face of the projecting observation deck on the seventh floor was brightly illuminated. It was until he unscrewed the offending flood at 2:30 A.M. He singed his fingertips, despite the protective padding of his handkerchief, but not enough to desensitize them for what he was about to do.

He took the elevator from the deserted lower level to the seventh floor. The corridor up here was empty, too. That was logical enough for this graveyard hour. His primary concern was that some amorous couple might have decided the open-air observation deck was just right for some wee-hour play.

But his luck held. The deck, too, was empty. Thanks to his work in the garden below, its face was now in as deep shadow as the lanai of Room 507, two floors down and to his right.

He paused at the deck's concrete parapet to tighten his belt another notch over the Bernardelli. Then he looped a leg over the waist-high wall and stretched down for a toehold.

The decorative concrete strip projected not quite two inches from the building's face. Leather-soled shoes would never have done it, but Prettykin's trade called for pliable rubber soles. His searching foot found the narrow ledge. He hoped the contractor hadn't cheated in the mix. He put his weight on it. Tested. It held nicely. The other leg came over, and he stood on the top strip.

Moving down the parallel strips of the relief work was a tricky bit of business. His left foot slipped on a patch of sand that had spalled loose. Sweat broke across his shoulders. Seven floors made it a long way down.

Then his scrabbling toe found a new hold and took the nearly unbearable weight off his straining fingers.

He moved crabwise along the face of the building projection that the observation deck surmounted. At the ell with the main structure, he edged across the corner and was above the vertical rows of lanai balconies.

Toes and fingers cramping with the strain, he dropped onto the sixth floor balcony directly below. He sank in a deep crouch to absorb the hard shock of the nine-foot plunge. No sound came from the darkened room beyond the glass doors.

Prettykin raised his head to parapet level. The garden with its carefully spaced floodlights—minus the unit he had disabled immediately below—was deserted, as was the crest of the lava cliffs beyond.

He swung over the sixth-floor-balcony parapet, let his body hang straight and looked down. He swung out, then in, and released. He nearly crashed into the glass-topped table, avoiding it an instant before disaster by twisting his body sideways and hitting the concrete floor shoulder first. He crumpled flat to absorb the shock and muffle the sound. Not so slick this time. He waited, frozen against the cool concrete floor.

A breeze rattled the palm fronds below the balcony. Beyond the irregular black shoulder of the lava cliffs, he heard the thump and wash of an occasional big one. He didn't hear a sound in 507.

He took a single-celled penlight from his pocket, shielded its tiny glow, and checked the lock on the sliding door. Standard up-and-down slider. And no charley bars. Those were for nervous homeowners and motels with less-than-three-figures-a-night rates.

He took out his wallet and extracted a plastic card. It fit the slot nicely. He angled it outward, got the bend he needed and pushed up with steady pressure. The bolt slid open with a slight metallic scratch, not enough to wake even a light sleeper.

He eased the door open less than eighteen inches. It moved noiselessly. Good maintenance. He stood against the closed drape, transferred the penlight to his left hand, and with his right, drew the Bernardelli from his waistband.

This had to be done right, and it had to be done fast. One shot each with the muzzle held tight against the blanket over chest or spine to muffle the sound. One precise shot each from between the two beds—unless they had made it easy for him by using one bed.

He wouldn't go back out over the balcony. He would slip out the door into the hall. He figured at least a twenty-second delay, maybe longer, before anyone reacted. If they heard the muffled shots at all. These high-ticket rooms had to be well insulated.

With the back of his left hand, he eased the drape aside and slid into the room. This was like edging into a mine. The blackest of blacks. He extended the tiny flashlight.

He had to be a camera now, remembering every detail he could pick up in the single tiny flash he would permit himself. He thumbed the contact button on the end of the penlight's barrel.

One quick flare. Not much more than the wink of a single candle. Limned against his retinas: a chair directly in front of him, dresser beyond. Escape route past them to the hall door beyond the jog in the wall for the closet. Beds on the left. Both with sheets and blankets thrown back. Both empty!

And something else had been caught in the penlight's wink, something that grabbed his gut. Climbing onto the far bed, a woman's naked butt, beyond it, her head just beginning to turn his way. What in hell was she—

Then he was struck by lightning, right in the curve of his neck. His left arm died from the shoulder out.

He ducked away and down, bunched his legs and shoved sideways. He crashed into hard legs in soft cloth. Pajamas. The guy had stood right here waiting for him. Bashed him with a big ashtray or something but missed his head.

They slammed together against the bed. Prettykin's gun hand was pinned under him. He'd lost the penlight, but he hadn't dropped the gun. He struggled to wrench it free.

An arm snaked around his head. He dipped under it. He could feel his left hand again, bunched his fingers and stabbed where the guy's gut should be. He hit mattress.

A fist sailed out of the darkness, crashed into his ribs. He lashed out with a foot, hit something soft, heard a grunt.

He back-pedaled on his hands and knees, leaped to his feet. He could hear the guy panting. Off to the left. What the hell was he—

Something flew at him, crunched into him like somebody had shoved parchment in his face. It fell away without making real impact. The guy must have thrown a lamp without unplugging it.

Prettykin lunged out, found an arm, guessed where the rest of him was, brought up the Bernardelli's muzzle, jerked the trigger.

The blast was louder than he'd expected. Its blue-white flash made another tableau. Guy falling back against the wall. Naked woman fumbling under a pillow on the other bed.

Hell of a mess now. With luck, he'd zapped Franklin and fulfilled his negocio. But naked Venus over there was a real threat to longevity. And his estimated countdown had begun with the .38's racket.

He could blunder around in the dark trying to get her, too. He could snap a shot at her bed and hope to hit home. If she was still where he'd seen her in the muzzle flash. Which he doubted.

Or he could get the hell out of here.

He took the last option, crashed between the dresser and the beds, misjudged the width of the closet's protrusion, slammed it hard, bounced free, found the door, and jerked it open. The brass security chain didn't mean a thing. He popped all four anchor screws, was momentarily blinded by the hallway fluorescents, then sprinted for the emergency stairs.

First there were a lot of police in the room. There was hotel security, two of them, one a red-faced, wrestler-chested, security-guard type; the other a buttoned-down understudy, no doubt just out of some college criminology course. There were two Hawaiian Police Department uniforms, locally assigned out of Hilo, one young and chunky; the other with gray stubble on his caramel jaws. There was a Lieutenant Mana in plainclothes, also out of Hilo, assigned to the Kona District. He was a Peter Lorre type, short, slight, soft-voiced, and darkly ominous.

Room 507 was a nut house of confusion until the hotel security duo shooed a knot of gawking guests on down the hall, then were shooed out themselves by the blue shirts, who in turn faded after Lieutenant Mana asserted himself.

When the door finally closed on just the three of them, Mana, in a tan suit, with the open collar of his cream shirt riding outside the lapels of his jacket, smiled benignly.

"Why do I have the feeling you're not being altogether open with me, Mrs. Franklin?"

She offered him an ingenuous gaze. "I don't understand, Lieutenant."

"Let me see if I have more-or-less straight what you told me," Mana said. "You are vacationing here. This perpetrator gets in off the balcony, apparently a pro hotel dipper. There's a struggle. The guy takes a shot at your husband. No doubt about that. Powder burned entrance and exit holes in the pajama top. Hole in the wall where the slug ended up. The lab boys'll dig it out. I'm more interested in what I can't see."

"For instance?"

Mana's dark, froggy eyes glittered without malice. She realized he relished this. "For instance," he said in his oily, subdued voice, "why would a B and E booster—sorry, that's breaking and entering—why would the guy take all the trouble to building-walk his way down to this room when there are a lot easier ways to score? You follow?"

"Building-walk?"

"He had to come off the observation deck on those decorative projections. Only way. No empty room adjacent to this one where he could have gone in and swung up or down. Too far laterally to swing over. When the lab guys check those concrete strips up there, they're going to find scratches. Bet on it."

Lieutenant Mana settled back in the chair by the lanai door, crossed his legs, smoothed his polyester thighs with his palms.

"Mr. Franklin, what do you people have that he'd want bad enough to hang by his toes and fingernails seventy feet up?"

He shrugged. "I have no idea."

She suppressed a gasp of relief. She hadn't been sure how he was going to react, what he was going to say. There had been hardly any time at all to coach him as she'd thrown on her nightgown and robe and he'd pulled on slacks and a shirt. She saw the two-inch scorch along the ribs beneath his left arm.

"You all right, Murtha?" It was still important to reinforce the Murtha concept.

He'd only growled. He was all right.

She wasn't so "all right" herself. Her heart still thudded loudly enough to wake the floor below. She could feel pulse wham in her throat. Too many decisions in too few seconds. When they'd heard the door lock open, she'd slid low for her S&W. It was under her farthest pillow. After the blond man aced Franklin-Murtha, she was going to let him have a 9mm. dead center as he went out the door. Just a matter of good timing would seal up the whole assignment in a neat package.

But she had gotten a surprise. Her subject had fought like a gorilla. That screwed up the whole sequence. Blondy had fired a speculative shot that missed. Barely, but it did miss. She'd thought, though, he'd made his hit. She had the door lined up. Then when the blond man yanked it open and stood in its bright rectangle for a split instant—all she needed—she heard the subject scrambling around behind her. Too damned alive.

Instead of firing, she had jumped out of her naked

crouch, let her feet tangle in the sheets and sprawled hard on the carpet between bed and door. The idea was to give the guy escape time.

Now she had to get Franklin-Murtha clear of this probing little island shield, then work out a way to expose him again. Blondy wouldn't evaporate. She knew that. Not with the kind of persistence he'd shown to date. Not with Sindicato Sud's rep for deadwood attrition.

Mana raised his pencil-line brows. "Mr. Franklin, you have no idea why the man selected this room on the fifth floor out of the five hundred hotel rooms he could have hit? A lot of them would have called for fewer acrobatics."

"No."

She had been afraid he would blurt out something stupid but not now. She wasn't sure what had turned him again. The blond man's attack on her out there on the Belt highway? Franklin-Murtha's acceptance of her bitter claim that she was "through with Sindicato Sud"? Or had she managed to regain control, or at least force him to rethink, with the most basic persuasion of all: the infinitely slow taking of him while he slept? That had been a calculated act of desperation. Who knew the psychological effect of such erotic manipulation of a man who'd been through what he had?

"Well, folks," Mana said affably, locking his fingers behind his head and stretching back comfortably, "I don't believe much of what you are telling me, you follow? I'm going to need witnessed statements, and that calls for steno work and that takes us across the island to Hilo."

She couldn't decide whether he was bluffing. But she didn't need even the possibility of this thing officially ballooning. All right, Mana, enough. She reached in the pocket of her robe.

"Lieutenant?" She handed him her Justice metal and ID. Mana lined them up in his palm.

"It's a federal matter, Lieutenant. Pure and simple."

Mana showed nice white teeth. "I suspect you're not so pure, Agent Burch. And I know I'm not simple. There's some text to go with this artwork?"

"The Federal Witness Protection Program, Lieutenant. You follow?"

"Ah, ha." Long pause between the ah and the ha. "And now they—whoever—know you're here."

"You're a fast learner, Mana. But it's my problem."

"You've done nicely so far." He turned to Franklin-Murtha. "You got a gash or scrape there under your shirt, my friend? I see you fingering it now and then."

"Powder burn."

"You leveling? If it's a gunshot wound, we got a complication."

"Show him," she said.

He lifted his shirt. The burn was a fading red streak.

"Okay, whatever your name might be. Unlike horseshoes and hand grenades, close doesn't count in this instance."

"Funny," she couldn't resist saying. "You don't talk like a Hawaiian."

"Four years at UCLA, three at Fort McNair. And what's a Hawaiian these days?" He stood. "It has been swell, guys. Just a routine B and E. Don't know yet how the guy got in. There was a struggle. The gun went off. Nobody hurt, but the police have several leads. Meanwhile, guests should make sure they securely lock their doors. How's that sound, Burch?"

"You should have been in PR, Mana."

"I am. This island lives off macadamia nuts and tourists. I try to help keep it safe for both. Now, if you will give me a description of your wall-scaling hit man, I'll help keep it safe for you, too."

"I never got a good look at him. Average height."

"Hair dark, light, what?"

"Couldn't tell in the dark."

"You're not a whole lot of help, Burch."

"Sorry, Lieutenant."

"Okay." He offered a wry expression. "Looks like all I have to do is some paperwork. Just don't have me filling out a requisition for two body bags, you follow?" The even teeth flashed. A little on the sharky side, she thought.

"Aloha," he said.

• • •

They went downstairs for breakfast. If she thought she had him back, she was wrong. In the soft dark when he'd glided awake to find himself possessed by her velvet aggression, she might have been able to clinch her break with Sindicato Sud, his ID as Frank Murtha, her determination to protect him—anything she had wanted to whisper with those satin lips brushing his ear. She might have done that while sandalwood and musk lingered in the air-conditioned dark.

Then. Not later. Not after he'd pushed himself up the wall to glimpse the partially open hallway door silhouetting the blond man into a perfect target with her crouched on the bed, the S&W locked in both hands and centered on that target only ten feet distant.

Then she had lunged forward, tripped on the sheet and sprawled flat.

Not convincing, Burch. Not at all. You *let* the guy get away.

He gave their little waitress with the Minnesota accent a desultory order. Pineapple juice, sweet roll, and coffee. No Pyremisine, please. The stuff, if it had any sort of lingering half-life, had surely worn off by now. Every one of his senses felt fine-tuned. He could see sails, tiny as baby sharks' teeth, on the sea's horizon, beyond the dining room's open-sided ocean exposure. He could hear the couple three tables away try to decide between a short drive north to Kailua or a much longer one south, around Mauna Loa's southwest rift to see if Kilauea was doing anything spectacular today.

When the waitress brought his Kona, it had a full, rich, benign savor. He could think. A lot. That made him nervous as hell.

"Murtha?"

"I don't want to hear it." That wasn't smart. He regretted the surly words the instant he'd snapped them at her.

"We shouldn't be down here. We shouldn't be out in public at all." She was still working on him.

"Fat lot of good that did us this morning." If only she hadn't so obviously bobbled her shot as the guy had gone out the door, he could have almost believed in her again.

Not now. Her complex game was blown, but into so many pieces that he still had no clear idea what he was enmeshed in. There were a lot of blanks. But he'd fill them in. He was sure he could fill them in. He needed time to think. Alone.

He finished the sweet roll, drained the coffee. "I'm going to the pool."

"There are two pools. Both exposed, Murtha." But he noticed she didn't seem overly concerned.

"Whichever has the most people. I'm going to sit with a lot of people out there in the sun and try to pull myself together."

"I'll go with you."

"Alone. I don't care what you do."

She threw him a curious glance, then sipped her coffee. A little stall to organize her thoughts?

"Murtha, that's against all FWPP procedures."

He glared across the table into those lovely deceitful eyes. "Don't talk to me about procedures."

"Murtha—"

"I suspect you can drop that crap, too."

Her whole face changed. The eyes, the set of her mouth, the abrupt slackening of her strong jaw gave it away. She sagged from earnest insistence to shock, though she tried hard to conceal her sudden emotional twist.

"I'll be up when the sun gets me," he said as consolation. It was a try to cover his second breakfast blunder. He knew he wasn't good at this. He wasn't Donald Franklin. He was pretty damned sure he wasn't Frank Murtha, either. He had to be somebody with a nice little office and a Princeton diploma. That was what had really felt like a fit. Somebody named Walter Rodney Putnam.

But who was Walter Putnam?

He gave her no choice. He signed the check with the "Don Franklin" cover name and got up from the table. He left the dining room abruptly and walked down the lobby steps to the south-pool corridor. Only when he reached the long, dimly lighted lower passageway did he realize how stupidly he might be behaving. The blond guy could be anywhere.

But apparently he wasn't here. Walter Putnam pushed open the pool-access exit door, then squinted against the bright late-morning sun. As he had anticipated, the pool deck was reassuringly crowded, mostly with middle-aged women and some men sedately sunning themselves on the green pads of the white, metal poolside chaises.

A striking redhead drew eyes as she paraded her paisley bikini along the pool's coping, toward the snack bar. A scatter of kids used the pool at the moment. He found an empty chaise in the shade of a tall palm whose slender, arched trunk brought its starburst crown well over the pool area's laced-canvas fencing.

He lay back, cushioning his head on interlaced fingers. The morning was reasonably cool, though the filtered sun was warm. For the first time, he appreciated the intoxicating lightness of the Hawaiian breeze. He stared up into the gently swaying palm fronds. Then he closed his eyes.

Not Franklin. Not Murtha. But Putnam. He was sure of that now. He silently mouthed the name. *Walter Rodney Putnam.* Yes, it did seem to click into place, unlike the alien feel of Franklin and Murtha. He had the pieces now. The problem was to assemble the puzzle.

Who was Walter Putnam? With no effort this time, he could recall the office with the plum drapes. His office. His office in— What was that building beyond the window? He knew that columned facade, had stared at it often enough while he pondered the implications of the ledgers and computer runouts. Gee . . . Geo? Geo, that was it. Geographic. The National Geographic Society Building!

Washington. Putnam's—his—office was in downtown Washington. M Street. The Miserable Misers of M Street. He and John . . . Elias. Jack. Elias and Putnam. C.P.A.s. Accountants, for God's sake. He was an accountant.

G.A.O. That had cropped up in his odd sleep visions. Of course! He and Jack Elias subcontracted to the General Accounting Office. The Navy's $1,730 wall-unit air-conditioners contract, when anyone could pick one up in a department store for $375. That one had been his. Jack worked mostly on G.A.O.-supplied Air Force procurement data.

They were whistle-blowers, professional whistle-blowers. The not-so-honorary title, Miserable Misers of M Street, had been leaked to them out of the Pentagon. Nobody liked a whistle-blower. Except the G.A.O., which liked Elias and Putnam well enough to make business downright lucrative. And Tomlinson of *The Washington Post*. He loved Elias and Putnam. They made damned good copy.

So how did *that* tie in with the Justice Department, the "Donald Franklin" deception, Lorraine Burch, and the blond man with the fast car and faster gun?

In sequence, now, Walter Rodney Putnam. Let's take it in meticulous sequence. You are at the Washington Hilton with a precise little round-headed man and a big one with stupid bangs. Invited there for a business lunch, he recalled now, presumably with a potential client . . . one who had managed to slip him something that made his guts turn inside out. That was clear enough. They walked him out of there and put him under with a needle.

Then came the ambulance ride. To Horger's remote clinic? Seemed logical. And up there, they—"They"?— Horger, a doctor named Krupas, and, yes, Lorraine Burch, too, had used some technique on him, something they called . . . What was that term that had come rolling out of his struggling memory? Chemohypnosis. That was it.

The term itself explained what they had done to him. Shot him full of some crud that paralyzed his thought processes and helped blank out his past. Then Krupas had gone to work on him. No bandages while they'd had at him. Didn't that mean no injuries? There hadn't been an accident! Washington Hilton to Horger Clinic with no stops between, except probably one brief delay for a rural transfer from the round-headed man's agency-pool car to a Horger Clinic ambulance. He'd bet on that.

Then why had he come out of it in that antique bedroom with his forehead, nose, and cheek swathed in gauze. Those had been real wounds. They'd hurt enough. But the "accident" had been a lie.

What had Dr. Fukada called his scars? Evidence of rhytid . . . Rhytidectomy. And rhino-something. Face lift and nose job. But if there had been no accident, then— My God, they rebuilt my brain and changed my face!

Why?

She had admitted the "Don Franklin" arrangement was a cover. Why the equally intricate "Murtha" business? It was full of holes, too. He didn't doubt that she was a J.D. special agent, but she sure hadn't done much of a job protecting her witness, had she? In fact, he'd accused her of being a Sindicato Sud payoff, and she had stunned him by going along with that. Then she claimed she had turned, after the little incident of the battering-ram Camaro up there on the Belt Road.

No good, Lorraine. Too many inconsistencies. You purposely missed a shot at the guy. Didn't want Lieutenant Mana's help this morning. Still played the Murtha game. Tried to simplify the whole thing down to man-woman-and-sex last night.

Whatever you are up to, lady, I'd guess it has come seriously unraveled.

But what in God's name was it?

Not Don Franklin, accident victim. Not Frank Murtha, federal witness. But Walter Putnam, whistle-blower with an altered face. Altered so he wouldn't look like Walter Putnam? A lot of brain cells were still suppressed in mental haze, but damned if he could remember even the threat of a threat to Walter Putnam.

Altered, then, to resemble someone else! *Who?*

From the pool rose a shriek. He jumped. But it was followed by laughter. Kids at play. He lay back again, closed his eyes.

Franklin, then Murtha. She'd let the Franklin cover blow without much anguish, but she had really hung in there with Murtha.

Showed him the badge and the ID. Then set him up for the blond man. Why in ruddy blazes would she do that? Only if she had been paid off by Sindicato Sud—if that truly was who the blond menace worked for. Nothing like keeping an open mind, Walt.

He thought back to her insistence that she had broken with Sindicato Sud when their man had gone at her, too, with his Camaro. Poor befuddled Walt Putnam would have been so much chopped meat up there if he'd still been on Pyremisine, wouldn't he?

The damned drug. She'd wanted to keep him on that stuff. When he had managed to cut it off, his brain began to clear. She had *needed* him on the Pyremisine to control him, to let her . . . set him up.

That was logical enough, if she was being bribed by the Colombian interests to do just that. But it made sense only if he indeed was Frank Murtha. And he knew now that he was not.

Work it another way, Walt. Suppose—this was monstrous—but suppose that what she had told him about Frank Murtha was true—but only to a point. Assume Murtha was indeed the Sindicato's procurador, their legal eagle. Assume he did make a deal, turned himself in for federal immunity and protection. Surely his Colombian employers would want him out of the picture as quickly as that could be arranged. The Justice Department would certainly be aware of that.

Assume some overeager amoral bureaucrat decided he would make Frank Murtha subtly available for killing, not the real Frank Murtha, but a reasonable facsimile thereof.

Walt Putnam's eyes snapped open. My God, it all fit!

No, no. This was too hideous to consider. No federal official would sanction such a deadly affront to morality.

Yet, hadn't a federal agency considered assassination of Castro through the Mafia? Wasn't it federal people who had commissioned the development of a dart gun that could kill silently from a startling distance? Hadn't it been a federal suggestion to dement a nationally syndicated columnist by placing a hallucinogenic drug on the steering wheel of his car? And just who was back in the nerve-gas-and-germ-warfare business?

It all fit.

Frank Murtha turns himself in. He's hidden away, but somebody at Justice is convinced that Sindicato Sud will successfully hunt him down before hearings can be scheduled. The solution: create a decoy Murtha. Let the Colombians find him, liquidate him. So endeth that risk to the real

Murtha. And imagine the Sindicato shock when he appears as scheduled. A wonder to behold. Only one small problem, guys. We'll have to find somebody who looks like the son of a bitch and throw him to those South American piranhas. Some nonentity. Some guy with no family to speak of . . . or to speak up. What have we got on the computer? Anybody know anybody who looks like this Murtha in the photo here?

Say, damned if he doesn't look a little like that pain in the ass who's giving Navy Procurement fits. You know, that C.P.A. who works under contract to the G.A.O. Walter something. Putnam. Walter Putnam. Yeah, bend his nose a little off-center, put that scar on his cheek, smooth the creases out of his forehead, and you've damned near got Murtha.

That bastard's one of those pro "whistle-blowers." That'll be a fringe benefit to the military complex.

Wry laughter.

I can go along with that, but *he* sure as hell won't.

Aren't you forgetting the Krupas File?

Wry grin, this time. That was laboratory controlled.

With one-hundred-percent success, you'll recall, as long as the subject stayed on the Pyro— What the hell was that stuff?

Pyremisine.

Right. Look, we blank the guy out, build a false background for him, send a phony wife along to keep him dosed, then leak that he's Murtha.

Goddamn beautiful, guy. Goddamn beautiful. I'll drink to that.

So will he. It's an oral medication.

Har-hars all around.

Those sons of bitches! It could have happened exactly that way. "Don Franklin" had been created as imperfect cover for a facsimile of Frank Murtha. Lorraine Burch was his Judas goat, the control to keep him on the disabling drug and to put him in the right place at the right time.

"May I get you something from the snack bar, sir?"

She stood over him in a scarlet, yellow, and blue sarong,

pad and pencil in hand, dark hair framing her delicate Polynesian features. A poolside waitress.

"What? No. No, thank you. Wait. Yes, you can."

He realized he was one extremely frightened man. His forearms were wringing wet. "You can bring me a telephone."

When D.C. Information had gotten as far as "The number for Elias and Putnam is two-oh-two, four-one—" (Thank God, there really is an Elias and Putnam!), the rest of the number popped into mind. He made it a collect call. He didn't want to leave a record of the number on the hotel's billing tally for Room 507, though he'd had to use the room number to call Information.

In Washington, it would be late afternoon. A Saturday. But he'd remembered that Jack Elias customarily worked on Saturdays and stayed fairly late to take advantage of the quiet. He was remembering a lot, in bits. A random scrap here, an occasional whole gob there. Walt Putnam was from Connecticut. Went to high school in Hartford, then on to Princeton. And Wharton. That diploma hung on the wall just inside the office door, didn't it? He could visualize it as easily as he could now picture the Hartford house, a big, white three-story frame with a lot of gables. Almost Victorian. There was a girl, younger than he. Bess. His sister.

Oh, he'd been a good risk for this. Parents dead and a sister way off in Oregon. No relatives close enough to Washington to put their hearts into an investigation of his disappearance. Only a hobby to keep him occupied outside the M Street office. Something borrowed . . . Something blue. He was rambling. Something old . . . Something— Hell, that was it. He collected antiques for his outsized apartment on upper Sixteenth. For himself. He had nobody. Only the people at work, a few friends. Jack Elias.

"Good afternoon. Elias and Putnam." The Saturday receptionist was still there.

"Will you take a collect call from Mr. Putnam in Hawaii?" the operator asked mechanically.

Had there been a little squeak of surprise? "Please hold.".

the receptionist five thousand miles distant asked. She would be the Saturday part-timer.

Click. Then silence. A long silence. "Hello?" the operator tried. "Hello?"

A second click. Then Jack Elias's meaty voice held a guarded note. "Hello? Can I help you?"

"Jack, I . . . It's—" His voice trembled, broke. Walt fought back tears. "Jack . . ."

He heard a gasp. Then Jack's tone was one of total incredulity. "Is this . . . That can't possibly be!" Jack Elias then got hold of himself. "Look, whoever the hell you are, this is one damned cruel joke."

"It's not a joke. It's Walt, Jack. It's Walt."

Stunned silence came from the distant Washington end. Then Jack Elias said, "What was the last job you were working on?"

Oh, God. Walt tried desperately to concentrate.

"They've done something with my brain, Jack. I can't—"

"Sure, fella."

"Jack, for God's sake!" What could have been a salvation phone call was turning into a bad dream of disbelief and challenge.

Then another tiny mental door opened. "The kitchen utensil purchase from Hevistone Products! That was—No, that wasn't the last. You'd just handed me a folder before lunch. A gray job jacket. Asked me to get at it as soon as I got back from the Hilton. The Meinhoff Corporation contract. I never got to look at it, Jack. I—"

"God Almighty!" Jack's voice was hoarse with shock. "I went to your funeral, Walt. All of us here went to your funeral."

—14—

If there was traffic worse than Washington's tourist crawl on a rainy Saturday afternoon, Richard Vandenhoff couldn't imagine where it would be. Maybe in Calcutta or Hong Kong. Certainly no other U.S. city could match D.C.'s wet Saturday sightseers' vehicular clog. Why couldn't he work five days a week like the rest of the country? But rainy Friday commuter traffic would be no better.

He snaked his brown LeBaron a couple of blocks east on Independence, then north on Seventh past the west end of the Air and Space Museum, up Seventh, across the Mall between the National Gallery and the Natural History Museum. The rain fell even heavier seven blocks later, when he gunned the LeBaron around Mt. Vernon Square to join the sluggish Massachusetts vehicular stream. God, what a city when rain caught the tourists by surprise. What an ending to a week of not knowing what in blue hell was going on in Hawaii.

The thing should have been over and done with days ago. Vandenhoff hated a project that ran over schedule. Intricate planning began to unravel. That was dangerous.

He trusted Burch, but only as far as he trusted any of his SAs. Under exceptional duress, who really knew what anyone would do?

Or was he imagining trouble where trouble did not yet exist? Her periodic check-ins had been on time until this week. The last call, two days ago, after a lengthy silence, had told him tersely, "We're on fallback."

That wasn't good, but it wasn't irrevocably disruptive, either. The Don Franklin cover was blown, but she was slick. What she had to do now was convince the man he was in reality Frank Murtha. The project would move ahead virtually uninterrupted.

Then, believing Murtha out of the picture, Sindicato Sud would call off what Vandenhoff assumed was a nationwide search for him, would call off whatever emergency procedures it had put in action, and would be a complacent sitting duck when Frank Murtha miraculously rose from the dead to take a stand at the forthcoming Senate hearing.

Despite Burch's need to revert to fallback, Vandenhoff assured himself that at this point in time, he had no concern causative, to put it in IMS jargon. But he did have one hell of a disturbing premonition. He hated premonitions. They were women's stuff.

A gray sedan with South Carolina plates cut in front of him as he picked his way around the tangled lanes of Dupont Circle.

"Bastard!"

His angry bark was confined to his air-conditioned capsule. Rain drummed the car's roof and danced across the hood. He switched on his headlights. At the Washington Cathedral, he almost missed the right turn into Wisconsin. Visibility was rotten.

He was an overaggressive driver. He knew it. But this twice-a-day rampant charge through D.C. and Maryland traffic was the only means of release he had. Well, almost. He worked hard to present an unruffled facade to his people. In his car, he had a half hour each way to vent. In cascading rain, it took longer.

Frustration poured into steering wheel and accelerator. Nobody understood. Oh, maybe Louisa. A little. But no one could fully comprehend the urgency, the need, the importance of what he did. He was in a war—a war!—against complacency, bureaucratic fiddle-faddle, and gross national ignorance. The country was going down the tubes.

He and his IMS stood virtually alone against the over-whelmingly powerful enemy.

Six clogged miles later, he fumed in the traffic snake on the bridge above the jammed lanes of the Capital Beltway. The crush didn't thin until he jerked the Chrysler off 240 into the rural outskirts of Rockville.

He raced the little car around the long curve that skirted familiar woods. When he reached the isolated split level (one of these days, he'd do better than this trite stone, brick, and clapboard builder's afterthought), he bounced onto the uptilted concrete apron and left the LeBaron in the rain. Louisa's old Datsun was awarded the one-car garage on rainy days because its trunk shipped water in a downpour. He grabbed his briefcase, ducked his head, dashed up the walk's three drenched concrete steps, and had his key ready when he reached the front door.

It wasn't locked. She'd hear about that. He slid his damp briefcase on the hall-closet shelf for now.

"Weeza!"

"In here, Richard."

She didn't call him uncle, and he didn't introduce her as his niece, but for different reasons. She had dropped the uncle appellation when she had moved to Maryland from Chicago, a self-liberated collegian. He'd learned that identifying her as "my niece" garnered too many likely-story glances, though God knew she wasn't the kind of twenty-two-year-old who raised eyebrows when she was with her twice-her-age uncle. She looked as if she had been built in a hurry from spare parts: slender at the shoulders and through a chest that still sported the pubescent breasts of her early teens. Yet the hips flared below her narrow waist to burgeon into bulging thighs supported on solid peasant legs.

She was in the living room, dressed—if you could call it that, he thought—in a frilled, white short-sleeved blouse and grapefruit-yellow short-shorts. She had propped her outsized bare feet on the coffee table, angling her upper legs to support her sociology text. A notebook lay open on the sofa beside her. His eyes slid unbidden to the creamy columns of her big legs, along the smooth inner thighs to the bunched fabric at their apex.

"Is it still raining?" She didn't look up.

"Still raining, and I'm soaked. Weeza, how many times have I told you to *lock* the doors? At all times."

She ignored that. "I've got a lasagna on, garlic bread and a salad ready."

She earned her keep as a basic but adequate cook, along with the other housework. She had proposed that arrangement to provide herself with room and board while she attended the University of Maryland in nearby College Park. When she'd moved in, he had thought there was something congenitally wrong with her or perhaps some birth injury. She was abject, disinterested, a lump.

Then he found the stuff. There was something wrong, indeed. He pleaded, railed, threatened to institutionalize her. She finally, incredibly, broke what was as yet a minor barbiturate habit. But by then he couldn't break his habit with her. Didn't want to. Felt rotten about it. Put the blame where he was convinced it belonged: not on her but on the animals that supplied her. Downers, uppers, coke, horse, he made no distinctions. It was all the same. All poison. All an assault on the people of the nation. War.

He tore his eyes from her bunched shorts. "I'll be down as soon as I get out of these wet clothes and take a shower."

When he reappeared in yellow slacks and a white T-shirt, she had set the kitchen table. She opened the oven with a mitted hand. The zesty aroma of lasagna filled the kitchen. He was hungry but preoccupied. Damned job. Damned Code Franklin, to be specific.

Or maybe it was the whole job.

"I don't think one lousy soul appreciates what I do," he blurted. His stolid niece, he had found, made a comfortable, if not overly perceptive, listener.

"I'm sure a lot of people do, Richard." She engulfed a sizable forkful of lasagna. She never nibbled or sipped. She gorged and guzzled with a youthful exuberance he somehow did not find repugnant.

"No, I'm afraid I'm doomed to be just another overlooked soldier in our current war."

She raised her heavy eyebrows. "War?"

"My God, you too? What do you call the multibillion-dollar tidal wave of cocaine that's rolling over us right this minute? What do you call *that*!"

She was silent.

"Weeza, I asked you a question."

"It's terrible, Richard. I know it's terrible. But you mustn't think you're the only one concerned. We've talked about all this before. A lot."

"So we have, Weeza. But it gets worse and worse." He broke off a piece of the crisp garlic bread and munched angrily. The sons of bitches were wrecking the nation. *Their* sons of bitches were out to scoop up American bucks in their filthy coke- and smack-stained fingers. And *our own* sons of bitches joined in the poison trade or didn't care enough of a damn to do much about it. The country was more concerned with the flavor formula of Coca-Cola than it was about the coke invasion from the Latins.

"Did you hear that the Senate is still fiddling over the constitutionality of assigning military units to drug enforcement? The *constitutionality* of it while kids are dying in the streets!"

"Awful. It's just awful, Richard. More salad?"

He shook his head. "You remember that guy who was indicted for running a fifty-million-dollar cocaine business from his house in Georgia?"

"I remember."

"Scot-free."

"Scot-free?"

"Illegal search and seizure, for God's sake. What kind of justice is that?"

"That's terrible, Richard."

"Damned right, that's terrible. You remember the Sindicato Sud I told you about?"

"Yes, Richard."

"We just might get those bastards." He longed to hint to her how clever Code Franklin was, but he always had to stop short of specifics. His federal clearance precluded his telling her anything but generalities about his work. That was frustrating as hell. God, would she be impressed with her fussy old unc if she knew what he'd thrown at El Fabricante and his damned Sindicato! But he couldn't breathe a word. Not that she was any kind of risk. Their own secret, now more than a year old, proved that.

"More lasagna, Richard?" Her voice, rich and syrupy smooth, was her one physical grace.

"No, thanks. Have you been listening to one damned thing I've been saying?"

"All of it. You know I listen."

He knew it, but it was like shooting arrows into cotton. She never reacted. Nobody gave him the support he deserved or the money he deserved or the recognition he deserved.

Well, they would when Frank Murtha walked into that big hearing room on the second floor of the Senate Office Building at Constitution and First and poured out chapter and verse. He'd give a lot to be able to see El Fabricante's face when the news of Murtha's appearance devastated him, weeks after he'd been assured that Murtha had been hit in Hawaii. Damn, that would be—

"Spumoni?" she asked over her shoulder as she cleared the kitchen table. "I picked up some at Venicelli's."

Spumoni. He worried about an engulfing wave of two-billion-dollars' worth of illegal South American coke; she was concerned with spumoni.

"A small dish." When she'd brought his ice cream and her own and sat across from him again, he compressed his lips and slowly shook his head.

"The job?"

He nodded. "The job. Can't do it all, can't get more help, can't talk about it."

She reached across the metal-topped kitchen table to touch his hand. "Richard," she said in her low, silky voice, "I could use some help with my Visa bill this month."

"The Visa bill."

"This time."

She always knew. She could read him so well.

"After I finish my sixty-day interim report narrative?"

"Sure. When you're ready."

He completed the draft at ten forty-five, threw the front-

and back-door deadbolts, set the alarm system, and turned out the downstairs lights. His legs felt wooden on the seven steps to the upper level. She was so damned perceptive. He was carrying the whole complicated IMS on his own shoulders, knowing that if the A.G. or any of his deputies got wind of Code Franklin—or any of many other Codes, past and present—he would be a small dead man on a long rope. Talk about your martyrs.

She was in her bathroom. He heard the shower stop. Then she came out in white terrycloth, her knot of brown hair loosened. It glistened with droplets. He liked her damp.

"Ta-dah!" she cried and flung off the robe. Water drops sparkled between the big thighs. Oh, yes, he did indeed like her damp. He was seized with his familiar disturbing and undeniable compulsion. He had no way to resist it; didn't want to resist it.

He was no longer sure who had made the first irrevocable step toward this, but he was certain he wouldn't have taken it had she not encouraged him to do so. Academic now. After a year, there were no real inhibitions left.

He stripped away shirt, slacks, shorts. "Ta-dah, yourself!"

She giggled and shoved beneath her sheet and blanket.

"It's warm," he said. He pulled the sheet and blanket away.

"I . . . Not with the lights on, Richard." Well, there was one tiny little inhibition, after all.

"Okay." He snapped down the wall switch. The room went velvety black.

She had arrived a virgin, aggressively independent, and eager to change that status, she blatantly told him. But her attitude turned men off. Her odd figure didn't help either. Her clandestine use of downers did. When Vandenhoff had counseled her, he had been both taken aback and stirred by her frankness.

She lacked modesty, except in the matter of in-flagrante-delicto lighting, curiously. Frequent glimpses of her exposed thighs had fascinated him. A rampantly eager young female, once he got her off the barbs, and a middle-aged, repressed bachelor belatedly discovering desire were too latently explosive a combination to circumvent the inevitable for many weeks. Ten, to be exact.

He recalled the date. A February blizzard. Fourteen inches of wet Maryland snow had exhausted them by the time they had cleared the driveway. They had gone upstairs to get out of sweat-soaked clothes. Then she walked past her open door, blatantly naked as he watched. He felt an unfamiliar surge. She noticed, had smiled. Had stood there. His instigation or hers?

Who cared now? In the dark, she was moistly soft, then fluidly warm, and in minutes, incredibly overwhelming, then beyond control herself. Her triumphant squeal was far from honey-voiced.

He lay back, slick with exertion. He'd just shot a hundred toward her Visa account. The financial aspect—her idea—excited him, thus enhanced the arrangement for them both. Biologically, he rationalized, he was not breaking a taboo. Sister Margaret's second husband had brought with him the baggage of a failed first marriage, much like her own, plus that marriage's sole fruit: bookish, fourteen-year-old Louisa. She was heavy-hipped even then.

So he wasn't lying here in the viscid afterglow of coupling with true kin. And she was scrupulously careful with her pills. That risk was minimal. Another kind of risk, though, was immense. He knew that if certain of his own people—LaBranche, for instance—were somehow to bug this bedroom—

Her bedside Princess phone erupted in a shrill cricketing that shattered his descent into ruminative torpor.

"For you," she said in the dark.

"Vandenhoff?" A female voice.

"Yes."

"Burch."

He had call forwarding from his office hotline and occasionally received circumspect messages at home. But only in emergencies, by his strict order. His skin congealed.

"What is it?"

"He's gone."

He wanted to shout: How? When? Why did you let him? But almost all long-distance calls now were satellite-relayed, certainly calls originating in Hawaii. God knew who might be using a skyward-aimed dish.

"Find him!" That wasn't enough. "I'll be there!" Holy Lord!

The bed lamp clicked on, blinded him. Louisa's head, her hair wildly mussed, was propped on an elbow.

"Not good?"

"Routine," he managed. He rolled out of bed, dressed in a hurry. "I'll be out of town for a while," he said at the door. Then he came back to the bed and pulled the sheet up over her big thighs and small breasts. "You're a sweet kid," he said.

"And a good lay?"

He wished she hadn't said that. His craving for the little pointed breasts and great thrashing legs was periodically irresistible, but he couldn't throw off his oppressive guilt after every compulsive welding to her resilient torso.

The omnipresent guilt had to be that. Surely he had been head of IMS too long to permit a professional conscience to cloud an operation like Code Franklin.

Because of the phone call, though, Vandenhoff's inevitable postcoital guilt was quickly overshadowed by a much more unpleasant emotional surge close to panic.

Putnam had disappeared at two-thirty P.M. More accurately, it was two-thirty when Lorraine Burch realized he'd been out by the pool one hell of a long time. She went looking for him.

He wasn't there. She walked back through the lower-level access corridor, apprehensive but not yet alarmed. She mounted the stairs to the lobby. He wasn't there, either. Nor did she find him lounging beside the north pool.

Now increasingly concerned, she hurried through the landscaped pathway through the garden that flanked the resort's ocean frontage. She eyed the hulking tops of the lava cliffs beyond. Not here, either. Yet the Kona Imperial was a big place.

She failed to find him in the coffee shop, the cocktail lounge, or the restaurant. She strode along the row of lobby shops and paused to inspect each through its broad display window. No sign of Putnam. Now she felt hot prickles across her shoulders.

The balcony end of the shopping arcade at the second-floor lobby level overlooked the parking area. He had the keys, damn it. She should have found a way to have gotten them back. Serious slip there, Burch. Yet the Toyota was still where they had left it.

That meant he was in the hotel. Or did it? Was he clever enough to use another way out of here and leave the car as a delaying tactic?

Come on, Lorraine. All his clothes are in the room. What's he got on him? Not much more than two hundred in cash plus the credit cards in the Franklin name. Vandenhoff could make certain Putnam would leave a trail wide as a computer run-out sheet if he used any of them.

Maybe she'd simply missed him in this stuccoed maze of a hotel. She retraced her search route.

An obvious checkpoint was the desk.

"Mr. Franklin?" the muumuu-clad clerk repeated. "I'm not sure I—"

"Tall man, dark hair, scar on his cheek, and a crooked nose. We're in Five-oh-seven." Increasing concern, she realized, was making her voice shrill.

"Sorry, Mrs. Franklin. Would you like him paged?"

"Yes, I would." She drummed impatient fingers on the registration counter's polished teak. The clerk's amplified voice echoed sibilantly through the lobby and its branching corridors.

Nothing.

"Would you like to leave a message for him, Mrs. Franklin? He may check the desk when he returns."

She shook her head. He had gone. She felt it in the queasy hollow of her stomach.

No, damn it! She would not let herself think that. He had probably returned to their room. She had passed him somehow. Maybe in different elevators. He was up there now, wondering where *she* had gone.

As she stepped off the elevator, then fitted her key in the lock of 507, she realized what a forlorn hope this was. Of course the room was empty. Nor was he on the lanai.

She slumped on her bed. She had really underestimated him. Vandenhoff would make her pay for this. You did not blow an IMS project and get away with a simple reprimand. She didn't know how, but the vindictive little creep would make her pay.

Where had the thing gone off track? When Putnam found out about the Pyremisine, for a starter. But he seemed to have accepted the fallback; had apparently been convinced he was Murtha.

The chemohypnosis itself? Krupas had warned them it was still experimental, though recent controlled experiments had proved highly successful. He and Horger and you, too, Lorraine, honey, had been convinced that they had erased the essential portion of Putnam's mind; had wiped out his biomemory, leaving basic skills and abilities intact. She had wondered about that until he had regained consciousness at the clinic, after Horger's facial manipulations. Krupas's work had been remarkable, or had seemed so then.

Her own efforts had not been so shoddy, either, she thought. She had done her level best to become, in Putnam's mind, his devoted and loving wife. In every way. How many points would that passionless little Vandenhoff allow her for that? She had given Putnam everything he'd wanted. Hadn't that meant anything to him? How could he dump her like this? How could he walk away without a single word?

My God, Burch, you were here to get him killed. Now you're feeling he let you down!

She had to report in. That was obvious. She reached for the phone. Her fingers trembled. Maybe a shower would help calm her.

Maybe when she came out, he would be there—out on their lanai, staring out to sea as if the answer to his layers of confusion were out there in the glittering Pacific.

But she emerged from the shower into an empty room. She felt alone and threatened. Still she delayed, hugged her robe tightly around her, then called room service for a mai tai.

Seven minutes later, a tap at the door made her heart surge. Maybe, just maybe— But it was the waiter.

At five-thirty, she faced facts. Reinforced by the mai tai's warming rum, she picked up the phone. With daylight saving, which Hawaii did not participate in, Washington time would be eleven thirty P.M., she realized with a crumb of satisfaction. This had been Vandenhoff's plan, not hers. Let him do some worrying.

When he blurted, "I'll be there," her chest thudded so hard she had to take a long, shivery breath before she could respond.

He had never, as best she could recall, gone into the field to try to salvage a blown operation. She hung up, breaking into ugly gooseflesh this time. Then she dialed room service again. Delivery of the second mai tai took eleven minutes. She thought she would die before it arrived.

The taxi had picked him up at the Kona Imperial's obscure parking-level entrance. It was a six-year-old Plymouth wagon with a ponderously heavy Hawaiian driver, his flowered shirt a mobile tent over rolls of fat.

Walt ducked into the rear seat as unobtrusively as he could. The blond man and his damned Camaro might be miles away, or far more likely in view of his past persistence, right out there in a hidden corner of the parking area.

"Where to, boss?"

"Airport." His mouth was dry, and his voice sounded strangled.

He sank low in the wagon's back seat and looked for the tan Camaro as the taxi rolled back through the parking lot.

Not there, thank God. Not there.

They emerged between the chunky lava columns and began the climb up the access drive.

The conversation with Jack Elias had been reassuring and unsettling at the same time. Certainly incredible.

"You never came back from lunch that day, Walt. Around three, we got a call. D.C. Police. They said you were crossing Connecticut and had been hit by a car. They wanted to know what to do with the body. . . . Sorry, Walt. They wanted me to tell them where to send you. I tried to get in touch with your sister, but she wasn't at the number we had on file here for next of kin."

"She'd moved. I forgot to update the file."

"I told them to send . . . the remains— Damn, this isn't easy, Walt. The company arranged the funeral. Closed casket." Jack paused. "Of course it was closed. The whole thing was a fake, wasn't it? The police report, the funeral. The story planted in the *Post*."

"They're very thorough, Jack. They faked the police call and got to the funeral director. Not too difficult when you're the federal government."

"But they can't do this sort of thing, for God's sake. They can't!"

"They have. But I'm going to bring the bastards down, I don't care who they are. They've kidnapped me, drugged me, operated on me, screwed up my brain, set me up for murder. I'm going to bring those bastards down. But I can't do it from here. I've got to get back to D.C. To *The Washington Post*. To Morris Tomlinson."

"Can't you call him from there?"

"You think he'll believe a phone call like this? He doesn't know my voice like you do."

"I could back you up."

"God, no, Jack! You think they'll stop with me? Don't say a damned word about this to anyone until I get back there."

"You got any money?"

"A couple hundred."

"That's not enough, Walt."

"And some credit cards. But I suspect they'll put a stop on the credit cards."

"Look, I can transfer a thousand in cash to . . . Wait a minute." Walt heard him flip through his Rolodex. "Canfield, Armor and Yamato. We've done some co-op military account work with them. They're in Honolulu, on Beretania."

"They're going to want ID, aren't they?"

"What have you got?"

"The credit cards. Oh, and a driver's license. All in the name of 'Donald R. Franklin.'"

"Right. Damn, tomorrow's Sunday. Monday morning's the earliest I can swing it. That'll have to do. But I'll call Harry Armor at home tomorrow to get it set up." Jack's voice suddenly choked. "I feel so damned *helpless*, Walt. Look, why don't I hop on a United flight out of Dulles—"

"No! These people have no conscience, no conscience at all, Jack. You're more help to me there."

"Walt—"

"I mean it! Canfield, Armor and . . . ?"

"Yamato. On Beretania Street. Monday morning."

"Once I have the money, Jack, I'll be set."

But would he? Halfway up the climb from the Kona Imperial to Alii Drive, he wondered whether he had acted with logic or in panic. Had Jack been right when he'd suggested flying out here himself? No, damn it! If they would expose their own agent to ultimate hazard, Jack Elias would be at peril the minute they made the connection.

Jack's suggestion that Walt call Tomlinson from here was equally futile. What hard-edged newsman would believe a telephone call like that one would have to be?

No, it wasn't possible to put an end to this without reaching Tomlinson in person, convincing him, giving him more than enough to enable him to launch a thorough, rapid, and complete investigation and full exposé. Anything less than that would make targets of Tomlinson, Elias, and God-knew-who-else while it dragged on.

At the top of the access road, the dusty blue wagon creaked northward into Alii Drive. Walt Putnam tried to settle back and control his racing thoughts. Was he acting out of logic? Or panic? Or an inevitably disastrous combination of both?

No, he had to put full confidence in what he was doing. He forced himself to loosen his leg and stomach muscles, to unclamp his fingers from the door handle. He would take a room in a moderately-priced Honolulu hotel tonight, lay low through tomorrow, then pick up the thousand Monday morning. After that, he would take the next flight to the Mainland. Cash for everything. No trail.

For the first time in he'd literally forgotten how long, he

began to feel a touch—just a touch—of security here in this squeaking, anonymous airport-bound station wagon.

His impression of security was false. Like a persistent jackal trailing doomed prey, a charcoal gray Reliant had emerged from the Kona Imperial's parking acreage. Now it matched the taxi's unhurried pace a half mile behind.

Prettykin wasn't sure whether he was motivated by guts, fear, or greed, but it all came down to the same need: Franklin had to go. Franklin had to go quickly, before this thing unraveled further.

What had begun as a fairly straightforward hit had now been complicated by two hideous blunders: the double miss up on the Belt Road and last night's fiasco in Room 507.

He had been lucky to get in there without being spotted, unlucky in that he'd missed what he had figured to be a point-blank shot, then lucky again when he'd gotten out of there. He could have sworn the broad had a gun on him when he'd found the hall door and yanked it open. Had it misfired or what? Some wife you've got there, Franklin. Or was there an angle to this he didn't know about?

He had charged down the corridor to the emergency stairs, taken them two at a time, emerged in the front garden. Raced around the south pool to the nearby Camaro. Driven out of the Kona Imperial with his mind galloping but the car cruising. That hadn't been easy. He wanted to blast up the hill, roar off on Alii. Get the hell out of here! But he couldn't. He'd heard Franklin getting to his feet again. With the negocio target still alive up there, Prettykin was held here as surely as if he were dragging an anchor. He needed that son of a bitch *dead*.

How much could Franklin and his wife—or whatever she was—tell the inevitable police? Apparently, they hadn't said a damned word about the Belt Road botch. But a guy in your hotel room taking a shot at you was quite another box of snakes. The cops would be there, all right.

Ahead in the tropical darkness, a red light winked. Headed this way. Oh, yes, the cops would be there. He dipped his high beams. The police car passed, making time south. Another whipped by a minute and a half later.

The Camaro was too risky. He pulled in at the first big hotel that had a Hertz sign still lighted out front. When he got out, he raised the hood and yanked a plug wire. He closed the hood and went inside.

The sleepy registration clerk, a middle-aged, balding man with a hard Massachusetts accent, was able to handle the problem with a single phone call, even at three in the morning.

"Man says it's running rough as hell. Needs to switch to another car . . . Yeah, we got one. . . . Yep. No problem."

It was a dark-gray K-car. No guts in its four cylinders, but he wasn't being choosy. He drove on to Kailua, parked the Reliant behind the King Kamehameha, and took the stairs to his floor.

He shaved quickly, packed, messed up one of the beds, then checked out. After two near-misses, the Franklins were certain to try to get the hell off the Big Island, probably as soon as the police had finished with them, and they were able to pack and check out.

That gave him, he estimated, just about time to get back there and set up watch. He was reasonably confident they would still be at the Kona Imperial when he arrived, just as gray-pink dawn began to melt away the shadows along Mauna Loa's long skirt. The ocean was a sheet of rippled cast iron to the emerging horizon, but the seaside cliffs below Alii Drive were scarved in ground fog.

He swung down the steep access road, snapped off the Reliant's lights as he entered the hotel's parking lot, and picked his way along the rows of dew-dampened cars. He found the Toyota. Now he was certain Franklin was still here.

The new sun began to dissolve the lingering fog swaths. A chilling morning breeze helped. Prettykin found a space near the parking area's lava-columned egress that offered clear views of the Toyota and both of the hotel's front exits: the ramped lobby-level access and the smaller, almost hidden, lower-level portico off the corridor that linked the south pool with stair-and-elevator access to the lobby. He backed in, switched off the engine and focused his powerful little Zeiss binoculars.

It was one hell of a long wait. He yearned for coffee. Should have picked up a cup in the King Kamehameha's all-night coffee shop. No, that would have created a subsequent problem. As it was, he could have used a men's room by late morning.

By noon, the sun beat strongly on the Reliant's roof. The breeze slowed to an occasional tepid drift. He was sticky, urgently in need of a bathroom, thirsty, hungry, and fighting an urge to lay his head back and just drift off.

What the hell you won't go through for forty Gs, he marveled. His head pounded. His eyes were gravelly from their binoculared concentration on every emergence from either exit. First out had been the police cars. He'd sunk below dashboard level as they passed. Then he studied tour buses, taxis, and the increasing outpour of guests' cars, some of them brought up from the parking area to the lobby level by a hard-working attendant for guests who didn't care to traverse the broad, hot pavement to access their cars themselves.

The tour buses gave him his worst moments. They did conveniently park several yards from the upper entrance, thus affording him a clear view of the emerging tour groups. But it wasn't easy to make an ID check of twenty or thirty people in a bunch.

Franklin, though, was a tall man. That helped. Prettykin was reasonably sure that he had not been among any of the half-dozen tours that boarded buses and vans through the morning, though that might not have been a bad way to get out of here.

The blond man laid his binoculars in his lap and massaged his aching eyes with thumb and forefinger. A Dodge station wagon rattled in from the access road. Its faded-blue front door was emblazoned with the huge white letters, TAXI. Hawaiian driver. Big one. Prettykin picked up his binoculars.

The taxi swung around to the lower entrance and obscured it. That was interesting. The other taxis all had gone to the upper-level lobby entrance.

One guy got in. Tall with dark hair. The vehicle's roof obscured his face, but Prettykin's adrenalin began to pump. Could be. Could be. . . .

He slid low in the seat but kept his binocs on the taxi as it rattled back past him.

Crooked nose. Scar. Got him!

Prettykin slammed the binoculars on the seat, twisted the key. The little engine ground to life. He waited until the taxi had begun its left turn into Alii at the top of the hill. Then he nosed the Reliant out of its slot and accelerated up the hill after it.

Headache, burning eyes, urgent bladder, exhaustion, all were forgotten. He had the bastard now. Good-bye, Mr. Franklin.

—15—

"Aloha Airlines, sir, will get you into Honolulu around five."

She was trying to help, Walt realized. Her pixie face had screwed into concern beneath her thin forehead fringe of orange hair.

"Sorry. I'm in a hell of a hurry." A moment ago, he had actually yelled at this little ticket agent, then was ashamed to see tears start in her pale eyes. "Give me a seat on that flight, then."

"Smoking or nonsmoking, Mr. Adams?"

That had been the first name that had popped into mind when she'd asked. Robert Adams. Hardly inspired, but damned if he would leave any more of a trail than he had to.

"I don't care," he said.

"W-window or—"

"Anywhere. Just get me on it."

The little jaw quivered.

He paid in cash. "Forgive me," he muttered as she handed him ticket and boarding pass. "It has been a hell of a day."

She avoided his eyes. "For me, too."

He left the counter and took a seat on a bench in the shade of a poinciana tree. The terminal was a parklike collection of huts. It could have been Fiji or New Guinea. He felt obvious and exposed, but that was unavoidable here.

He tapped his boarding pass on his knee as he glanced

around the little open square. Only one blond man, and he appeared to be in his fifties. Surely, Walt realized, I've gotten paranoid. But who wouldn't, after what he had been through?

It was almost over now. He would hole up in Honolulu through tomorrow, pick up the thousand Monday, pay cash for his Mainland ticket—using another cover name—and be high over the Pacific by Monday afternoon, securely headed for Washington and rationality.

He sat back, feeling almost his own man for the first time since this hideous experience had begun.

Walt Putnam felt this deceptive impression of release not because of what he saw here in this remote little Keahole Airport, but because of what he had not seen.

Prettykin had had an easy time trailing the Dodge wagon north on the sparsely traveled Queen Kaahumanu Highway to the airport. He was able to drop more than a mile behind at times and still keep his quarry in sight across the lava flats. Even when he lost the old taxi momentarily, just past the side road to Kaloko Point, he wasn't disturbed. It was obviously headed for the airport. He was confident that he had locked in on Franklin's thinking now. Without the woman to confuse the situation, Prettykin felt he could now read his man like a timetable.

He followed the taxi along the lengthy airport access road, allowing another car to edge between them and serve as unwitting cover. Beyond the low Polynesian-style buildings in their sheltering grove of tropical trees, the airport ramp was empty except for a small twin-engine prop-driven plane. No jetliners in sight. He had time to do this right.

"When's the next plane out?"

"Where to, sir?"

The only logical move for Franklin to make was a straight line for Oahu. The only flights to the Mainland departed from Honolulu International.

"Next flight to Honolulu?" he asked the wispy ticket agent. Her odd orange hair was getting away from her, and she looked like she'd had a rough day.

"Aloha Airlines at three-forty-seven, with a fifteen-minute stop at Maui. Luggage, sir?"

When he had pulled the Reliant into the rental-car return area, Prettykin had realized he had to dump the Bernardelli or take a chance. This out-of-the-way Hawaiian airport in all probability did not have the equipment to scan checked luggage, though U.S. regulations for screening carry-on bags surely were in effect. He parked in a quiet corner of the rental lot and slipped the automatic from under his Hawaiian shirt. Then he snapped open his briefcase and shoved the pistol beneath soiled laundry. He had closed the case and thumbed its combination lock.

"Luggage, sir?" the girl repeated.

Prettykin broke his gaze from the stack of luggage near the chainlink fence that separated the aircraft parking apron from the open-air security checkpoint. This place was like an airport in an old Bogart movie.

"I'd like to check this bag through." He handed her the briefcase.

"It has to have a tag, sir. Your name and address." She reached in a drawer behind the counter and gave him a blank baggage tag of tough clothlike plastic.

He had already provided her with a cover name. He used her pen to write "Edward Leonard" and a fake St. Louis address on the tag, stripped off the backing, and secured the tag around the briefcase's handle.

He spotted Franklin easily. Off-center nose, scarred cheek, tan slacks, short-sleeved white Hawaiian shirt patterned with vines of tan leaves. You're an easy man to tail, friend.

Prettykin found a bench well away from the little open square where Franklin and most of the other passengers waited. He wondered why the man was traveling without his wife, then realized there could be a lot of reasons. Maybe the police had urged him to leave the island alone. Maybe he'd sent her to some refuge on the Big Island, then had cut and run. If that was the case, could Prettykin be wrong? Could Franklin be headed elsewhere than Oahu to wait in some Molokai or Kauai refuge until she joined him? Or maybe she wasn't his wife at all.

None of that mattered now, did it? Franklin was his negocio, and Franklin was here. All Prettykin needed was retrieval of his briefcase at Honolulu International, then the opportunity.

Right in the crowded, confusing terminal? Better in a men's room, if he could maneuver Franklin and himself in there as the sole occupants. Or in a darkened lower-level corridor. In desperation, he could palm the gun, jam it in Franklin's ribs and force him to a secluded area.

Even if Franklin managed to slip past him at the Inter-Island Terminal, there was the shuttle bus. If his assumption that Franklin was headed for the Mainland was correct, the man would have to change terminals at Honolulu International.

The shuttle—what did they call it . . . the wiki-wiki bus?—was a trainlike arrangement of three trolleys pulled by the lead car. Could he blast Franklin right on the bus, then bail out of the slowly moving car, and disappear before the rest of the riders realized what had happened? A long chance there, but it was another possibility for a bold gun.

The Aloha 737 landed before he heard it, turned off the north-south runway, taxied to the apron. Its two turbofans sighed metallically, then died to hot ticking. Among the trees, an amplified female voice announced the imminent boarding of Aloha Airlines Maui-Oahu flight. The group in the square began to move toward the screening station near the gate.

Prettykin worked into the line a dozen people behind Franklin. He wanted the man to be occupied with settling in and adjusting his belt when he passed in the aisle headed for his own seat far to the rear. He hoped fate hadn't placed Franklin back there, too.

His target reached the top of the boarding steps and entered the plane as Prettykin began the climb. Inside, Prettykin closely followed a young mother with a five- or six-year-old who wasn't at all happy about any of this. His squalls riveted attention as his part of the shuffling line neared Franklin's seat—happily midway down the aisle, Prettykin noted with relief. Prettykin used the distraction to push past. It was a potentially risky moment, but Prettykin could thank the kid.

He found his seat and buckled the belt. He had debated wearing the planter's hat or buying a cap to cover his cornsilk hair, but he felt that might draw more attention than the hair itself. The broad-brimmed straw had ended up in the trash bin near the rental-return lot.

How great was the risk? Franklin, after all, had not gotten a real look at him. All the man could have seen on the Belt Road, or in the split second in the hotel room doorway, was a flash of blond hair. There were a lot of blond men in the world. Two others, in fact, right here on the plane.

The muumuued flight attendant closed the cabin door. The 737's engines whined to life. Seven minutes later, the stubby jet climbed northwestward over Kiholo Bay.

The brief stop at Maui's Kahului Airport was uneventful—until the jet drew up to the terminal, and the Maui-bound passengers debarked. Prettykin glanced at Franklin's seat.

Empty! The dumb bastard wasn't so dumb. He'd managed to slip into the line of departing passengers, probably when Prettykin's view had been momentarily blocked by a wide middle-aged woman wearing a vivid and voluminous yellow caftan.

He snapped open his seat belt and began to rise. Then a disturbing realization hit him. The damned briefcase would ride on to Honolulu, would be expelled onto the baggage pickup belt, and there would circle around and around, unclaimed until some baggage handler finally took it to Aloha Air's Lost and Found.

Would they send it on to the nonexistent Edward Leonard in St. Louis? When it arrived there, and proved undeliverable, then what? At some point, somebody was going to open the thing, find the loaded Bernardelli and notify the St. Louis police. The weapon, he was sure, was untraceable. But his fingerprints were on it and surely all over the interior of the case. And he had been printed during that one unfortunate incident in Cedar City, Utah.

What had Utah done with his prints? Torn up the sheet after the charges had been dropped? Filed them? Sent them on to the print-hungry Identification Divison of the F.B.I. in Washington, where computerized matching was a matter of minutes?

Prettykin sat back down. Hell of a decision. He had assumed Franklin was headed for Oahu, not Maui. And here the son of a bitch had thrown him a real problem. Take the chance, get off here, stick with Franklin, and carry out the contract without a piece? He abhorred the idea of physical-contact killing, had never done it, and he could not imagine closing his fingers on a throat clammy with terror as it retched for air or feeling a knife rip through clothes, sink into flesh, and grate on bone.

He needed a handgun, and he didn't know how to get one in a hurry on Maui. Even if he did, there would remain the disturbing potential of his abandoned briefcase.

Another alternative would be to stay aboard, retrieve the Bernardelli on Oahu, then charter a flight back here. Sightseeing helicopters, he had noticed, left from certain hotels on the Big Island. No doubt he would be able to make similar arrangements on Oahu, and hotel heliports did not have passenger-screening requirements.

The problem with that alternative was finding Franklin again. The man might have business here on Maui, might stay, might leave on the next plane for Oahu, or even return to the Big Island. How was Prettykin supposed to outguess this suddenly unpredictable quarry?

Was the guy a pro or a clown who didn't know what was underway here and was shot with dumb luck? In one simple move, just stepping off the plane here, he had plunged Prettykin from the elation of impending success to the desperation of an agonizing decision. Forty Gs had just walked out that cabin door and left behind them the chilling possibility of Sindicato termination for failure.

Was there one other possibility? Hold up this flight to have his briefcase extracted from the cargo bay, one small bag from the dozens, maybe hundreds, crammed in there? No, that would focus too much attention on him, would undoubtedly require a lengthy delay, and Franklin would be long gone.

The only rational plan he could come up with had to be

based on the assumption that Franklin had made him, had realized who he was, and had left the plane because of that. At Keahole Airport, Franklin had exhibited the mannerisms of a nervous man. He had glanced around too frequently in the waiting area, had drummed his fingers on the bench, had tapped the boarding pass on his knee, had eyed every fellow passenger in the tree-shaded square. Conclusion? Franklin had to be putting distance between himself and the threat on the Big Island. It was a safe bet that he was headed for the Mainland. Safe? Ninety percent? Seventy? Fifty-five? It was Prettykin's bet now, the only one he had.

The hunted had reduced the hunter to speculation over percentages. Prettykin had to assume that Franklin had gotten off in an amateurish move to break his trail. That panicky maneuver wouldn't have had a prayer of working except for the damned potential hazard of the briefcase with its loaded pistol, checked through to Honolulu.

Even as he peered through the 737's little oblong window and spotted Franklin entering the terminal beyond an ineffective screen of fellow passengers, Prettykin forced himself to stay put. Twelve minutes later, he looked down from the steeply climbing jet at Maui's emerald-blanketed West Mountains as they drifted aft.

He had been reduced to a single option. He had no choice but to set up a vigil at Honolulu International and wait. And hope he was right. Otherwise he soon would be looking over his own shoulder.

Fifty minutes later on Oahu, Prettykin had retrieved his briefcase without incident, had ridden the shuttle to the John Rodgers Main Terminal and had taken up the vigil that he realized could evolve into a mini-hell of its own.

His initial plan had been to set up watch in the Inter-Island Terminal, but he had soon realized there were two problems with that. It was sparsely populated between arrivals and departures. He would quickly become far too conspicuous. The other problem was more troublesome.

Franklin knew he was a marked man. Might he have the smarts to charter a sightseeing helicopter that would land elsewhere? Or even a boat? That way, Franklin could bypass the Inter-Island Terminal. But if Prettykin was right, the man could not avoid the Main Terminal. Not if he was Mainland-bound.

When he'd gotten off the wiki-wiki shuttle, Prettykin had walked quickly through the Main Terminal's various levels and realized his initial thoughts of zeroing Franklin somewhere in the building were impractical. Too busy. Too exposed. He'd need several hours' recon to find a safe site here, but he suspected he didn't have much time at all.

Change of plan. He descended to the baggage-pickup-and-car-rental level, used his Edward Leonard license and a large cash deposit to arrange for an unremarkable looking Avis Nissan, then walked across the exit lanes to locate the light-gray car in the nearby parking garage. Bay 34.

He returned to the terminal building and located himself near the upper-level entrance. Of concern were the groups of passengers who alighted periodically from the three-unit wiki-wikis from the Inter-Island Terminal. Lulls in activity gave him chances to study the Oahu map he'd picked up at the car-rental counter.

Also of concern, not at first, but if this thing dragged on too long, would be airport security. He had a cover story ready if he was asked why he was hanging around here hour after hour: his business partner, a Roland Johnson, was due here today or tomorrow but had run into travel complications. They had lost contact with each other. Since Prettykin-Leonard had already checked out of his Honolulu hotel in anticipation of joining Johnson for an essential hop to the Kona Coast, he had no alternative but to wait here until Johnson showed up. That might be a thin cover, but Prettykin knew that if he spoke earnestly enough and made it complicated enough and offered more than the security people would want, he could get away with it.

A third troublesome aspect of this public ambush was the matter of personal needs. A snack bar was reasonably close by. No problem. The men's room was across the way. He would have to use it quickly so as not to leave the area unobserved long enough for Franklin to slip past. Fortunately, Prettykin's blond stubble would not require a shave for another twenty-four hours, maybe longer. Even then, airport travelers could get away with considerable seediness.

He pushed back against the hard formed-plastic seat and crossed his legs, briefcase in his lap. This was one hell of a gamble, but it was the only one he had left.

In the small Kahului Terminal on Maui, Walt Putnam had concealed himself behind a news kiosk and watched the Aloha Airlines 737 out there on the ramp. The terminal was partly open-sided. That gave him an unsettling feeling of exposure. But that was a couple of steps down the panic scale from his reaction on the plane. He had seen the blond man slip past the woman and her misbehaving boy. He might not have tumbled except for the man's slick professional move. In that instant, Walt knew. He felt it in his gut, and his gut froze.

He dared not crane his head around to see where the guy sat. All through the twenty-minute flight to Maui, Walt was sick with helplessness, trapped in this damned airborne tube, hurtling toward disaster.

It wasn't fair! He'd been through hell, had struggled out of a nightmare, had broken the chain the Justice Department had locked around his neck. Now this piranha of a hit man was twenty or ten or three feet behind him.

He stared out the little window at the rough slate of the Pacific and bit the ball of his thumb. Better than shouting in frustration. Beside him, a fiftyish gray-haired man in a mustard-yellow polo shirt calmly leafed through an in-flight magazine. Lucky bastard. All he had to worry about was making connections.

When the flaps and landing gear rumbled down and the jet whistled into Kahului, edged to the terminal, and stopped, the polo shirt stood, reached overhead for his sports coat. Now Walt hazarded a glance aft. The blond man was not in any of the seats on this side. The view from the rearward seats on the other side of the aisle was blocked by the line of departing passengers. Blocked . . .

Two chances. Fat and slim. Hunched low, he edged into the departing line, keeping to the right. Just a little touch of luck, please God.

The worst of it was walking from the bottom of the exit stairs to the terminal in full view of the 737's left-side windows. Walt managed to walk to the right of a tall elderly man and ahead of a sizable woman. Shaky cover. He felt naked.

But the blond man had failed to follow him. A blessed miracle in view of the guy's ability to materialize out of thin air. Now from behind the kiosk deep in the terminal, Walt watched the big plane until the door closed, and the engines wound into their departing howl.

On to Oahu and out of my life, you persistent son of a bitch!

He felt a surge of elation. He had outsmarted the blond man, had gotten the upper hand, had taken control at long last. From here on, his problems were clear-cut and understandable. Get on the next plane to Oahu. Keep out of sight tomorrow. Monday morning, pick up the cash Jack had arranged to transfer, then buy a ticket home—all the while obliterating the dangerous Donald Franklin identity.

His elation was short-lived. He had shaken off the blond man, but that wasn't the only threat, was it? The federal people had far more resources. *You are still way out on a very shaky limb, Walt Putnam.*

He changed airlines and bought an Oahu ticket on Hawaiian Air. Forty minutes later, the DC-9 with the bright-red hibiscus on its vertical fin banked past Diamond Head and descended into the deepening gold of late afternoon. The flight had been routine except for a minute or two of turbulence over Kalohi Channel, between Molokai and Lanai, just after he had been served a brimming cup of coffee. Before he could drink it down to a manageable level, it had sloshed over the rim and down the left leg of his trousers in a broad six-inch-long streak. Compared to his overriding trauma, the coffee stain seemed incidental at the time.

Walt deplaned warily, his Maui-generated confidence ebbing as he probed the reaches of the Inter-Island Terminal for a half-expected glimpse of yellow hair. In the air, he had realized the man could be waiting for him here. As he walked into the terminal, growing apprehension pressed down on him like damp heat. But the blond man was nowhere to be seen.

Walt almost laughed with relief. Out front, he signaled a taxi. In minutes, they rolled east on the Nimitz Highway toward the brightening glow of downtown Honolulu at dusk.

His cash had dwindled fast, eaten away by the taxi to Keahole Airport and two airline tickets. This ride was already past the eleven-dollar tally. He would have only some one hundred and fifty bucks plus change when he reached hotel row, where he would be forced to stay two nights. And he realized that he looked like a tramp. He needed toilet articles, a respectable pair of trousers to replace his rumpled and badly stained gabardines. He could certainly use a clean shirt. And a change of underwear.

As they neared the big Ala Moana Shopping Center, he remembered the place from a hazy day Lorraine had dragged him around Oahu. A huge impersonal Deardorff International store anchored one end of the enclosed mall.

"This'll be fine," he told the wide-faced, brown driver. Walt was forced to go easy on the tip, got a surly "mahalo," and was left on the sidewalk that edged Ala Moana Park across from the mall.

He was tired and felt disoriented. He crossed at the light at Piikoi, walked through the south parking area and entered the big department store. When he checked out wearing new dark-gray pants and a light-blue shirt, his purchases—clothing, a travel kit, and a small suitcase he'd decided he'd better carry to facilitate hotel registration—came to more than he'd anticipated, close to sixty dollars. Paying cash would reduce his reserve to less than a hundred. Hell, below ninety. He wouldn't have enough cash to pay for even a moderately priced hotel room. Using a credit card when he registered, as hotel procedure would undoubtedly insist, would provide too much checking time if the Franklin accounts had been closed out.

The chance had to be taken here, with the Deardorff card they had so thoughtfully provided him. If the account was closed, he'd be forced to pay in cash and the cash he would have left wouldn't see him through to Monday morning. God, wouldn't this nerve-stretching strain ever end?

He slipped the blue-and-gold plastic wafer from his

wallet and handed it to the small dark-haired clerk behind the cashier counter. His teeth clenched his lower lip.

She punched the account number into her pinging computer-register. He waited, tried to feign unconcern. A muscle beneath his left eye jittered. A woman behind him sighed.

Then the register flashed a new set of numbers. She ran the slip through, had him sign, gave him back the card, bagged the underwear packets—he'd had to buy T-shirts and shorts in packages of three—and dismissed him with a Mainland-accented "Have a nice evening."

He'd gotten away with it. Feeling deceptively cash-flush now, he hailed another cab at Piikoi and Ala Moana and rode into Kalakaua Avenue's tourist rush. He got out at Lewers and walked north, away from the beach. Room rates dropped back here.

He found a quiet hotel a couple of blocks back, registered as "John Roberts" of Seattle, pulling name and address out of the warm lobby air and paid $69.50 in advance for the first night.

Monday's checkout would just about wipe out his cash, but then he would pick up the thousand from Canfield, Armor and Yamato. In his plain but adequate room, he checked the Honolulu phone book. Yes, they were on Beretania, as Jack had told him. Downtown. Quick stop there, then back to the airport, cash for a one-way coach ticket to D.C., Jack Elias, Morrie Tomlinson, and an end to this haunting dread.

No more problems. Unless he had slipped somewhere.

In a one-story sculptured cement-block building in an industrial park between Kansas City, Missouri, and Independence, the night-shift manager of the computer bank that serviced Deardorff International outlets west of the Mississippi was diverted from her Janet Dailey paperback by the insistent dinging of the electronically actuated alert signal.

Another deadbeat was trying to slip a charge through. At 1:00 A.M., CDST? Had to be Hawaii or even further west.

She brushed back a tendril of gray. Funny how you let yourself go on this shift. Too hard to get to the Blue Summit beautician when you were forced to sleep away most of the day. She punched the read-out code on the console in front of her. The CRT doled out its amber block letters.

FRANKLIN, DONALD R . . . ACCT 339-747-8160 EXP 6/88 ACTVD ALA MOANA BR, HI. CLEAR AND NOTIFY IMMED SPEC DC OP . . . DIRECT DIAL 212-28.

This was odd. Her standard duty was to check blocked accounts against computerized late-payment records. This was quite a different instruction, one she had never seen before.

She read the glowing letters again. Then she shrugged and dialed 212-28, feeling a bit foolish.

The efficiency with which her information was taken by the distant female voice left her with a curiosity that was never to be relieved. She tried to get back into her book, but even the earthy parts seemed pallid now.

—16—

For God's sake, Vandenhoff was forced to tell himself, you're flopping around like a hawk with a broken wing! Sit down and think, man. Think!

After Burch's tense phone call, he had yanked on his clothes. Then he realized he had no place to go. Not until morning, and it would be tough then. Government, like commerce, closed down on Sunday. A dozen things had to be done, but he had no way to do them until tomorrow morning.

In frustration, he grabbed a yellow pad and began to make a list:

—Contact American Express, Visa, MasterCard, Deardorff International, Shell, Texaco . . . Every Donald Franklin credit card issuer. Demand immediate notification if any of them are used.

—Insist that Hertz, Avis, all other car-rental agencies immediately notify IMS in D.C. of a Donald Franklin rental. All offices, entire U.S.

—Telex all Hawaiian P.D.s (there's no state police organization out there, damn it) to report presence of Donald R. Franklin, but do not apprehend. Include detailed description.

• • •

Was there more? In the shadowed living room, Vandenhoff's chest pounded. This was going to be a tricky piece of business. He wanted Putnam personally, not in the hands of Hawaiian police. God knew what damaging accusations that man might blurt out, what dangerous investigations that might precipitate. It was essential that he and Burch alone—

"Richard?" Louisa's voice behind him was almost a whisper. "Was it something I—"

"No, no. You were sweet, Weeza."

"But it's nearly two."

"The damned phone call. Something I'll have to handle personally. In Hawaii. I'll be leaving in a few hours. Go back to bed, Weeza."

His need to fly out there told him how critical this thing had become. He was being pulled into it irresistibly when he should be cutting connections, reassigning, shifting responsibility, setting up a surrogate in the event that control was irrevocably lost. Laundering himself.

But the potential for organizational injury was already too frighteningly high for that. His fault. He had conceived Code Franklin. He had retained its control. He had run Burch and LaBranche personally. There was no way out except the prompt and efficient elimination of the unfortunate Mr. Putnam. A deserted Hawaiian valley. One shot in the head. He'd see that Burch was irrevocably involved. Tropical growth and jungle rot should quickly obliterate what was left of their man who never was. He'd already had his funeral and no longer existed, anyway. Neat. Risky, callous, but terrifying if they failed.

Dawn's early light found him tapping his ruled pad with his ballpoint, the problem still there. But now he could begin to do something about it. He stuffed the pad in his briefcase, then realized he was dressed in his lemon slacks and rumpled T-shirt, unshaven. He felt unacceptably grubby. First outward sign of inward disintegration, wasn't it? The deterioration of dress and physical appearance.

He rushed upstairs, shaved, dressed properly in federal gray, with a white shirt and maroon tie. He packed a bag. Had he been about to run out of here without a bag? He checked his wallet. No banks open today, but he had enough for incidentals. Credit cards would have to carry him through. He'd have to make his own flight reservations and pick up the ticket at Dulles or National or Baltimore-Washington International, whichever had the flight that would get him out there fastest.

Now you're clicking, Vandenhoff. Burdened with briefcase and suitcase, he tried to shut the front door quietly. The central Maryland morning was humid with dew and already warm. Another Sunday scorcher in Washington.

There was almost no traffic on the Rockville Pike this early morning, and he used a heavy foot. The influx of tourists was building in the city itself, though, and he fumed down Massachusetts, then Seventh. Despite his lack of sleep, anxiety kept him scalpel sharp, he thought, as he parked under L'Enfant Plaza, hurried through the deserted underground shopping arcade to open the dark IMS office. He clicked on his desk lamp and began his phone calls.

The first Hawaiian flight he could catch left BWI, thirty miles up the Baltimore-Washington Parkway, in just under an hour and a half. That turned out to be a hell of a demanding drive out East Capitol Street, then up Kenilworth to the Parkway in thickening Sunday sightseeing traffic.

But he made it. Not until United's Los Angeles-bound 727 was thirty thousand feet over western Maryland and still climbing did he realize how exhausted he was. He slept all the way to the Rockies.

Lorraine Burch had spent one bitch of a day in Room 507. Absolutely nothing had happened. First she had hoped, against all common sense and instinct, that a discreet rap on the door would bring Walter Putnam back. Then she realized how inept she would appear when Vandenhoff showed up and found Putnam here and Code Franklin apparently back on schedule after she had pulled the disaster switch.

Yet, with Putnam missing, she would have to put up with Vandenhoff until they somehow found him. She did not look forward to that! She was a loser either way.

She took two showers, did her nails, watched TV without any retention of what she saw. She fretted, worried, *hated* this, ordered a mai tai at noon, then a room service meal late in the afternoon with another. Her stomach rebelled, but she ate what she could.

Well, after dark, there did come a tapping at the door. Oh God!

She squinted through her room's security peephole. Standing too close, thus distorted by the wide-angle lens, Vandenhoff in his sterile steel rims looked like an ugly bug with a long, shiny proboscis. She opened the door.

"Burch." More a statement of fact than a greeting.

"Welcome to Kona." She had no enthusiasm for this, either.

He strode past her, found the phone, and called room service. "Scotch and soda, and expedite it." He plunked down the handset without concerning himself whether she wanted anything. He gazed at her with sleep-robbed eyes. He needed a bath.

"You look like the wrath of God," she said with a touch of satisfaction.

"You don't look so shipshape yourself."

"I didn't sleep much last night." Not with this whole assignment falling apart; not with Vandenhoff blundering into the field with her. Had he ever been a field man? She'd thought she had concealed the shadowed hollows beneath her lusterless eyes, but she hadn't fooled him.

"You know any more than you did when you called me?"

"No. He never came back. He's gone."

"We'll find him." He sketched out the steps he'd taken before leaving D.C. "I've directed that all pertinent information be relayed here, to this room, from IMS sources the instant it is received. Regardless of the hour."

"Thanks."

He peered at her through his damned mad-doctor glasses. "What is it, Burch?"

"Why are you here? Don't you think I'm capable?"

"You lost him."

She didn't have a response. He slid open the lanai door and walked out there. When the room service waiter arrived, Vandenhoff didn't come back in. She signed the check, then took the tray out to him. Then she stood at the low concrete parapet, tapped a Casino out of a new pack, and lit it with fingers that threatened to betray her unease.

She had to break the hard silence. "What's your room number?"

"Six forty-four." He let the curtain drop again.

"Good trip?" Why was she offering these nervous inanities?

"If you call an endless wait in the L.A. takeoff line, a thunderstorm an hour out of California, and a kid kicking your seat for three hours straight, good, then I had a good trip."

"So now what?" She could be just as sour.

"So now we wait. I checked in only fifteen minutes ago. I'm going to my room to shower, clean up, then I'm coming back here. This is HQ, Burch, until I direct otherwise. You are to stay right here, monitoring the phone. It is not possible for that man to move very far without tripping over some strand of the net that I've thrown around these islands."

Insufferable little ass! She was relieved when he left.

When the phone shrilled. Lorraine Burch and Vandenhoff were finishing a room service supper in 507. A salad was all she could manage. Since Vandenhoff had arrived on the scene, her stomach had drawn into an even tighter knot. He had ordered lobster, a baked potato, and macadamia nut pie, and he'd eaten everything but the lobster shells. Yet he didn't look so damned carefree himself.

She had just lighted a Casino, still desperately controlling the tremor in her fingers. He had leaned back, tossed his napkin over the table debris, and cocked his head.

"Your problem, Burch, is—"

That was when the phone rang. He was nearest.

"Five-oh-seven," he said. Then his face sagged. "That's a whole *day's* delay, for God's sake! What in hell is the matter—I know it's Sunday. What difference does that make!"

He slammed down the handset, and his mean little mouth

twisted. "Your boy is in Honolulu. Used his Deardorff card last night. *Last night!* What in *hell* have they been doing with that information all day!"

Poor dumb Putnam. Lighting his own signal fire with a credit card.

"There was something else," Vandenhoff said. "There was a D. Franklin American Express charge a couple days ago, put through Dr. Fukada here on Kona."

Not such a dumb son of a bitch after all, she realized. "That's interesting."

"This is *it!* And we're already running a day behind. Get yourself in gear, Burch. We're checking out right now."

He grabbed the phone again and dialed at length. Waited. . . . Banged his fist on the night table. "Come on! Come *on!* Oh, sorry, This is Vandenhoff. I want the Honolulu Main Terminal under tight surveillance ASAP. Issue a description. . . . I *know* we already issued one. Do it again. And remember—he is not, repeat *not* to be apprehended. Observe and report only. To me. . . . Yes, damn it. I'll still be accessible through Honolulu P.D. I know you're at home, but *do it*, Surjin. Now!"

He hung up. "It's essential that you and I get him at this end or that you and I get him at the other end. Nobody else—unless we are lucky enough to have Sindicato Sud do our work for us. We're down to CYA procedures now, Burch." Then he turned ashen.

"What is it?"

"I just realized that phone call was a satellite relay."

She felt a little flutter of satisfaction. "You can't win 'em all, Vandenhoff."

He pursed thin lips into an expression of prissy concern. "It was routine departmental traffic, wasn't it? Did I say anything that could backbite?"

She smiled for the first time since he had arrived. "I don't remember," she said sweetly.

At Keahole, well after nightfall, they had to charter a flight out with an unhappy lean pilot in an eight-passenger twin-prop Piper Navajo.

"You could wait for the eight A.M. Oahu shuttle, you know."

Vandenhoff shoved his J.D. badge under the pilot's thin nose.

"Uh, huh," the grumbling man in the leather jacket said. "I guess you couldn't."

The accounting firm was in a glass-and-steel highrise with a startling view of the ornate Iolani Palace eleven stories below, through the Canfield, Armor and Yamato lobby window.

The pretty honey-haired Caucasian receptionist repeated the name with Deep South languor. "Donald Franklin?" She checked her appointments list. "Did you want to see Mr. Canfield, Mr. Armor, or Mr. Yamato?"

"I'm not certain who—"

"Oh, here's a note." She punched buttons. "Mr. Armor?" she said into the tiny stalk microphone clipped to the band across her smooth hair, "there's a Mr. Franklin here to see you?" She looked up at Walt. "You can go right on in, Mr. Franklin."

Armor was a big man in brown: brown suit coat, brown trousers, brown vest, brown striped tie, all violently out of place in casual, colorful Hawaii.

"Mr. Franklin?" No hand offered. "Sit down, please. You have some identification?" Armor remained standing.

Walt handed him the false driver's license.

Armor studied the photo, Walt's own photo, transferred no doubt from his legitimate license, a photo of Walter Putnam before the ministrations of Elmo Horger.

Armor scowled. "This doesn't look a hell of a lot like you, Mr. Franklin."

"I've had an accident since, with plastic surgery." His palms were suddenly damp against the chair arms. To come this far and run into a technical roadblock was unthinkable.

"That's why I'm in Hawaii," he added. "To recuperate."

"Jack did mention something about that." Armor tapped the driver's license on his palm.

"You can call him to verify. I'll talk to him, get confirmation."

To Walt's relief, Armor shrugged. "Not necessary." He handed back the license and bent down to open the middle drawer of his desk. "I don't know why I'm guarding this so damned zealously. It's Jack's money, not ours. I would appreciate your signing the receipt."

Walt scrawled "Donald R. Franklin" on the typed receipt form.

"One grand, Mr. Franklin, in tens and twenties. Fairly bulky packet."

It was that. Alone in the elevator, Walt stuffed his wallet with as many bills as it would take and shoved the balance in its white envelope in a trouser pocket.

He had to fight a nutty impulse to grin. Yesterday had been a Sunday of lonely apprehension spent holed up in his drab hotel room. He'd dared emerge only for three quick meals. But Armor's white envelope did it! He was free of the Donald Franklin terror, free of Judas Burch, free of the blond man and his killer car and eager pistol.

He stepped into busy Beretania and waved a cab to the curb. Just another tourist now, Walt Putnam. It felt damned good.

Prettykin had made it through the night on coffee and doughnuts. His stomach felt as if it had been pumped full of hot acid. He needed a shower, and he needed a shave. And clean clothes. And a decent breakfast.

Most of all, he needed Donald Franklin to walk through that damned wiki-wiki shuttle-bus entrance. And he needed to stop thinking that Franklin wouldn't.

But by 10:00 A.M., he knew Franklin wouldn't. Prettykin had underestimated him again. That was unsettling. He was accustomed to rational assignments, people who acted out of habit and in predictable behavior patterns. Franklin was like a rabbit, running here, jumping there. Not a dumb rabbit, either. As the morning grew older Prettykin was forced to an unwanted conclusion: surer than hell, Franklin was not going to show up on that shuttle.

Now what?

All right, Prettykin could still make a much-better-than-fifty-fifty bet that Franklin was headed for the Mainland. Which airline was the most traveled Hawaii-Mainland carrier? United. Simple as that. Unless the predictable bastard had already made an end run.

Prettykin left the now all-too-familiar wiki-wiki bus entrance and hurried to the United ticket counter area. The change of scene sharpened his senses for some minutes, but he knew the deadening effects of no sleep and monotony would soon blanket him again. He forced back the nagging worry that Franklin might have bypassed him, might have gone from the Inter-Island Terminal into Honolulu for some reason, then back here to the Main Terminal. That way, he would not have used the shuttle and would not have appeared at the wiki-wiki bus stop at the terminal's upper level.

Prettykin refused to believe that, because he had no real alternative to what he was doing now. He had to bet forty thousand dollars—and in all probability his life—on his conviction that Franklin would show up here in the United ticket area.

His stomach churned and rumbled. Its distress proved an asset now. He was exhausted, but his sour stomach kept him wide awake. He found an empty plastic chair and lit a Raleigh.

For some unfathomable reason, Vandenhoff wanted to talk. She didn't want to listen. Maybe that in itself was the reason for his unexpected garrulousness. He had an absolute gift for driving her up the wall.

He'd been near-silent as she had raced them to Keahole in the rented Toyota and hurriedly checked it in. The delay caused by the need for delivery of replacement keys from the Keahole rental office infuriated Vandenhoff, but they were trapped by the absence of late-night taxi service. The wait had been an uncomfortable one made even more so by her opportunity to glance over the hotel bill. She discovered not only the expected call to a local number she assumed was Dr. Fukada's. There was also listed a call to D.C. information.

"Not your call?" Vandenhoff scowled over the itemized runout. "Now just what could that mean?"

Her conception of Walter Putnam as a docile man without purpose was fast evaporating.

Getting to a near-deserted airport late at night was not her favorite idea of how to end a day. Getting there with this demon-driven little bureaucrat made it a nerve-twisting experience.

He had been mercifully silent during the fast drive up ink-black Queen Kaahumanu Highway, but on the noisy little charter plane, three seats separated them from the pilot. Vandenhoff seemed compelled to talk. It had to be tension combined with the aural insulation of the engine noise.

"Did you know I started in government service as a clerk?" he said abruptly as the Navajo reduced its steep takeoff angle to a steady westward climb.

Oh, Lord, she thought, he's going to tell me his life's story.

"Came out of Northwestern in sixty-two with a B.A. and a heart murmur. Couldn't get into the service, but the Department of Commerce had an opening. You have any idea what it's like to work for Commerce for fifteen years, top floor of that huge obsolete hulk at Fourteenth and Constitution? They had maps on every floor so visitors wouldn't get lost, but the offices were little holes. Furniture from the thirties and forties."

She stared out at stars and knew the sea began where they stopped. But this was her superior prattling away. She turned away from the window's escape and said, "It must have been dreary."

"Good word for it." He cocked his head her way. Sign of a long seige? "It took some doing to get a transfer to Justice. And a lot more to organize and split out the IMS."

"And still more to make the IMS into what it is, I'm sure."

"You have no idea what I went through—what I still go through in terms of worry, overwork, and actual physical strain."

A dirty job, Vandenhoff, but somebody has to do it, right? "I have an inkling," she said. "A lot of it rubs off on your field people."

"It's a thankless job, Burch, but somebody—"

"No medals," she said. Damned if she'd let him finish the cliché.

"What?"

"The real aggravation is that there's never any public thanks." She was speaking for herself now. And damned little private thanks, either, you cold little schemer.

"That's absolutely correct. You're quite perceptive, Burch. But you do realize how important our work is." He glanced forward. The pilot wore earphones and couldn't possibly overhear them. "Take this case. The DEA is overwhelmed by the very immensity of the drug invasion. The military is hamstrung by a constitutional interpretation. Too many agencies are more concerned with PR than with the public good."

She must have let her eyes stray off his face. He cocked his head in that odd way of his.

"Maybe I'm not getting through to you with these generalities, Burch. Here's a story that might bring it home to you. Happened a couple days ago in Baltimore. A woman was using a pay phone on a downtown street while her three-year-old daughter waited beside her. A stranger stood at a nearby corner. Suddenly, a man across the street pulled an automatic and banged away at the man on the corner. He fired back. It was a merry little duel between rival cocaine pushers. That would have been fine if they had managed to kill each other, but when they both ran out of ammo and ran off, there was only one casualty. The three-year-old had taken a thirty-eight slug right through her stomach."

She didn't know how to react or what he wanted from her.

"It's not just the drugs that kill, Burch. It's the people who sell them, the officials who turn the other way, the complacent public. So what does that leave?"

"A hell of a problem."

"It leaves us, Burch—one tiny hidden-away section. A handful of people with real guts. You know what a brown recluse is?"

"A brown what?" He had a knack for keeping people off balance.

"It's a spider that prefers dark, out-of-the-way places. An overlooked species for years. But its bite is devilish. Just a pinprick, but the effect spreads. Eventually, the necrotic tissue must be excised by surgery. You see the parallel? The bite of the IMS can conceivably destroy Sindicato Sud. You understand my personal concern for this project?"

She nodded. She had noticed a disturbing, slightly unfocused glare in his pale-ginger-ale eyes. Bland little zealots made her flesh crawl.

But the pay is good, isn't it, Lorraine? You do what the man says, don't you? Orders are orders. That hadn't washed at Nuremberg, but the world had been different then. Hadn't it?

She wanted to get him off his IMS track. He had come too close to her.

"You never married?"

He shot her an odd look. "No. No time for that, I'm afraid."

No time while he clerked away at Commerce and plodded up the GS ladder? No time while he cajoled, pleaded, and conned to split out his seemingly innocuous and budget-conserving Internal Management Section at Justice? No time to find a woman to share his drive and dedication?

"You live with your niece."

He seemed startled at that common knowledge. He actually began to color above his collar before he controlled it.

Ah, so.

"She boards at my home while she attends the University of Maryland."

"I see." And that was the only sliver of humanity she did see in Richard Vandenhoff. Maybe he had an incestuous little yen for his boarder, but otherwise he was a dour, dedicated administrator, uncomfortable and overbearing with women, considered dull by those who knew him outside IMS. But he sent people out to do the unthinkable.

"I've arranged for a Honolulu P.D. unit for our use," he said as the small plane began its long descent past the darkened hulk of Diamond Head and Waikiki's glittering strip. "Radio contact will be a necessity."

She was beat. "Where do we sleep?"

"In the car. Now, if only the guy hasn't left the islands . . ."

He kept talking of arrangements and necessities while her adrenalin began to surge. The man they had rebuilt into Donald Franklin was somewhere down there in the streets jeweled with strings of golden lights, and they were coming to kill him.

—17—

Prettykin's exhaustion-tinged eyes burned from his unremitting surveillance of the United ticket area. Twice he had caught himself beginning to slip into the compelling numbness of pre-sleep. He dug his nails into his palms. The discomfort quickly brought him back to wakefulness.

He had been here all of frigging yesterday, all last night, and now it was late morning of a second day. He was disgusted, exhausted, and a touch panicky, all at the same time. The briefcase in his lap concealed the Bernardelli's pocket bulge, but it felt like it weighed a half-ton. The coffee he'd grabbed at a nearby snack shop was working on him. He had to take another chance at the men's room.

He hurried across the ticket lobby holding the briefcase close and dodged the scattered foot traffic. Then his ears thudded. His legs threatened to give way and drop him on the hard floor.

After thirty-eight hours of scanning hundreds of people for a glimpse of Franklin, he'd almost fallen over him.

The man who rushed in front of him had to be the guy! Scar on cheek, bent nose, right height, dark hair.

Prettykin was off balance, but he recovered quickly.

"Mr. Franklin!"

The name, rapped out with authority, served as Prettykin had hoped. The guy stopped dead, then jerked his head around. Then he turned away. But the delay had already served its purpose. Prettykin stood at his side. Close. No space between them. His right hand was in his pocket.

"Mr. Franklin, I have a thirty-eight-caliber automatic aimed straight at your groin. I'm willing to use it right here unless you'd prefer to turn around slowly and casually and walk ahead of me down to the baggage pick-up level, then across the service road, and into the rental garage. Are we going to have fatal trouble here, or are we going to take a walk together?"

Walt had spotted the blond man an instant too late, the same moment he had heard the abruptly spoken name, "Mr. Franklin!"

He knew he should have kept walking, but an uncontrollable reflex had stopped him dead. Only for a split second. But that was enough. His knees suddenly were gelatin. He fought not to show it. Then the man was right beside him, touching him, his voice rough in Walt's ear, his breath sour with old coffee and morning dank.

The desperate, seedy look, but most of all the hard, unblinking eyes, told Walt the blond man was perfectly capable of doing as he threatened: gun him down here and take a chance at escape through the inevitable confusion, unless Walt complied with his order to leave with him. The gun was no bluff. He felt its muzzle against his thigh through the blond man's pocket.

Walt turned as he had been told and took the escalator to the lower level. Somewhere down there must be an airport security officer, a cop, somebody to stop this. He couldn't accept as a fact that he was being abducted from a busy airport terminal and no one would take any notice of what was happening to him.

But this persistent blond bastard had planned well. From the escalator to the exit was only a few paces. They emerged into bright sunshine. Several knots of departing passengers awaited rides. A man in a green and yellow Hawaiian shirt, with a red, white, and blue United tote bag dangling from one hand, lounged against the building front, disinterested.

No help here.

"Across the road, Franklin. Into the garage. Bay number thirty-four."

Like everyone who lived in a major, high-crime city, Walt had wondered what he would do if he were ever confronted by a mugger with a gun. Fantasy had him swing his briefcase upward in an unerringly accurate arc, knock the weapon aside and with the toe of his shoe, slam into an unprotected groin, leaving the assailant groveling helplessly on the sidewalk in nauseating pain.

Even if he had fully trusted his reflexes, that mentally rehearsed scenario would not work here. The man was behind him, the gun was not in sight, and Walt's lightly loaded cheap bag wouldn't knock a ten-year-old off balance.

"Reach behind you." The guy had a soft southern accent, all the more unnerving because it lacked any hint of nervousness.

He thrust back his hand and felt car keys drop in his palm.

"You're doing the driving. It's the gray Nissan there. The two-door. Get in the right side, toss your bag in the back, slide over. Buckle your seat belt."

That way, he'll be beside me all the time, Walt realized.

Now the gun was out, no bluff for sure in this deserted corner of the Avis garage. The guy held it casually at seat level between them. It was satiny black with an ugly tapered muzzle, somehow foreign looking. The blond man kept it aimed into Walt's gut as he fastened his own seat-and-shoulder belts with his free hand.

So much for Walt's half-formed thought of getting up to speed then jamming the brakes to throw the guy into the windshield. And Walt's own safety restraints squelched the possibility of opening his door to roll out at a crowded intersection. The guy was chillingly efficient.

There was a sharp left turn just beyond the garage exit. Walt slid his eyes toward the terminal. Not a sign of hope. Only more impatient arrivals and the unconcerned man with the tote bag.

He turned and left the terminal behind. The garage lane joined the exit road. He swung the Nissan right to follow the light exiting traffic. When the road branched left toward

Pearl Harbor and right toward downtown Honolulu, the blond man said, "Left lane, Franklin."

They merged into the faster and heavier traffic on the westbound Kamehameha Highway, swung around the long curve above Hickam Air Force Base, then skirted the east side of Pearl Harbor.

Never had air smelled sweeter, even in this industrial and military clutter. Never had the sky seemed so clear a blue, nor the sun so caressingly warm. Walt's senses had been brought to excruciating sharpness by the rush of blood from his banging heart. He'd never known fear like this, and he had no choice but to drive on toward certain disaster.

The highway cut through dense industrial development, past drab military installations, then blocks of cramped housing. The blond man said nothing until they neared a sprawling interchange past Pearl City.

He glanced at the map he had spread across his knees. "Split off on Farrington at the Wahiawa Interchange."

Four miles later, he said, "Take a right on Seven-fifty." His voice was emotionless, like that of a judge passing sentence.

KUNIA ROAD announced the directional sign. Then Walt was struck with the absurdity of trying to memorize their route. This was a one-way trip.

"Listen—" He cleared his parched throat. "Listen to me. I don't know who you're after, but I'm not him. My name is Walter Putnam. I work for a C.P.A. firm in Washington. I'm—"

"Shut up, Franklin. Drive."

The man at the lower level of the John Rodgers Main Terminal in the green-and-yellow Hawaiian shirt was far from a disinterested idler. He was Sergeant Julio Ramos, H.P.D., and his tote bag contained a radio handset. He yanked it out only a few seconds after the gray Nissan had turned left and exited the parking garage.

"Ramos, Position Six. Subject just departed terminal in a gray Nissan sedan, accompanied by white male Caucasian, blond hair. May have concealed weapon. Subject appeared to be under strain. License number—" He cursed his short memory and consulted his pocket notebook to read off the number.

An acknowledgement grated in the handset's little speaker.

Two-and-one-half minutes later, Ramos heard, "We got him. Headed west on the Kam Highway. Unit Eight on his tail. Do you copy, Unit Four?"

And in their borrowed cruiser, an unmarked blue Dodge with an excellent radio, Lorraine Burch glanced at Vandenhoff, who now showed a scruff of pale beard.

"Ten four," Vandenhoff barked into his mike with obvious relish. The little creep was enjoying this. "Do not apprehend," Vandenhoff said. "Repeat, do not apprehend."

He screeched the Dodge out of its space beside the airport's public-parking section, raced down the exit road, then gunned the overpowered cruiser west on Kamehameha.

"One unit between us and them, Burch. We've got to get past it. Who's the blond guy?"

"It has to be Sindicato Sud. Their cannon. That confuses—"

"No, it doesn't at all!" Vandenhoff grinned. "That could make it a very neat package. Gift-wrapped."

He managed to pass the H.P.D. unit at the Pearl Harbor Interchange, gunning recklessly around them just before they hit the Kamehameha off-ramp.

Then they had a bad moment. "Damn! Lost him!" Then she was able to pick the Nissan out of the traffic ahead by its very drabness and its frequent lane changing. It was driven by an extremely nervous man.

"There! Just behind the van."

"Got it!" Vandenhoff slowed the unmarked loaner and held position a quarter-mile behind.

Only a few miles up Kunia, Walt noted with growing dismay that the landscape had changed drastically. They had skirted the east, then north, perimeter of Pearl, through heavy development. Along Farrington, the clutter had eased into less dense commercial blocks, then merged into residential areas that themselves fell behind when he had been ordered to swing north on Kunia. Now they rushed along a stretch of isolated blacktop that gradually climbed up the broad saddle between two flanking mountain ranges.

The road became a channel between stands of towering sugar cane, taller than a man, a sea of giant grass bisected by the strip of narrow pavement. It was a lonely road. In the rearview mirror, Walt could see only one other car, far behind. Behind that solitary traveler, he caught a final glimpse of Honolulu's white clutter. Then it dwindled to heat shimmer and disappeared beyond a slight bend in the road. Walt and the blond man sped through a breeze-ruffled Sargasso of towering cane.

The blond man peered ahead at a break in the green wall on the left. A dirt service road wound westward into the cane fields.

"Turn in there."

Walt's chest thudded. His new undershirt was already soaked. His hands slipped on the wheel as he braked to turn into the narrow lane. This cold assassin with his two days' of blond stubble, who smelled of too many hours without a bath, whose red-rimmed eyes saw Walt's every twitch and tremor, was about to slam a bullet in Walt's head or heart and leave him deep in this remote cane field.

Walt's visit to Fukada and that doctor's startling revelation, Walt's escape from the Big Island, Jack's prompt help through the Honolulu C.P.A. affiliation—all of it meant nothing now. Nothing. The grotesque plan put in motion, apparently by the Justice Department, had rolled relentlessly to this inevitable and fatal moment. He had been hopelessly bouncing around in a huge, inescapable trap—like a mouse that had cleverly avoided a series of snares and snags only to discover that all the time it had been locked in a cage with a king snake.

A half mile in, the blond man said, "Park it here."

Adjacent to the dirt service lane that had been bulldozed through the cane was a small clearing, perhaps a holding point for field machinery.

"Get out."

"You've got the wrong man, damn it!"

"Get out." The muzzle of the automatic prodded him just below his right armpit. If he refused, he would be shot right here. If he complied, he would gain a moment or two more.

Walt released the seat-belt catch. He opened the door. These could be the few seconds, the only few seconds, when he and the blond man would be separated: the moment when the man got out on his own side, a clumsy moment when he would be off balance. How good was he with that gun? If Walt could make it to the dense cane . . .

Standing beside the open door, Walt tensed his leg muscles.

"Hold it right there."

The blond man slid out the driver's side. His gun muzzle never wavered.

And Walt Putnam knew he was about to die.

"No sirens," Vandenhoff said into the mike. "And do not, repeat, do not close in on me."

He glanced at his rearview mirror. Lorraine twisted around and saw the police cruiser almost a mile behind fall back a bit further.

What, she wondered, is the little man up to? They'd had the Nissan in sight for the past twelve miles, had tailed it past Pearl, through Waipahu's suburban sprawl, lost it once on a Kunia curve but had it in sight now, about a mile ahead on this secondary road's straight stab through these acres of swaying sugar cane. Just what in hell was Vandenhoff up to?

Then she knew. And the instant she realized that he was still intent on salvaging his damned Code Franklin project, the car ahead disappeared.

"Where did—"

"Turned off," he said. His voice was tight with excitement. "There must be a side road up ahead."

He hunched over the wheel. She had to give the little creep one thing. He could handle a car. He had zipped through the clotted Pearl Harbor area like an Indy qualifier. Never lost the Nissan for a second through there. Only lost it once on Kunia, but that hadn't mattered because they were driving up a channel.

They hadn't lost it this time, because there certainly was a side road here, just as Vandenhoff had predicted, a narrow dirt lane off to the left. Now, she suddenly realized, Vandenhoff himself was trapped in a way. The island police were not far behind, though twisting around again, she didn't yet spot them. If Vandenhoff parked out here on Kunia Road, there were sure to be questions about procedure. But he did need delay.

Almost leisurely, he bent the Dodge off the pavement and nosed into the dirt trail, careful not to rev the engine. The unmarked police car's excellent maintenance, the heavy cane growth, and the deadening effect of the pumicelike dirt surface muffled their approach. The Dodge rounded a ragged bend, and Vandenhoff nearly rear-ended the Nissan.

A hundred feet off to the left, the startled blond man whirled toward them. His weapon, she saw, was dead center on Putnam's spine.

Lorraine leaped out while Vandenhoff fumbled with his seat belt, stepped through the dust drift they had kicked up, then she and Vandenhoff stood together at the edge of the clearing.

"Drop it," the blond man called. His voice was controlled. A pro, even now. She looked down at the S&W in her right hand. She didn't remember taking it out of her purse.

"Drop it or I drop him."

"We can save it!" Vandenhoff's voice was low but charged with excitement. "Force him. Force him. He nails Putnam, then you nail him. A beautiful package!"

She raised the S&W, took the prescribed straddle, steadied her right wrist with the grip of her left hand.

"You heard me," the hit man called. "You've got five seconds, then he goes."

She knew his position was not as hopeless as it looked. The blond man was only a few yards from the cane. Once he'd dived into that dense cover, they'd never find him.

Putnam stood rigid, staring at her. His face was the color of egg shells.

She centered the sight. Squeezed.

The gun bucked upward. The flat detonation was swallowed by the encircling sugar cane. A flock of bright yellow birds whirred across the clearing and away.

The blond man's face held its fixed stare as his head flew back. His automatic fell from nerveless fingers. There was a neat hole above his left eye. He fell stiffly backward, dead before he hit the bulldozed ground.

Putnam looked down at the dropped Bernardelli.

"We can still save it!" Vandenhoff's voice was shrill. "Get that gun, pick it up without disturbing the prints, then use it on Putnam."

"Where's your own piece, Vandenhoff?" She knew what that comment could cost her, but she couldn't keep the disgust out of her voice.

"I don't use a gun. I don't use one." His voice had a manic edge.

Putnam just stood out there, arms slack at his sides. He looked like a man in shock.

"Tell him to stay right where he is. Then *get that gun.* Use a handkerchief. Don't you understand? The guy got him, then you got the guy. It'll wash. I'll make it wash."

"Oh, *God!*" She thrust her S&W at Vandenhoff. "It's all yours. Let's see you make it wash."

"I'm an administrator," he shrilled. "An administrator!" He shrank back toward the open door of the Dodge.

Behind them, vehicles had entered the narrow lane. No sirens, as Vandenhoff had directed. But their red-and-blue flashers danced through the cane. They came in fast, three cars in close tandem, and braked abruptly. A towering dust cloud rolled past them and obscured the tiny clearing.

Out of it walked Walter Putnam. He held Prettykin's Bernardelli at waist level. He glanced at Vandenhoff who hunkered sideways, head down, in the Dodge's driver seat. Then his eyes met Lorraine's.

"My prints are on it now." His voice was peculiar, toneless. "Maybe he'll think you could get away with a suicide coverup."

He'd been ahead of Vandenhoff through it all. She couldn't read his look. Hatred? Not hatred, but surely not forgiveness. She couldn't read him.

He dropped the pistol in front of her and walked past to the waiting police.

Vandenhoff's head rose slowly. His eyes held venom. "My failure was in not realizing who my real enemies are, Burch."

"No, Vandenhoff. Our failure was ourselves."

She followed Walt Putnam toward the flashing lights.

—Epilogue—

Walter Putnam was turned over to the Honolulu Field Office of the Federal Bureau of Investigation. He was returned to Washington and accepted restorative plastic surgery at government expense, but he refused psychiatric treatment. He disclosed very little to Hawaiian and federal authorities, but immediately following his release from George Washington University Hospital, he sought out Morris Tomlinson.

He rejected any compensation for his revelations. Subsequently, he testified as an unfriendly witness in the case of *The People of the United States* vs *Lorraine Burch*. Reporters covering the trial were struck by the fact that he showed no visible emotion. He has rejoined his C.P.A. firm and is currently at work investigating cost overruns in the U.S. Navy's "Starlock" astronavigation program.

Morris Tomlinson of *The Washington Post* was awarded a Pulitzer Prize for his exposé of the IMS Code Franklin project.

Lorraine Burch reported a sanitized version of the killing of Arthur Prettykin to Honolulu police. They notified the Justice Department and were instructed to hold her until a federal marshal arrived to take custody. At her trial, she was commended for her full disclosure of the facts surrounding

Code Franklin, but she was nevertheless convicted of conspiracy to deprive Walter Putnam of his civil rights.

She was sentenced to ten years in the Maryland Correctional Institution for Women at Jessup. Walter Putnam's corroborating testimony contributed much to the jury's guilty verdict after only three hours of deliberation.

Lorraine felt no animosity toward him. She thought she felt nothing at all until one April evening when a soft breeze drifted across the Maryland farmland and through the open window at the end of the exercise corridor. Something in that breath of cool evening air—some elusive scent perhaps—reminded her of the Big Island, its exotic fragrances, its pounding surf against the lava cliffs . . . and the only man from whom she had ever received tenderness.

Dr. Elmo Horger, following an abortive investigation by the New York State Medical Licensing Authority, is still active as director of the Horger Clinic. There was speculation, never substantiated, that the investigation was terminated at the request of the F.B.I.

Richard Vandenhoff was incoherent when police reached him in the Kunia Road cane field. He was taken to the hospital at Fort Shafter Military Reservation, where authorities contacted the Justice Department. Returned to Washington with a federal escort, Vandenhoff was evaluated at Walter Reed Army Medical Center and judged unfit to stand trial. He was remanded to Sheppard and Enoch Pratt Hospital, Baltimore County, Maryland, where he is currently a resident psychiatric patient. Vandenhoff, though he had never used anything stronger than aspirin, himself had become an indirect victim of the international drug trade.

He has only one frequent visitor, Ms. Louisa Alvoort, a niece, who, following her graduation from the University of Maryland, is a sociologist with the Department of the Interior.

Frank Murtha, who had been sequestered with a crack team of federal marshals in a privately owned vacation lodge on

Michigan's Upper Peninsula, testified before the Senate Commission on Drug Control as scheduled. He identified the shadowy crime figure "El Fabricante," as Gaspar Heredero, a Key Biscayne resident of Bolivian descent, with import-export offices in Miami.

The Miami activity, subsequently proven to be a major cocaine conduit into the United States, was shut down by the Drug Enforcement Administration. Seven men and three women arrested by the D.E.A. were tried and convicted for their involvement in the Miami operation.

Heredero has not been located as of this writing. His disappearance has led to speculation that Sindicato Sud remains in operation, despite the loss of its Miami connection.

Frank Murtha was provided with a new identity and lives somewhere in the Midwest under the auspices of the Federal Witness Protection Program.

In the wake of the sensational disclosures of the Burch Trial and a resulting interdepartmental investigation, the Internal Management Section (IMS) of the Justice Department was slated for dissolution. That action was forestalled only two days before it was to take effect. The deciding factor was an impassioned plea on the Senate floor by Senator Osborne "Shoutin" Shorten, North Carolina, reinforced with the bipartisan support of Massachusetts Senator Jensen LaBranche. Together, they convinced a majority that the IMS was an essential part of the Federal Departmental Self-Regulatory Program (FEDSERP).

The IMS survived and is today headed by Stanley N. Surjin, formerly the section's financial chief.

Bestselling Thrillers —
action-packed for a great read

___ $4.50 0-425-10477-X **CAPER**
Lawrence Sanders

___ $3.95 0-515-09475-7 **SINISTER FORCES**
Patrick Anderson

___ $4.95 0-425-10107-X **RED STORM RISING**
Tom Clancy

___ $4.50 0-425-09138-4 **19 PURCHASE STREET**
Gerald A. Browne

___ $4.95 0-425-08383-7 **THE HUNT FOR RED OCTOBER**
Tom Clancy

___ $3.95 0-441-77812-7 **THE SPECIALIST** Gayle Rivers
___ $3.95 0-441-58321-0 **NOCTURNE FOR THE GENERAL**
John Trenhaile

___ $3.95 0-425-09582-7 **THE LAST TRUMP**
John Gardner

___ $3.95 0-441-36934-0 **SILENT HUNTER**
Charles D. Taylor

___ $4.50 0-425-09884-2 **STONE 588** Gerald A. Browne
___ $3.95 0-425-10625-X **MOSCOW CROSSING**
Sean Flannery

___ $3.95 0-515-09178-2 **SKYFALL** Thomas H. Block